The New Zealand Book of the Beach

Also by Graeme Lay

NOVELS AND SHORT STORY COLLECTIONS
The Mentor
The Fools on the Hill
Temptation Island
Dear Mr Cairney
Motu Tapu: Stories of the South Pacific
The Town on the Edge of the World
Alice & Luigi

YOUNG ADULT NOVELS
The Wave Rider
Leaving One Foot Island
Return to One Foot Island
The Pearl of One Foot Island

CHILDREN
Nanny Potaka's Birthday Treat

TRAVEL
Passages: Journeys in Polynesia
Pacific New Zealand
The Cook Islands (with Ewan Smith)
New Zealand – A Visual Celebration (with Gareth Eyres)
Samoa (with Evotia Tamua)
Feasts & Festivals (with Glenn Jowitt)
The Globetrotter Guide to New Zealand
Are We There Yet? A Kiwi Kid's Holiday Exploring Guide
The Best of Auckland
The Miss Tutti Frutti Contest – Travel Tales of the South Pacific
New Zealand – the Magnificent Journey (with Gareth Eyres)
Inside the Cannibal Pot

EDITOR
Metro Fiction
100 New Zealand Short Short Stories
Another 100 Short Short Stories
The Third Century
Boys' Own Stories
50 Short Short Stories by Young New Zealanders
An Affair of the Heart: A Celebration of Frank Sargeson's Centenary
(with Stephen Stratford)
Golden Weather: North Shore Writers Past & Present
(with Jack Ross)
Home: New Short Short Stories by New Zealand Writers
(with Stephen Stratford)

The New Zealand Book of the Beach

Edited by Graeme Lay

Front cover: Back Beach Bach, limited edition screenprint 2006, acrylic on archival paper, New Zealand artist Tony Ogle

David Ling Publishing Limited
PO Box 34601, Birkenhead
Auckland 0746, New Zealand
www.davidling.co.nz

ISBN 978-1-877378-16-4

First Published 2007

Typeset by Express Communications Limited
Printed in China

Contents

Introduction ... 7
Graeme Lay

At the Bay (slightly abridged) ... 9
Katherine Mansfield

(from) The End of the Golden Weather ... 43
Bruce Mason

Entanglements ... 45
Kevin Ireland

The Tsunami ... 47
Owen Marshall

Holly ... 53
Tina Shaw

The Seahorse and the Reef ... 61
Witi Ihimaera

A Great Day ... 66
Frank Sargeson

self-catering ... 74
Emily Perkins

Broken Rhythms.....76
Sarah Quigley

(from) The Lonely Margins of the Sea.....82
Shonagh Koea

The Outsider.....90
Graeme Lay

The Picnic Virgin.....99
Victoria McHalick

My Late Father.....111
Kevin Ireland

The Line.....121
Rhonda Bartle

Bitten Tongue.....127
Norman Bilbrough

Only Waving.....136
Sue Emms

Storms.....142
Charlotte Grimshaw

The History Of.....160
Jenah Shaw

Water Bores.....166
Linda Niccol

Swimming to Australia.....178
Lloyd Jones

At Waimama Bay.....193
Annamarie Jagose

Contributors.....216

Acknowledgements.....223

Introduction

New Zealand has a 6000km-long coastline and nowhere in the country is more than a two-hour drive from the sea. Consequently its people have an abiding love of the beach and the sea, both of which have become an integral part of the country's consciousness. Novelist Maurice Shadbolt put it well. 'New Zealand', he wrote, 'begins with the sea and ends with the sea. Understand this and you begin to comprehend New Zealand and the New Zealander'. Sharing a border with no other country, New Zealand's coastline is its defining frontier.

From the last years of the nineteenth century, when sea bathing first became acceptable, the coast has drawn New Zealanders to it, for excursions and family holidays. The evolution of a beach cult can be traced from the writing of one our earliest literary chroniclers, Katherine Mansfield, whose story 'At the Bay' is republished in this collection. The emotions invoked by this story, with its seaside games, flirtations and family tensions, carry reverberations which today's New Zealanders can still recognise, although 'At the Bay' is set well over a century ago. This resonance is counter-pointed by Annamarie Jagose's story, a contemporary equivalent, 'At Waimama Bay'.

As the beach became more and more popular in the twentieth century, rudimentary dwellings were built in clusters around the coasts of New Zealand, making a base for family holidays, often for several generations. (Significantly, a recurring noun in this collection, along with 'beach', is the word which is only one letter removed from it – 'bach'). For a few hectic weeks between Christmas and the resumption of work and school, most New Zealanders flee to the coast, and for the rest of the year the beach is seldom far from their thoughts. To the bathing, rock pool exploring, dalliances and other seaside pastimes in Katherine Mansfield's 'At the Bay', have been added many other beach-based recreational activities, including surfing, sailing, barbecuing, fishing, strolling and picnicking. Most of these pursuits are incorporated into the twenty stories in the collection.

It is unsurprising that the beach has long provided fertile ground for our fiction. The beach, like its sister the sea, plays a powerful role in the human imagination. As a setting for informal human contact, the beach is like no other natural arena. Sea, sun, sand and sky comprise a potent sensual mix. As well as providing balm to the troubled spirit, the beauty and mystery of the seashore quicken the senses. The beach is a natural aphrodisiac. Young love at the beach in high summer has been a rite of passage for New Zealanders for generations and it is likely that a significant percentage of New Zealanders have been conceived within earshot of the sea. Accordingly, it is no coincidence that several of the stories in *The New Zealand Book of the Beach* involve transgressions of one sort or another. At the beach, temptations beckon.

And as we grow older, the beach still has a role to play – in our memories. In other of the stories, a contemporary beach setting triggers recollections of childhood. Part of the power of beaches present is their ability to invoke memories of beaches past.

Although the traditional Kiwi bach is now an endangered species, a consequence of the value of coastal land soaring, the love of New Zealanders for the beach is undiminished. Our beaches belong to all of us, from the indigenous Maori people – the tangata whenua – to fifth-generation Kiwis to the most recent immigrants. The common love of all New Zealanders – Polynesian, Pakeha, Asian Kiwis, West and East European Kiwis – for the beach is what unites us more than anything else. Like a natural lodestone, the beach draws all people to it. The writers represented in this anthology recognise this gravitational pull, and their writing reflects its power. *The New Zealand Book of the Beach* is a tribute to the beach's enduring allure, and the literature this fascination has inspired.

– Graeme Lay

At the Bay (slightly abridged)

Katherine Mansfield

I

Very early morning. The sun was not yet risen, and the whole of Crescent Bay was hidden under a white sea-mist. The big bush-covered hills at the back were smothered. You could not see where they ended and the paddocks and bungalows began. The sandy road was gone and the paddocks and bungalows the other side of it; there were no white dunes covered with reddish grass beyond them; there was nothing to mark which was beach and where was the sea. A heavy dew had fallen. The grass was blue. Big drops hung on the bushes and just did not fall; the silvery, fluffy toi-toi was limp on its long stalks, and all the marigolds and the pinks in the bungalow gardens were bowed to the earth with wetness. Drenched were the cold fuchsias, round pearls of dew lay on the flat nasturtium leaves. It looked as though the sea had beaten up softly in the darkness, as though one immense wave had come rippling, rippling – how far? Perhaps if you had waked up in the middle of the night you might have seen a big fish flicking in at the window and gone again ...

II

A few moments later the back door of one of the bungalows opened, and a figure in a broad-striped bathing suit flung down the paddock, cleared the stile, rushed through the tussock grass into the hollow, staggered up the sandy hillock, and raced for dear life over the big porous stones, over the cold, wet pebbles, on to the hard sand that gleamed like oil. Splish-Splosh! Splish-Splosh! The water bubbled round his legs as Stanley Burnell waded out exulting. First man in as usual! He'd beaten them all again. And he swooped down to souse his head and neck.

'Hail, brother! All hail, Thou Mighty One!' A velvety bass voice came booming over the water.

Great Scott! Damnation take it! Stanley lifted up to see a dark head bobbing far out and an arm lifted. It was Jonathan Trout – there before him! 'Glorious morning!' sang the voice.

'Yes, very fine!' said Stanley briefly. Why the dickens didn't the fellow stick to his part of the sea? Why should he come barging over to this exact spot? Stanley gave a kick, a lunge and struck out, swimming overarm. But Jonathan was a match for him. Up he came, his black hair sleek on his forehead, his short beard sleek.

'I had an extraordinary dream last night!' he shouted.

What was the matter with the man? This mania for conversation irritated Stanley beyond words. And it was always the same – always some piffle about a dream he'd had, or some cranky idea he'd got hold of, or some rot he'd been reading. Stanley turned over on his back and kicked with his legs till he was a living waterspout. But even then ...

'I dreamed I was hanging over a terrifically high cliff, shouting to some one below.' You would be! thought Stanley. He could stick no more of it. He stopped splashing. 'Look here, Trout,' he said, 'I'm in rather a hurry this morning.'

'You're *what*?' Jonathan was so surprised – or pretended to be – that he sank under the water, then reappeared again blowing.

'All I mean is,' said Stanley, 'I've no time to – to – to fool about. I want to get this over. I'm in a hurry. I've work to do this morning – see?'

Jonathan was gone before Stanley had finished. 'Pass, friend!' said the bass voice gently, and he slid away through the water with scarcely a ripple... But curse the fellow! He'd ruined Stanley's bathe. What an unpractical idiot the man was! Stanley struck out to sea again, and then as quickly swam in again, and away he rushed up the beach. He felt cheated.

Jonathan stayed a little longer in the water. He floated, gently moving his hands like fins, and letting the sea rock his long, skinny body. It was curious, but in spite of everything he was fond of Stanley Burnell. True, he had a fiendish desire to tease him sometimes, to poke fun at him, but at bottom he was sorry for the fellow. There was something pathetic in his determination to make a job of everything. You couldn't help feeling he'd be caught out one day, and then what an almighty cropper he'd come! At that moment an immense wave lifted Jonathan, rode past him, and broke along the beach with a joyful sound. What a beauty! And now there came another. That was the way to live – carelessly, recklessly, spending oneself. He got on to his feet and began to wade towards the shore, pressing his toes into the firm, wrinkled sand. To take things easy, not to fight against the ebb and flow of life, but to give way to it – that was what was needed. It was this tension that was all wrong. To live – to live! And the perfect morning, so fresh and fair, basking in the light, as though laughing at its own beauty, seemed to whisper, 'Why not?'

But now he was out of the water Jonathan turned blue with cold. He ached all over; it was as though some one was wringing the blood out of him. And stalking up the beach, shivering, all his muscles tight, he too felt his bathe was spoilt. He'd stayed in too long.

III

Beryl was alone in the living-room when Stanley appeared, wearing a blue serge suit, a stiff collar and a spotted tie. He looked almost uncannily clean and brushed; he was going to town for the day. Dropping into his chair, he pulled out his watch and put it beside his plate.

'I've just got twenty-five minutes,' he said. 'You might go and see if the porridge is ready, Beryl?'

'Mother's just gone for it,' said Beryl. She sat down at the table and poured out his tea.

'Thanks!' Stanley took a sip. 'Hallo!' he said in an astonished voice, 'you've forgotten the sugar.'

'Oh, sorry!' But even then Beryl didn't help him; she pushed the basin across. What did this mean? As Stanley helped himself his blue eyes widened; they seemed to quiver. He shot a quick glance at his sister-in-law and leaned back.

'Nothing wrong, is there?' he asked carelessly, fingering his collar.

Beryl's head was bent; she turned her plate in her fingers.

'Nothing,' said her light voice. Then she too looked up, and smiled at Stanley. 'Why should there be?'

'O-oh! No reason at all as far as I know. I thought you seemed rather –'

At that moment the door opened and the three little girls appeared, each carrying a porridge plate. They were dressed alike in blue jerseys and knickers; their brown legs were bare, and each had her hair plaited and pinned up in what was called a horse's tail. Behind them came Mrs. Fairfield with the tray.

'Carefully, children,' she warned. But they were taking the very greatest care. They loved being allowed to carry things. 'Have you said good morning to your father?'

'Yes, grandma.' They settled themselves on the bench opposite Stanley and Beryl.

'Good morning, Stanley!' Old Mrs. Fairfield gave him his plate.

'Morning, mother! How's the boy?'

'Splendid! He only woke up once last night. What a perfect morning!' The old woman paused, her hand on the loaf of bread, to gaze out of the open door into the garden. The sea sounded. Through the wide-open window streamed the sun on to the yellow varnished walls and bare floor. Everything on the table flashed and glittered. In the middle there was an old salad bowl filled with yellow and red nasturtiums. She smiled, and a look of deep content shone in her eyes.

'You might cut me a slice of that bread, mother,' said Stanley. 'I've only twelve and a half minutes before the coach passes. Has anyone given my shoes to the servant girl?'

'Yes, they're ready for you.' Mrs. Fairfield was quite unruffled.

'Oh, Kezia! Why are you such a messy child!' cried Beryl despairingly.

'Me, Aunt Beryl?' Kezia stared at her. What had she done now? She had only dug a river down the middle of her porridge, filled it, and was eating the banks away. But she did that every single morning, and no one had said a word up till now.

'Why can't you eat your food properly like Isabel and Lottie?' How unfair grown-ups are!

'But Lottie always makes a floating island, don't you, Lottie?'

'I don't,' said Isabel smartly. 'I just sprinkle mine with sugar and put on the milk and finish it. Only babies play with their food.'

Stanley pushed back his chair and got up.

'Would you get me those shoes, mother? And, Beryl, if you've finished, I wish you'd cut down to the gate and stop the coach. Run in to your mother, Isabel, and ask her where my bowler hat's been put. Wait a minute – have you children been playing with my stick?'

'No, father!'

'But I put it here.' Stanley began to bluster. 'I remember distinctly putting it in this corner. Now, who's had it? There's no time to lose. Look sharp! The stick's got to be found.'

Even Alice, the servant-girl, was drawn into the chase. 'You haven't been using it to poke the kitchen fire with by any chance?'

Stanley dashed into the bedroom where Linda was lying. 'Most extraordinary thing. I can't keep a single possession to myself. They've made away with my stick, now!'

'Stick, dear? What stick?' Linda's vagueness on these occasions could not be real, Stanley decided. Would nobody sympathize with him?

'Coach! Coach, Stanley!' Beryl's voice cried from the gate.

Stanley waved his arm to Linda. 'No time to say good-bye!' he cried. And he meant that as a punishment to her.

He snatched his bowler hat, dashed out of the house, and swung down the garden path. Yes, the coach was there waiting, and Beryl, leaning over the open gate, was laughing up at somebody or other just as if nothing had happened. The heartlessness of women! The way they took it for granted it was your job to slave away for them while they didn't even take the trouble to see that your walking-stick wasn't lost. Kelly trailed his whip across the horses.

'Good-bye, Stanley,' called Beryl, sweetly and gaily. It was easy enough to say good-bye! And there she stood, idle, shading her eyes with her hand. The worst of it was Stanley had to shout good-bye too, for the sake of appearances. Then he saw her turn, give a little skip and run back to the house. She was glad to be rid of him!

Yes, she was thankful. Into the living-room she ran and called 'He's gone!' Linda cried from her room: 'Beryl! Has Stanley gone?' Old Mrs. Fairfield appeared, carrying the boy in his little flannel coatee.

'Gone?'

'Gone!'

Oh, the relief, the difference it made to have the man out of the house. Their very voices were changed as they called to one another; they sounded warm and loving and as if they shared a secret. Beryl went over to the table. 'Have another cup of tea, mother. It's still hot.' She wanted, somehow, to celebrate the fact that they could do what they liked now. There was no man to disturb them; the whole perfect day was theirs.

'No, thank you, child,' said old Mrs. Fairfield, but the way at that moment she tossed the boy up and said 'a-goos-a-goos-a-ga!' to him meant that she felt the same. The little girls ran into the paddock like chickens let out of a coop.

Even Alice, the servant-girl, washing up the dishes in the kitchen, caught the infection and used the precious tank water in a perfectly reckless fashion.

'Oh, these men!' said she, and she plunged the teapot into the bowl and held it under the water even after it had stopped bubbling, as if it too was a man and drowning was too good for them.

IV

'Wait for me, Isa-bel! Kezia, wait for me!'

There was poor little Lottie, left behind again, because she found it so fearfully hard to get over the stile by herself. When she stood on the first step her knees began to wobble; she grasped the post. Then you had to put one leg over. But which leg? She never could decide. And when she did finally put one leg over with a sort of stamp of despair – then the feeling was awful. She was half in the paddock still and half in the tussock grass. She clutched the post desperately and lifted up her voice. 'Wait for me!'

'No, don't you wait for her, Kezia!' said Isabel. 'She's such a little silly. She's always making a fuss. Come on!' And she tugged Kezia's jersey. 'You can use my bucket if you come with me,' she said kindly. 'It's bigger than yours.' But Kezia couldn't leave Lottie all by herself. She ran back to her. By this time Lottie was very red in the face and breathing heavily.

'Here, put your other foot over,' said Kezia.

'Where?'

Lottie looked down at Kezia as if from a mountain height.

'Here where my hand is.' Kezia patted the place.

'Oh, there do you mean!' Lottie gave a deep sigh and put the second foot over.

'Now – sort of turn round and sit down and slide,' said Kezia.

'But there's nothing to sit down on, Kezia,' said Lottie.

She managed it at last, and once it was over she shook herself and began to beam.

'I'm getting better at climbing over stiles, aren't I, Kezia?'

Lottie's was a very hopeful nature.

The pink and the blue sunbonnet followed Isabel's bright red sunbonnet up that sliding, slipping hill. At the top they paused to decide where to go and to have a good stare at who was there already. Seen from behind, standing against the skyline, gesticulating largely with their spades, they looked like minute puzzled explorers.

The whole family of Samuel Josephs was there already with their lady-help, who sat on a camp-stool and kept order with a whistle that she wore tied round her neck, and a small cane with which she directed operations. The Samuel Josephs never played by themselves or managed their own game. If they did, it ended in the boys pouring water down the girls' necks or the girls trying to put little black crabs into the boys' pockets. So Mrs. S. J. and the poor lady-help drew up what she called a 'brogramme' every morning to keep them 'abused and out of bischief.' It was all competitions or races or round games. Everything began with a piercing blast of the lady-help's whistle and ended with another. There were even prizes – large, rather dirty paper parcels which the lady-help with a sour little smile drew out of a bulging string kit. The Samuel Josephs fought fearfully for the prizes and cheated and pinched one another's arms – they were all expert pinchers. The only time the Burnell children ever played with them Kezia had got a prize, and when she undid three bits of paper she found a very small rusty button-hook. She couldn't understand why they made such a fuss ...

But they never played with the Samuel Josephs now or even went to their parties. The Samuel Josephs were always giving children's parties at the Bay and there was always the same food. A big washhand basin of very brown fruit-salad, buns cut into four and a washhand jug full of something the lady-help called 'Limonadear.' And you went away in the evening with half the frill torn off your frock or something spilled all down the front of your open-work pinafore, leaving the Samuel Josephs leaping like savages on their lawn. No! They were too awful.

On the other side of the beach, close down to the water, two little boys, their knickers rolled up, twinkled like spiders. One was digging, the other pattered in and out of the water, filling a small bucket. They were the Trout boys, Pip and Rags. But Pip was so busy digging and Rags was so busy helping that they didn't see their little cousins until they were quite close.

'Look!' said Pip. 'Look what I've discovered.' And he showed them an old wet, squashed-looking boot. The three little girls stared.

'Whatever are you going to do with it?' asked Kezia.

'Keep it, of course!' Pip was very scornful. 'It's a find – see?'

Yes, Kezia saw that. All the same ...

'There's lots of things buried in the sand,' explained Pip. 'They get chucked up from wrecks. Treasure. Why – you might find – '

'But why does Rags have to keep on pouring water in?' asked Lottie.

'Oh, that's to moisten it,' said Pip, 'to make the work a bit easier. Keep it up, Rags.'

And good little Rags ran up and down, pouring in the water that turned brown like cocoa.

'Here, shall I show you what I found yesterday?' said Pip mysteriously, and he stuck his spade into the sand. 'Promise not to tell.'

They promised.

'Say, cross my heart straight dinkum.'

The little girls said it.

Pip took something out of his pocket, rubbed it a long time on the front of his jersey, then breathed on it and rubbed it again.

'Now turn round!' he ordered.

They turned round.

'All look the same way! Keep still! Now!'

And his hand opened; he held up to the light something that flashed, that winked, that was a most lovely green.

'It's a nemeral,' said Pip solemnly.

'Is it really, Pip?' Even Isabel was impressed.

The lovely green thing seemed to dance in Pip's fingers. Aunt Beryl had a nemeral in a ring, but it was a very small one. This one was as big as a star and far more beautiful.

V

As the morning lengthened whole parties appeared over the sand-hills and came down on the beach to bathe. It was understood that at eleven o'clock the women and children of the summer colony had the sea to themselves. First the women undressed, pulled on their bathing dresses and covered their heads in hideous caps like sponge bags; then the children were unbuttoned. The beach was strewn with little heaps of clothes and shoes; the big summer hats, with stones on them to keep them from blowing away, looked like immense shells. It was strange that even the sea seemed to sound differently when all those leaping, laughing figures ran into the waves. Old Mrs. Fairfield, in a lilac cotton dress and a black hat tied under the chin, gathered her little brood and got them ready. The little Trout boys whipped their shirts over their heads, and away the five sped, while their grandma sat with one hand in her knitting-bag ready to draw out the ball of wool when she was satisfied they were safely in.

The firm compact little girls were not half so brave as the tender, delicate-looking little boys. Pip and Rags, shivering, crouching down, slapping the water, never hesitated. But Isabel, who could swim twelve strokes, and Kezia, who could nearly swim eight, only followed on the strict understanding they were not to be splashed. As for Lottie, she didn't follow at all. She liked to be left to go in her own way, please. And that way was to sit down at the edge of the water, her legs straight, her knees pressed together, and to make vague motions with her arms as if she expected to be wafted out to sea. But when a bigger wave than usual, an old whiskery one, came lolloping along in her direction, she scrambled to her feet with a face of horror and flew up the beach again.

'Here, mother, keep those for me, will you?'

Two rings and a thin gold chain were dropped into Mrs Fairfield's lap.

'Yes, dear. But aren't you going to bathe here?'

'No-o,' Beryl drawled. She sounded vague. 'I'm undressing farther along. I'm going to bathe with Mrs Harry Kember.'

'Very well.' But Mrs. Fairfield's lips set. She disapproved of Mrs Harry Kember. Beryl knew it.

Poor old mother, she smiled, as she skimmed over the stones. Poor old mother! Old! Oh, what joy, what bliss it was to be young ...

'You look very pleased,' said Mrs Harry Kember. She sat hunched up on the stones, her arms round her knees, smoking.

'It's such a lovely day,' said Beryl, smiling down at her.

'Oh my *dear*!' Mrs Harry Kember's voice sounded as though she knew better than that. But then her voice always sounded as though she knew something better about you than you did yourself. She was a long, strange-looking woman with narrow hands and feet. Her face, too, was long and narrow and exhausted-looking; even her fair curled fringe looked burnt out and withered. She was the only woman at the Bay who smoked, and she smoked incessantly, keeping the cigarette between her lips while she talked, and only taking it out when the ash was so long you could not understand why it did not fall. When she was not playing bridge – she played bridge every day of her life – she spent her time lying in the full glare of the sun. She could stand any amount of it; she never had enough. All the same, it did not seem to warm her. Parched, withered, cold, she lay stretched on the stones like a piece of tossed-up driftwood. The women at the Bay thought she was very, very fast. Her lack of vanity, her slang, the way she treated men as though she was one of them, and the fact that she didn't care twopence about her house and called the servant Gladys 'Glad-eyes,' was disgraceful. Standing on the veranda steps Mrs Kember would call in her indifferent, tired voice, 'I say, Glad-eyes, you might heave me a handkerchief if I've got one, will you?' And Glad-eyes, a red bow in her hair instead of a cap, and white shoes, came running with an impudent smile. It was an absolute scandal! True, she had no children, and her husband... Here the voices were always raised; they became fervent. How can he have married her? How can he, how can he? It must have been money, of course, but even then!

Mrs Kember's husband was at least ten years younger than she was, and so incredibly handsome that he looked like a mask or a most perfect illustration in an American novel rather than a man. Black hair, dark blue eyes, red lips, a slow sleepy smile, a fine tennis player, a perfect dancer, and with it all a mystery. Harry Kember was like a man walking in his sleep. Men couldn't stand him, they couldn't get a word out of the chap; he ignored his wife just as she ignored him. How did he live? Of course there were stories, but such stories! They simply couldn't be told. The women he'd been seen with, the places he'd been seen in... but nothing was ever certain, nothing definite. Some of the women at the Bay privately thought he'd commit a murder one day. Yes, even while they talked to Mrs Kember and took in the awful concoction she was wearing, they saw her, stretched as she lay on the beach; but cold, bloody, and still with a cigarette stuck in the corner of her mouth.

Mrs Kember rose, yawned, unsnapped her belt buckle, and tugged at the tape of her blouse. And Beryl stepped out of her skirt and shed her jersey, and stood up in her short white petticoat, and her camisole with ribbon bows on the shoulders.

'Mercy on us,' said Mrs Harry Kember, 'what a little beauty you are!'

'Don't!' said Beryl softly; but, drawing off one stocking and then the other, she felt a little beauty.

'My dear – why not?' said Mrs Harry Kember, stamping on her own petticoat. Really – her underclothes! A pair of blue cotton knickers and a linen bodice that reminded one somehow of a pillow-case...'And you don't wear stays, do you?' She touched Beryl's waist, and Beryl sprang away with a small affected cry. Then 'Never!' she said firmly.

'Lucky little creature,' sighed Mrs Kember, unfastening her own.

Beryl turned her back and began the complicated movements of some one who is trying to take off her clothes and to pull on her bathing-dress all at one and the same time.

'Oh, my dear – don't mind me,' said Mrs Harry Kember. 'Why be shy? I shan't eat you. I shan't be shocked like those other ninnies.' And she gave her strange neighing laugh and grimaced at the other women.

But Beryl was shy. She never undressed in front of anybody. Was that silly? Mrs Harry Kember made her feel it was silly, even something to be ashamed of. Why be shy indeed! She glanced quickly at her friend standing so boldly in her torn chemise and lighting a fresh cigarette; and a quick, bold, evil feeling started up in her breast. Laughing recklessly, she drew on the limp, sandy-feeling bathing-dress that was not quite dry and fastened the twisted buttons.

'That's better,' said Mrs Harry Kember. They began to go down the beach together. 'Really, it's a sin for you to wear clothes, my dear. Somebody's got to tell you some day.'

The water was quite warm. It was that marvellous transparent blue, flecked with silver, but the sand at the bottom looked gold; when you kicked with your toes there rose a little puff of gold-dust. Now the waves just reached her breast. Beryl stood, her arms outstretched, gazing out, and as each wave came she gave the slightest little jump, so that it seemed it was the wave which lifted her so gently.

'I believe in pretty girls having a good time,' said Mrs Harry Kember. 'Why not? Don't you make a mistake, my dear. Enjoy yourself.' And suddenly she turned turtle, disappeared, and swam away quickly, quickly, like a rat. Then she flicked round and began swimming back. She was going to say something else. Beryl felt that she was being poisoned by this cold woman, but she longed to hear. But oh, how strange, how horrible! As Mrs Harry Kember came up close she looked, in her black waterproof bathing-cap, with her sleepy face lifted above the water, just her chin touching, like a horrible caricature of her husband.

VI

In a steamer chair, under a manuka tree that grew in the middle of the front grass patch, Linda Burnell dreamed the morning away. She did nothing. She looked up at the dark, close, dry leaves of the manuka, at the chinks of blue between, and now and again a tiny yellowish flower dropped on her. Pretty – yes, if you held one of those flowers on the palm of your hand and looked at it closely, it was an exquisite small thing. Each pale yellow petal shone as if each was the careful work of a loving hand. The tiny tongue in the centre gave it the shape of a bell. And when you turned it over the outside was a deep bronze colour. But as soon as they flowered, they fell and were scattered. You brushed them off your frock as you talked; the horrid little things got caught in one's hair. Why, then, flower at all? Who takes the trouble – or the joy – to make all these things that are wasted, wasted … It was uncanny.

On the grass beside her, lying between two pillows, was the boy. Sound asleep he lay, his head turned away from his mother. His fine dark hair looked more like a shadow than like real hair, but his ear was a bright, deep coral. Linda clasped her hands above her head and crossed her feet. It was very pleasant to know that all these bungalows were empty, that everybody was down on the beach, out of sight, out of hearing. She had the garden to herself; she was alone.

Dazzling white the picotees shone; the golden-eyed marigold glittered; the nasturtiums wreathed the veranda poles in green and gold flame. If only one had time to look at these flowers long enough, time to get over the sense of novelty and strangeness, time to know them! But as soon as one paused to part the petals, to discover the under-side of the leaf, along came Life and one was swept away. And, lying in her cane chair, Linda felt so light; she felt like a leaf. Along came Life like a wind and she was seized and shaken; she had to go. Oh dear, would it always be so? Was there no escape?

... Now she sat on the veranda of their Tasmanian home, leaning against her father's knee. And he promised, 'As soon as you and I are old enough, Linny, we'll cut off somewhere, we'll escape. Two boys together. I have a fancy I'd like to sail up a river in China.' Linda saw that river, very wide, covered with little rafts and boats. She saw the yellow hats of the boatmen and she heard their high, thin voices as they called ...

'Yes, Papa.'

But just then a very broad young man with bright ginger hair walked slowly past their house, and slowly, solemnly even, uncovered. Linda's father pulled her ear teasingly, in the way he had.

'Linny's beau,' he whispered.

'Oh, Papa, fancy being married to Stanley Burnell!'

Well, she was married to him. And what was more she loved him. Not the Stanley whom every one saw, not the everyday one; but a timid, sensitive, innocent Stanley who knelt down every night to say his prayers, and who longed to be good. Stanley was simple. If he believed in people – as he believed in her, for instance – it was with his whole heart. He could not be disloyal; he could not tell a lie. And how terribly he suffered if he thought any one – she – was not being dead straight, dead sincere with him! 'This is too subtle for me!' He flung out the words, but his open, quivering, distraught look was like the look of a trapped beast.

But the trouble was – here Linda felt almost inclined to laugh, though heaven knows it was no laughing matter – she saw her Stanley so seldom. There were glimpses, moments, breathing spaces of calm, but all the rest of the time it was like living in a house that couldn't be cured of the habit of catching on fire, on a ship that got wrecked every day. And it was always Stanley who was in the thick of the danger. Her whole time was spent in rescuing him, and restoring him, and calming him down, and listening to his story. And what was left of her time was spent in the dread of having children.

Linda frowned; she sat up quickly in her steamer chair and clasped her ankles. Yes, that was her real grudge against life; that was what she could not understand. That was the question she asked and asked, and listened in vain for the answer. It was all very well to say it was the common lot of women to bear children. It wasn't true. She, for one, could prove that wrong. She was broken, made weak, her courage was gone, through child-bearing. And what made it doubly hard to bear was, she did not love her children. It was useless pretending. Even if she had had the strength she never would have nursed and played with the little girls. No, it was as though a cold breath had chilled her through and through on each of those awful journeys; she had no warmth left to give them. As to the boy – well, thank Heaven, mother had taken him; he was mother's, or Beryl's, or anybody's who wanted him. She had hardly held him in her arms. She was so indifferent about him that as he lay there ... Linda glanced down.

The boy had turned over. He lay facing her, and he was no longer asleep. His dark-blue, baby eyes were open; he looked as though he was peeping at his mother. And suddenly his face dimpled; it broke into a wide, toothless smile, a perfect beam, no less.

'I'm here!' that happy smile seemed to say. 'Why don't you like me?'

There was something so quaint, so unexpected about that smile that Linda smiled herself. But she checked herself and said to the boy coldly, 'I don't like babies.'

'Don't like babies?' The boy couldn't believe her. 'Don't like me?' He waved his arms foolishly at his mother.

Linda dropped off her chair on to the grass.

'Why do you keep on smiling?' she said severely. 'If you knew what I was thinking about, you wouldn't.'

But he only squeezed up his eyes, slyly, and rolled his head on the pillow.

He didn't believe a word she said.

'We know all about that!' smiled the boy.

Linda was so astonished at the confidence of this little creature … Ah no, be sincere. That was not what she felt; it was something far different, it was something so new, so … the tears danced in her eyes; she breathed in a small whisper to the boy, 'Hallo, my funny!'

But by now the boy had forgotten his mother. He was serious again. Something pink, something soft waved in front of him. He made a grab at it and it immediately disappeared. But when he lay back, another, like the first, appeared. This time he determined to catch it. He made a tremendous effort and rolled right over.

VII

The tide was out; the beach was deserted; lazily flopped the warm sea. The sun beat down, beat down hot and fiery on the fine sand, baking the grey and blue and black and white-veined pebbles. It sucked up the little drop of water that lay in the hollow of the curved shells; it bleached the pink convolvulus that threaded through and through the sand-hills. Nothing seemed to move but the small sand-hoppers. Pit-pit-pit! They were never still.

Over there on the weed-hung rocks that looked at low tide like shaggy beasts come down to the water to drink, the sunlight seemed to spin like a silver coin dropped into each of the small rock pools. They danced, they quivered, and minute ripples laved the porous shores. Looking down, bending over, each pool was like a lake with pink and blue houses clustered on the shores; and oh! the vast mountainous country behind those houses – the ravines, the passes, the dangerous creeks and fearful tracks that led to the water's edge. Underneath waved the sea-forest – pink thread-like trees, velvet anemones, and orange berry-spotted weeds. Now a stone on the bottom moved, rocked, and there was a glimpse of a black feeler; now a thread-like creature wavered by and was lost. Something was happening to the pink, waving trees; they were changing to a cold moonlight blue. And now there sounded the faintest 'plop'. Who made that sound? What was going on down there? And how strong, how damp the seaweed smelt in the hot sun ...

The green blinds were drawn in the bungalows of the summer colony. Over the verandas, prone on the paddock, flung over the fences, there were exhausted-looking bathing-dresses and rough striped towels. Each back window seemed to have a pair of sand-shoes on the sill and some lumps of rock or a bucket or a collection of pawa shells. The bush quivered in a haze of heat; the sandy road was empty except for the Trouts' dog Snooker, who lay stretched in the very middle of it. His blue eye was turned up, his legs stuck out stiffly, and he gave an occasional desperate-sounding puff, as much as to say he had decided to make an end of it and was only waiting for some kind cart to come along.

'What are you looking at, my grandma? Why do you keep stopping and sort of staring at the wall?'

Kezia and her grandmother were taking their siesta together. The little girl, wearing only her short drawers and her under-bodice, her arms and legs bare, lay on one of the puffed-up pillows of her grandma's bed, and the old woman, in a white ruffled dressing-gown, sat in a rocker at the window, with a long piece of pink knitting in her lap. This room that they shared, like the other rooms of the bungalow, was of light varnished wood and the floor was bare. The furniture was of the shabbiest, the simplest. The dressing-table, for instance, was a packing-case in a sprigged muslin petticoat, and the mirror above was very strange; it was as though a little piece of forked lightning was imprisoned in it. On the table there stood a jar of sea-pinks, pressed so tightly together they looked more like a velvet pincushion, and a special shell which Kezia had given her grandma for a pin-tray, and another even more special which she had thought would make a very nice place for a watch to curl up in.

'Tell me, grandma,' said Kezia.

The old woman sighed, whipped the wool twice round her thumb, and drew the bone needle through. She was casting on.

'I was thinking of your Uncle William, darling,' she said quietly.

'My Australian Uncle William?' said Kezia. She had another.

'Yes, of course.'

'The one I never saw?'

'That was the one.'

'Well, what happened to him?' Kezia knew perfectly well, but she wanted to be told again.

'He went to the mines, and he got a sunstroke there and died,' said old Mrs. Fairfield.

Kezia blinked and considered the picture again … a little man fallen over like a tin soldier by the side of a big black hole.

'Does it make you sad to think about him, grandma?' She hated her grandma to be sad.

It was the old woman's turn to consider. Did it make her sad? To look back, back. To stare down the years, as Kezia had seen her doing. To look after them as a woman does, long after they were out of sight. Did it make her sad? No, life was like that.

'No, Kezia.'

'But why?' asked Kezia. She lifted one bare arm and began to draw things in the air.

'Why did Uncle William have to die? He wasn't old.'

Mrs. Fairfield began counting the stitches in threes. 'It just happened,' she said in an absorbed voice.

'Does everybody have to die?' asked Kezia.

'Everybody!'

'*Me*?' Kezia sounded fearfully incredulous.

'Some day, my darling.'

'But, grandma.' Kezia waved her left leg and waggled the toes. They felt sandy. 'What if I just won't?'

The old woman sighed again and drew a long thread from the ball.

'We're not asked, Kezia,' she said sadly. 'It happens to all of us sooner or later.'

Kezia lay still thinking this over. She didn't want to die. It meant she would have to leave here, leave everywhere, for ever, leave – leave her grandma. She rolled over quickly.

'Grandma,' she said in a startled voice.

'What, my pet!'

'*You're* not to die.' Kezia was very decided.

'Ah, Kezia' – her grandma looked up and smiled and shook her head – ' don't let's talk about it.'

'But you're not to. You couldn't leave me. You couldn't not be there.'

This was awful. 'Promise me you won't ever do it, grandma,' pleaded Kezia.

The old woman went on knitting.

'Promise me! Say never!'

But still her grandma was silent.

Kezia rolled off her bed; she couldn't bear it any longer, and lightly she leapt on to her grandma's knees, clasped her hands round the old woman's throat and began kissing her, under the chin, behind the ear, and blowing down her neck.

'Say never...say never...say never –' She gasped between the kisses. And then she began, very softly and lightly, to tickle her grandma.

'Kezia!' The old woman dropped her knitting. She swung back in the rocker. She began to tickle Kezia. 'Say never, say never, say never,' gurgled Kezia, while they lay there laughing in each other's arms. 'Come, that's enough, my squirrel! That's enough, my wild pony!' said old Mrs. Fairfield, setting her cap straight. 'Pick up my knitting.'

Both of them had forgotten what the 'never' was about.

VIII

The sun was still full on the garden when the back door of the Burnells' shut with a bang, and a very gay figure walked down the path to the gate. It was Alice, the servant-girl, dressed for her afternoon out. She wore a white cotton dress with such large red spots on it and so many that they made you shudder, white shoes and a leghorn turned up under the brim with poppies. Of course she wore gloves, white ones, stained at the fastenings with iron-mould, and in one hand she carried a very dashed-looking sunshade which she referred to as her *perishall.*

Beryl, sitting in the window, fanning her freshly-washed hair, thought she had never seen such a guy. If Alice had only blacked her face with a piece of cork before she started out, the picture would have been complete. And where did a girl like that go to in a place like this? The heart-shaped Fijian fan beat scornfully at that lovely bright mane. She supposed Alice had picked up some horrible common larrikin and they'd go off into the bush together. Pity to have made herself so conspicuous; they'd have hard work to hide with Alice in that rig-out.

But no, Beryl was unfair. Alice was going to tea with Mrs Stubbs, who'd sent her an 'invite' by the little boy who called for orders. She had taken ever such a liking to Mrs. Stubbs ever since the first time she went to the shop to get something for her mosquitoes.

'Dear heart!' Mrs. Stubbs had clapped her hand to her side. 'I never seen anyone so eaten. You might have been attacked by canningbals.'

Alice did wish there'd been a bit of life on the road though. Made her feel so queer, having nobody behind her. Made her feel all weak in the spine.

She couldn't believe that someone wasn't watching her. And yet it was silly to turn round; it gave you away. She pulled up her gloves, hummed to herself and said to the distant gum-tree, 'Shan't be long now.' But that was hardly company.

Mrs. Stubbs's shop was perched on a little hillock just off the road. It had two big windows for eyes, a broad veranda for a hat, and the sign on the roof, scrawled MRS. STUBBS'S, was like a little card stuck rakishly in the hat crown.

On the veranda there hung a long string of bathing-dresses, clinging together as though they'd just been rescued from the sea rather than waiting to go in, and beside them there hung a cluster of sand-shoes so extraordinarily mixed that to get at one pair you had to tear apart and forcibly separate at least fifty. Even then it was the rarest thing to find the left that belonged to the right. So many people had lost patience and gone off with one shoe that fitted and one that was a little too big ... Mrs. Stubbs prided herself on keeping something of everything. The two windows, arranged in the form of precarious pyramids, were crammed so tight, piled so high, that it seemed only a conjurer could prevent them from toppling over. In the left-hand corner of one window, glued to the pane by four gelatine lozenges, there was – and there had been from time immemorial – a notice:

LOST! HANSOME GOLE BROOCH
SOLID GOLD
ON OR NEAR BEACH
REWARD OFFERED

Alice pressed open the door. The bell jangled, the red serge curtains parted, and Mrs. Stubbs appeared. With her broad smile and the long bacon knife in her hand, she looked like a friendly brigand. Alice was welcomed so warmly that she found it quite difficult to keep up her 'manners.' They consisted of persistent little coughs and hems, pulls at her gloves, tweaks at her skirt, and a curious difficulty in seeing what was set before her or understanding what was said.

Tea was laid on the parlour table – ham, sardines, a whole pound of butter, and such a large johnny cake that it looked like an advertisement for somebody's baking-powder. But the Primus stove roared so loudly that it was useless to try to talk above it. Alice sat down on the edge of a basket-chair while Mrs. Stubbs pumped the stove still higher. Suddenly Mrs. Stubbs whipped the cushion off a chair and disclosed a large brown-paper parcel.

'I've just had some new photers taken, my dear,' she shouted cheerfully to Alice. 'Tell me what you think of them.'

In a very dainty, refined way Alice wet her finger and put the tissue back from the first one. Life! How many there were! There were three dozzing at least. And she held it up to the light.

Mrs. Stubbs sat in an arm-chair, leaning very much to one side. There was a look of mild astonishment on her large face, and well there might be. For though the arm-chair stood on a carpet, to the left of it, miraculously skirting the carpet-border, there was a dashing water-fall. On her right stood a Grecian pillar with a giant fern-tree on either side of it, and in the background towered a gaunt mountain, pale with snow.

'It is a nice style, isn't it?' shouted Mrs. Stubbs; and Alice had just screamed 'Sweetly' when the roaring of the Primus stove died down, fizzled out, ceased, and she said 'Pretty' in a silence that was frightening.

'Draw up your chair, my dear,' said Mrs. Stubbs, beginning to pour out. 'Yes,' she said thoughtfully, as she handed the tea, 'but I don't care about the size. I'm having an enlargemint. All very well for Christmas cards, but I never was the one for small photers myself. You get no comfort out of them. To say the truth, I find them dis'eartening.'

Alice quite saw what she meant.

'Size,' said Mrs. Stubbs. 'Give me size. That was what my poor dear husband was always saying. He couldn't stand anything small. Gave him the creeps. And, strange as it may seem, my dear' – here Mrs. Stubbs creaked and seemed to expand herself at the memory – 'it was dropsy that carried him off at the larst. Many's the time they drawn one and a half pints from 'im at the 'ospital...It seemed like a judgmint.'

Alice burned to know exactly what it was that was drawn from him. She ventured, 'I suppose it was water.'

But Mrs. Stubbs fixed Alice with her eyes and replied meaningly, 'It was liquid, my dear.'

Liquid! Alice jumped away from the word like a cat and came back to it, nosing and wary.

'That's 'im!' said Mrs. Stubbs, and she pointed dramatically to the life-size head and shoulders of a burly man with a dead white rose in the buttonhole of his coat that made you think of a curl of cold mutting fat. Just below, in silver letters on a red cardboard ground, were the words, 'Be not afraid, it is I.'

'It's ever such a fine face,' said Alice faintly.

The pale-blue bow on the top of Mrs. Stubbs's fair frizzy hair quivered. She arched her plump neck. What a neck she had! It was bright pink where it began and then it changed to warm apricot, and that faded to the colour of a brown egg and then to a deep creamy.

'All the same, my dear,' she said surprisingly, 'freedom's best!' Her soft, fat chuckle sounded like a purr. 'Freedom's best,' said Mrs. Stubbs again.

Freedom! Alice gave a loud, silly little titter. She felt awkward. Her mind flew back to her own kitching. Ever so queer! She wanted to be back in it again.

IX

A strange company assembled in the Burnells' washhouse after tea. Round the table there sat a bull, a rooster, a donkey that kept forgetting it was a donkey, a sheep and a bee. The washhouse was the perfect place for such a meeting because they could make as much noise as they liked, and nobody ever interrupted. It was a small tin shed standing apart from the bungalow. Against the wall there was a deep trough and in the corner a copper with a basket of clothes-pegs on top of it. The little window, spun over with cobwebs, had a piece of candle and a mouse-trap on the dusty sill. There were clotheslines criss-crossed overhead and, hanging from a peg on the wall, a very big, a huge, rusty horseshoe. The table was in the middle with a form at either side.

'You can't be a bee, Kezia. A bee's not an animal. It's a ninseck.'

'Oh, but I do want to be a bee frightfully,' wailed Kezia… A tiny bee, all yellow-furry, with striped legs. She drew her legs up under her and leaned over the table. She felt she was a bee.

'A ninseck must be an animal,' she said stoutly. 'It makes a noise. It's not like a fish.'

'I'm a bull, I'm a bull!' cried Pip. And he gave such a tremendous bellow – how did he make that noise? – that Lottie looked quite alarmed.

'I'll be a sheep,' said little Rags. 'A whole lot of sheep went past this morning.'

'How do you know?'

'Dad heard them. Baa!' He sounded like the little lamb that trots behind and seems to wait to be carried.

'Cock-a-doodle-do!' shrilled Isabel. With her red cheeks and bright eyes she looked like a rooster.

'What'll I be?' Lottie asked everybody, and she sat there smiling, waiting for them to decide for her. It had to be an easy one.

'Be a donkey, Lottie.' It was Kezia's suggestion. 'Hee-haw! You can't forget that.'

'Hee-haw!' said Lottie solemnly. 'When do I have to say it?'

'I'll explain, I'll explain,' said the bull. It was he who had the cards. He waved them round his head. 'All be quiet! All listen!' And he waited for them. 'Look here, Lottie.' He turned up a card. 'It's got two spots on it – see? Now, if you put that card in the middle and somebody else has one with two spots as well, you say 'Hee-haw,' and the card's yours.'

'Mine?' Lottie was round-eyed. 'To keep?'

'No, silly. Just for the game, see? Just while we're playing.' The bull was very cross with her.

'Oh, Lottie, you *are* a little silly,' said the proud rooster.

Lottie looked at both of them. Then she hung her head; her lip quivered. 'I don't not want to play,' she whispered. The others glanced at one another like conspirators. All of them knew what that meant. She would go away and be discovered somewhere standing with her pinny thrown over her head, in a corner, or against a wall, or even behind a chair.

'Yes, you *do*, Lottie. It's quite easy,' said Kezia.

And Isabel, repentant, said exactly like a grown-up, 'Watch me, Lottie, and you'll soon learn.'

'Cheer up, Lot,' said Pip. 'There, I know what I'll do. I'll give you the first one. It's mine, really, but I'll give it to you. Here you are.' And he slammed the card down in front of Lottie.

Lottie revived at that. But now she was in another difficulty. 'I haven't got a hanky,' she said; 'I want one badly, too.'

'Here, Lottie, you can use mine.' Rags dipped into his sailor blouse and brought up a very wet-looking one, knotted together. 'Be very careful,' he warned her. 'Only use that corner. Don't undo it. I've got a little starfish inside I'm going to try and tame.'

'Oh, come on, you girls,' said the bull. 'And mind – you're not to look at your cards. You've got to keep your hands under the table till I say "Go."'

Smack went the cards round the table. They tried with all their might to see, but Pip was too quick for them. It was very exciting, sitting there in the washhouse; it was all they could do not to burst into a little chorus of animals before Pip had finished dealing.

'Now, Lottie, you begin.'

Timidly Lottie stretched out a hand, took the top card off her pack, had a good look at it – it was plain she was counting the spots – and put it down.

'No, Lottie, you can't do that. You mustn't look first. You must turn it the other way over.'

'But then everybody will see it the same time as me,' said Lottie.

The game proceeded. Mooe-ooo-er! The bull was terrible. He charged over the table and seemed to eat the cards up.

Bss-ss! said the bee.

Cock-a-doodle-do! Isabel stood up in her excitement and moved her elbows like wings.

Baa! Little Rags put down the King of Diamonds and Lottie put down the one they called the King of Spain. She had hardly any cards left.

'Why don't you call out, Lottie?'

'I've forgotten what I am,' said the donkey woefully.

'Well, change! Be a dog instead! Bow-wow!'

'Oh yes. That's much easier.' Lottie smiled again. But when she and Kezia both had a one Kezia waited on purpose. The others made signs to Lottie and pointed. Lottie turned very red; she looked bewildered, and at last she said, 'Hee-haw! Ke-zia.'

'Ss! Wait a minute!' They were in the very thick of it when the bull stopped them, holding up his hand. 'What's that? What's that noise?'

'What noise? What do you mean?' asked the rooster.

'Ss! Shut up! Listen!' They were mouse-still. 'I thought I heard a – a sort of knocking,' said the bull.

'What was it like?' asked the sheep faintly.

No answer.

The bee gave a shudder. 'Whatever did we shut the door for?' she said softly. Oh, why, why had they shut the door?

While they were playing, the day had faded; the gorgeous sunset had blazed and died. And now the quick dark came racing over the sea, over the sand-hills, up the paddock. You were frightened to look in the corners of the washhouse, and yet you had to look with all your might. And somewhere, far away, grandma was lighting a lamp. The blinds were being pulled down; the kitchen fire leapt in the tins on the mantelpiece.

'It would be awful now,' said the bull, 'if a spider was to fall from the ceiling on to the table, wouldn't it?'

'Spiders don't fall from ceilings.'

'Yes, they do. Our Min told us she'd seen a spider as big as a saucer, with long hairs on it like a gooseberry.'

Quickly all the little heads were jerked up; all the little bodies drew together, pressed together.

'Why doesn't somebody come and call us?' cried the rooster.

Oh, those grown-ups, laughing and snug, sitting in the lamp-light, drinking out of cups! They'd forgotten about them. No, not really forgotten. That was what their smile meant. They had decided to leave them there all by themselves.

Suddenly Lottie gave such a piercing scream that all of them jumped off the forms, all of them screamed too. 'A face – a face looking!' shrieked Lottie.

It was true, it was real. Pressed against the window was a pale face, black eyes, a black beard.

'Grandma! Mother! Somebody!'

But they had not got to the door, tumbling over one another, before it opened for Uncle Jonathan. He had come to take the little boys home.

X

He had meant to be there before, but in the front garden he had come upon Linda walking up and down the grass, stopping to pick off a dead pink or give a top-heavy carnation something to lean against, or to take a deep breath of something, and then walking on again, with her little air of remoteness. Over her white frock she wore a yellow, pink-fringed shawl from the Chinaman's shop.

'Hallo, Jonathan!' called Linda. And Jonathan whipped off his shabby panama, pressed it against his breast, dropped on one knee, and kissed Linda's hand.

'Greeting, my Fair One! Greeting, my Celestial Peach Blossom!' boomed the bass voice gently. 'Where are the other noble dames?'

'Beryl's out playing bridge and mother's giving the boy his bath ... Have you come to borrow something?'

The Trouts were for ever running out of things and sending across to the Burnells' at the last moment.

But Jonathan only answered, 'A little love, a little kindness'; and he walked by his sister-in-law's side.

Linda dropped into Beryl's hammock under the manuka tree, and Jonathan stretched himself on the grass beside her, pulled a long stalk and began chewing it. They knew each other well. The voices of children cried from the other gardens. A fisherman's light cart shook along the sandy road, and from far away they heard a dog barking; it was muffled as though the dog had its head in a sack. If you listened you could just hear the soft swish of the sea at full tide sweeping the pebbles. The sun was sinking.

'And so you go back to the office on Monday, do you, Jonathan?' asked Linda.

'On Monday the cage door opens and clangs to upon the victim for another eleven months and a week,' answered Jonathan.

Linda swung a little. 'It must be awful,' she said slowly.

'Would ye have me laugh, my fair sister? Would ye have me weep?'

Linda was so accustomed to Jonathan's way of talking that she paid no attention to it.

'I suppose,' she said vaguely, 'one gets used to it. One gets used to anything.'

'Does one? Hum!' The 'Hum' was so deep it seemed to boom from underneath the ground. 'I wonder how it's done,' brooded Jonathan; 'I've never managed it.'

Looking at him as he lay there, Linda thought again how attractive he was. It was strange to think that he was only an ordinary clerk, that Stanley earned twice as much money as he. What was the matter with Jonathan? He had no ambition; she supposed that was it. And yet one felt he was gifted, exceptional. He was passionately fond of music; every spare penny he had went on books. He was always full of new ideas, schemes, plans. But nothing came of it all. The new fire blazed in Jonathan; you almost heard it roaring softly as he explained, described and dilated on the new thing; but a moment later it had fallen in and there was nothing but ashes, and Jonathan went about with a look like hunger in his black eyes. At these times he exaggerated his absurd manner of speaking, and he sang in church – he was the leader of the choir – with such fearful dramatic intensity that the meanest hymn put on an unholy splendour.

'It seems to me just as imbecile, just as infernal, to have to go to the office on Monday,' said Jonathan, 'as it always has done and always will do. To spend all the best years of one's life sitting on a stool from nine to five, scratching in somebody's ledger! It's a queer use to make of one's … one and only life, isn't it? Or do I fondly dream?' He rolled over on the grass and looked up at Linda. 'Tell me, what is the difference between my life and that of an ordinary prisoner. The only difference I can see is that I put myself in jail and nobody's ever going to let me out. That's a more intolerable situation than the other. For if I'd been – pushed in, against my will – kicking, even – once the door was locked, or at any rate in five years or so, I might have accepted the fact and begun to take an interest in the flight of flies or counting the warder's steps along the passage with particular attention to variations of tread and so on. But as it is, I'm like an insect that's flown into a room of its own accord. I dash against the walls, dash against the windows, flop against the ceiling, do everything on God's earth, in fact, except fly out again. And all the while I'm thinking, like that moth, or that butterfly, or whatever it is, 'The shortness of life! The shortness of life!' I've only one night or one day, and there's this vast dangerous garden, waiting out there, undiscovered, unexplored.'

'But, if you feel like that, why – ' began Linda quickly.

'*Ah*!' cried Jonathan. And that 'ah!' was somehow almost exultant. 'There you have me. Why? Why indeed? There's the maddening, mysterious question. Why don't I fly out again? There's the window or the door or whatever it was I came in by. It's not hopelessly shut – is it? Why don't I find it and be off? Answer me that, little sister.' But he gave her no time to answer.

'I'm exactly like that insect again. For some reason' – Jonathan paused between the words – 'it's not allowed, it's forbidden, it's against the insect law, to stop banging and flopping and crawling up the pane even for an instant. Why don't I leave the office? Why don't I seriously consider, this moment, for instance, what it is that prevents me leaving? It's not as though I'm tremendously tied. I've two boys to provide for, but, after all, they're boys. I could cut off to sea, or get a job up-country, or – ' Suddenly he smiled at Linda and said in a changed voice, as if he were confiding a secret, 'Weak... weak. No stamina. No anchor. No guiding principle, let us call it.' But then the dark velvety voice rolled out:

'Would ye hear the story
How it unfolds itself ...'

and they were silent.

The sun had set. In the western sky there were great masses of crushed-up rose-coloured clouds. Broad beams of light shone through the clouds and beyond them as if they would cover the whole sky. Overhead the blue faded; it turned a pale gold, and the bush outlined against it gleamed dark and brilliant like metal. Sometimes when those beams of light show in the sky they are very awful. They remind you that up there sits Jehovah, the jealous God, the Almighty, Whose eye is upon you, ever watchful, never weary. You remember that at His coming the whole earth will shake into one ruined graveyard; the cold, bright angels will drive you this way and that, and there will be no time to explain what could be explained so simply ... But to-night it seemed to Linda there was something infinitely joyful and loving in those silver beams. And now no sound came from the sea. It breathed softly as if it would draw that tender, joyful beauty into its own bosom.

'It's all wrong, it's all wrong,' came the shadowy voice of Jonathan. 'It's not the scene, it's not the setting for ... three stools, three desks, three inkpots and a wire blind.'

Linda knew that he would never change, but she said, 'Is it too late, even now?'

'I'm old – I'm old,' intoned Jonathan. He bent towards her, he passed his hand over his head. 'Look!' His black hair was speckled all over with silver, like the breast plumage of a black fowl.

Linda was surprised. She had no idea that he was grey. And yet, as he stood up beside her and sighed and stretched, she saw him, for the first time, not resolute, not gallant, not careless, but touched already with age. He looked very tall on the darkening grass, and the thought crossed her mind, 'He is like a weed.'

Jonathan stooped again and kissed her fingers.

'Heaven reward thy sweet patience, lady mine,' he murmured. 'I must go seek those heirs to my fame and fortune ...' He was gone.

XI

Light shone in the windows of the bungalow. Two square patches of gold fell upon the pinks and the peaked marigolds. Florrie, the cat, came out on to the veranda, and sat on the top step, her white paws close together, her tail curled round. She looked content, as though she had been waiting for this moment all day.

'Thank goodness, it's getting late,' said Florrie. 'Thank goodness, the long day is over.' Her greengage eyes opened.

Presently there sounded the rumble of the coach, the crack of Kelly's whip. It came near enough for one to hear the voices of the men from town, talking loudly together. It stopped at the Burnells' gate.

Stanley was half-way up the path before he saw Linda. 'Is that you, darling?'

'Yes, Stanley.'

He leapt across the flower-bed and seized her in his arms. She was enfolded in that familiar, eager, strong embrace.

'Forgive me, darling, forgive me,' stammered Stanley, and he put his hand under her chin and lifted her face to him.

'Forgive you?' smiled Linda. 'But whatever for?'

'Good God! You can't have forgotten,' cried Stanley Burnell. 'I've thought of nothing else all day. I've had the hell of a day. I made up my mind to dash out and telegraph, and then I thought the wire mightn't reach you before I did. I've been in tortures, Linda.'

'But, Stanley,' said Linda, 'what must I forgive you for?'

'Linda!' – Stanley was very hurt – 'didn't you realize – you must have realized – I went away without saying good-bye to you this morning? I can't imagine how I can have done such a thing. My confounded temper, of course. But – well' – and he sighed and took her in his arms again – 'I've suffered for it enough to-day.'

'What's that you've got in your hand?' asked Linda. 'New gloves? Let me see.'

'Oh, just a cheap pair of wash-leather ones,' said Stanley humbly. 'I noticed Bell was wearing some in the coach this morning, so, as I was passing the shop, I dashed in and got myself a pair. What are you smiling at? You don't think it was wrong of me, do you?'

'On the con-trary, darling,' said Linda, 'I think it was most sensible.'

She pulled one of the large, pale gloves on her own fingers and looked at her hand, turning it this way and that. She was still smiling.

Stanley wanted to say, 'I was thinking of you the whole time I bought them.' It was true, but for some reason he couldn't say it. 'Let's go in,' said he.

XII

Why does one feel so different at night? Why is it so exciting to be awake when everybody else is asleep? Late – it is very late! And yet every moment you feel more and more wakeful, as though you were slowly, almost with every breath, waking up into a new, wonderful, far more thrilling and exciting world than the daylight one. And what is this queer sensation that you're a conspirator? Lightly, stealthily you move about your room. You take something off the dressing-table and put it down again without a sound. And everything, even the bed-post, knows you, responds, shares your secret ...

You're not very fond of your room by day. You never think about it. You're in and out, the door opens and slams, the cupboard creaks. You sit down on the side of your bed, change your shoes and dash out again. A dive down to the glass, two pins in your hair, powder your nose and off again. But now – it's suddenly dear to you. It's a darling little funny room. It's yours. Oh, what a joy it is to own things! Mine – my own!

'My very own for ever?'

'Yes.' Their lips met.

No, of course, that had nothing to do with it. That was all nonsense and rubbish. But, in spite of herself, Beryl saw so plainly two people standing in the middle of her room. Her arms were round his neck; he held her. And now he whispered, 'My beauty, my little beauty!' She jumped off her bed, ran over to the window and kneeled on the window-seat, with her elbows on the sill. But the beautiful night, the garden, every bush, every leaf, even the white palings, even the stars, were conspirators too. So bright was the moon that the flowers were bright as by day; the shadow of the nasturtiums, exquisite lily-like leaves and wide-open flowers, lay across the silvery veranda. The manuka tree, bent by the southerly winds, was like a bird on one leg stretching out a wing.

But when Beryl looked at the bush, it seemed to her the bush was sad.

'We are dumb trees, reaching up in the night, imploring we know not what,' said the sorrowful bush.

It is true when you are by yourself and you think about life, it is always sad. All that excitement and so on has a way of suddenly leaving you, and it's as though, in the silence, somebody called your name, and you heard your name for the first time. 'Beryl!'

'Yes, I'm here. I'm Beryl. Who wants me?'

'Beryl!'

'Let me come.'

It is lonely living by oneself. Of course, there are relations, friends, heaps of them; but that's not what she means. She wants some one who will find the Beryl they none of them know, who will expect her to be that Beryl always. She wants a lover.

'Take me away from all these other people, my love. Let us go far away. Let us live our life, all new, all ours, from the very beginning. Let us make our fire. Let us sit down to eat together. Let us have long talks at night.'

And the thought was almost, 'Save me, my love. Save me!'

'Oh, go on! Don't be a prude, my dear. You enjoy yourself while you're young. That's my advice.' And a high rush of silly laughter joined Mrs Harry Kember's loud, indifferent neigh.

You see, it's so frightfully difficult when you've nobody. You're so at the mercy of things. You can't just be rude. And you've always this horror of seeming inexperienced and stuffy like the other ninnies at the Bay. And – and it's fascinating to know you've power over people. Yes, that is fascinating ... Oh why, oh why doesn't 'he' come soon?

If I go on living here, thought Beryl, anything may happen to me.

'But how do you know he is coming at all?' mocked a small voice within her.

But Beryl dismissed it. She couldn't be left. Other people, perhaps, but not she. It wasn't possible to think that Beryl Fairfield never married, that lovely fascinating girl.

'Do you remember Beryl Fairfield?'

'Remember her! As if I could forget her! It was one summer at the Bay that I saw her.

She was standing on the beach in a blue – no, pink – muslin frock, holding on a big cream' – no, black – 'straw hat. But it's years ago now.'

'She's as lovely as ever, more so if anything.'

Beryl smiled, bit her lip, and gazed over the garden. As she gazed, she saw somebody, a man, leave the road, step along the paddock beside their palings as if he was coming straight towards her. Her heart beat. Who was it?

Who could it be? It couldn't be a burglar, certainly not a burglar, for he was smoking and he strolled lightly. Beryl's heart leapt; it seemed to turn right over, and then to stop. She recognized him.

'Good evening, Miss Beryl,' said the voice softly.

'Good evening.'

'Won't you come for a little walk?' it drawled.

Come for a walk – at that time of night! 'I couldn't. Everybody's in bed. Everybody's asleep.'

'Oh,' said the voice lightly, and a whiff of sweet smoke reached her. 'What does everybody matter? Do come! It's such a fine night. There's not a soul about.'

Beryl shook her head. But already something stirred in her, something reared its head.

The voice said, 'Frightened?' It mocked, 'Poor little girl!'

'Not in the least,' said she. As she spoke that weak thing within her seemed to uncoil, to grow suddenly tremendously strong; she longed to go!

And just as if this was quite understood by the other, the voice said, gently and softly, but finally, 'Come along!'

Beryl stepped over her low window, crossed the veranda, ran down the grass to the gate. He was there before her.

'That's right,' breathed the voice, and it teased, 'You're not frightened, are you? You're not frightened?'

She was; now she was here she was terrified, and it seemed to her everything was different. The moonlight stared and glittered; the shadows were like bars of iron. Her hand was taken.

'Not in the least,' she said lightly. 'Why should I be?'

Her hand was pulled gently, tugged. She held back.

'No, I'm not coming any farther,' said Beryl.

'Oh, rot!' Harry Kember didn't believe her. 'Come along! We'll just go as far as that fuchsia bush. Come along!'

The fuchsia bush was tall. It fell over the fence in a shower. There was a little pit of darkness beneath.

'No, really, I don't want to,' said Beryl.

For a moment Harry Kember didn't answer. Then he came close to her, turned to her, smiled and said quickly, 'Don't be silly! Don't be silly!'

His smile was something she'd never seen before. Was he drunk? That bright, blind, terrifying smile froze her with horror. What was she doing? How had she got here? the stern garden asked her as the gate pushed open, and quick as a cat Harry Kember came through and snatched her to him.

'Cold little devil! Cold little devil!' said the hateful voice.

But Beryl was strong. She slipped, ducked, wrenched free.

'You are vile, vile,' said she.

'Then why in God's name did you come?' stammered Harry Kember.

Nobody answered him.

XIII

A cloud, small, serene, floated across the moon. In that moment of darkness the sea sounded deep, troubled. Then the cloud sailed away, and the sound of the sea was a vague murmur, as though it waked out of a dark dream. All was still.

(from) The End of the Golden Weather

Bruce Mason

I invite you to join me in a voyage into the past, to that territory of the heart we call childhood. Consider, if you will, Te Parenga. A beach, three-quarters of a mile long, a hundred yards wide at low water. Rocks at either end: on the east, chunky and rounded, a squat promontory. The 'king' and 'queen' stand a few yards from the shore: two squashed rock pillars with steps cut into their sides for diving in the summer. At high water, the sea will cover more than half of them. The rocks on the west are shallow, spreading into a terraced reef, shelving far out to sea. Here there is no smoothness. The surface of these rock shelves is jagged, cutting and tearing at the bare foot, fretted away by the corrosive sea. The receding tide leaves deep pools here where sea anemones with fronts of red and black jelly wave coloured strings to entice the shrimps, and sometimes a lone starfish lies marooned, diminishing in the sun. Ahead, across a narrow channel, central to vision and imagination, Rangitoto, enormous, majestic, spread-eagled on the skyline like a sleeping whale, declining from a central cone to the water in two huge flanges, meeting the sea in a haze of blue and green. It guards Te Parenga from wind and tempest: it has a brooding splendour.

The beach is fringed with pohutukawa trees, single and stunted in the gardens, spreading and noble on the cliffs, and in the empty spaces by the foreshore. Tiny red coronets prick through the grey-green leaves. Bark, flower and leaf seem overlaid by smoke. The red is of a dying fire at dusk, the green faded and drab. Pain and age are in these gnarled forms, in bare roots, clutching at the earth, knotting on the cliff-face, in tortured branches, dark against the washed sky.

Beside this majesty, the houses of Te Parenga have a skimped look. A low ridge curls upwards from the beach, flattening to accept the concrete ribbon of the main road north, an intermittent rash of shops on its margins, then the ridge rolls on and down to the mud-flats and mangroves of the upper harbour. The houses of Te Parenga face the sea, unlovely bungalows of wood and tin, painted red and brown to thwart the rodent air. At the end of the beach, before the main road leaves it for ever a clot of buildings: shops, banks, the Council Chambers, the Anglican church in wooden Gothic, cheek by jowl with the cinema – built to last – in brick.

It's only a hundred years since men dressed as chimneys, in top hats and black stove-pipes, women dressed as great bells, tiny feet as clappers, stepped ashore at Te Parenga from a broad-bellied, wind-billowed ship. They brought with them grain and root, tilling and harvest; timber trees, fruit trees, flowers, shrubs, grass; sheep, cows, horses, deer, pigs, rabbits, fish, bees; language, law, custom, clocks and coinage; Queen Victoria and her views on Heaven and Earth; the Trinity; Santa Claus and the imagery of snow where no snow will ever fall at Christmas; a thousand years of history, a shoal of shibboleths, taboos and prohibitions and the memory of a six months' voyage. They threw them all together in a heap and stepped ashore to slash the bush, banish the natives and pray silently far into the night. They left some of the pohutukawas, and Rangitoto was beyond their reach.

This is Te Parenga: my heritage, my world.

Entanglements

(from *Under the Bridge and Over the Moon*)

Kevin Ireland

The lighter side of the Year of the Japanese [1942] didn't seem funny during the worst weeks of the invasion scare, but it didn't take long for at least some – including the children – to realise that we'd all gone more than slightly mad.

Who would ever forget that day that an assortment of soldiers and civilians arrived on Takapuna beach, with hundreds of rolls of barbed wire and great stacks of wooden stakes? In no time at all there was a formidable system of entanglements running right along the beach at the high-tide mark. There were also five or six concrete pillboxes with gunslits to allow rifles and Bren guns to cover the whole length of the sea front. Every so often a defile was left, presumably to allow concentrated fire, but more conveniently from our point of view, they made it possible for us to get through the barbed wire to go for a swim.

How these entanglements could ever have impeded a full-scale amphibious invasion was never explained. They ran only from the coastal defence battery at North Head to Milford beach – perhaps five or six kilometres in all. The long stretches of rocks were entirely undefended, as were most of the other thousands of kilometres of the New Zealand coastline. Those living in the seaside suburbs of Auckland city had been offered a visual palliative. They could look at the barbed wire and know that someone was doing something to make them feel safer. The whole thing could only have been done to raise civilian morale, for its practical value was nil.

Our schoolboy gangs took over the concrete pillboxes along Takapuna beach as soon as the Home Guard deserted them, and we used to squint through the gun slits and joke about the way even the Japanese would have had the brains to land on a nice long beach up the coast, such as Orewa or Waiwera, where there was no barbed wire and only a token force to confront them. After all, they'd managed to work that one out when they took Singapore.

We also used to fall about laughing at the way that, if the Japanese had really been mad enough to land on Takapuna beach, it would have taken them all day to form in ranks, answer a rollcall and pump up the tyres of their pushbikes, and by the time they got themselves organised to pedal down to Devonport wharf they would probably have found they'd missed the last ferry. And that meant they would have had to hang about looking silly, whistling, with their hands in their pockets, while they waited an hour for the first night launch to get them over to town, one platoon at a time.

The Tsunami

Owen Marshall

I remember it was the day of the tidal wave from Chile. 'A tsunami,' Peter had said yet again, angrily, as we stood by the bench at breakfast. 'Nothing to do with the tide, nothing at all. A tsunami's a shock wave.'

Yet there it was in the paper of the night before; all about the Chilean tidal wave and how it was expected to be up to twenty-five feet high, and might sweep right over low-lying areas. Peter was doing a third unit of geography, and he took it as an academic affront that even the newspaper talked about the tsunami as a tidal wave instead of a tsunami. Raf and I agreed, of course.

'A tsunami, right,' we said, but we still thought about it as the tidal wave. In all of us is the perversity to resist correction.

We had tacitly decided that the tidal wave would be a big thing in our day. This wasn't a compliment to Chile or the wave. As students we found almost every day some preoccupation to shield us from our studies. Even now I have a fellow feeling when I read of prisoners who tamed cockroaches, or devised whole new political systems in their heads to pass the time. Thoreau knew that most of mankind understand a prisoner's world.

The newspaper said that the wave was expected between noon and two p.m., and over the radio there were warnings to farmers and property owners to be prepared. It was a compelling notion: the great wave sweeping majestically across thousands of miles of ocean, to fall with thunderous devastation on our New Zealand. It quite captured the imagination of the city, and before midday the cars were streaming out to the coast.

We bought pies and a half-gallon jar of apple wine on our way to the estuary. 'A carafe, you mean,' said the pale man in the bottle store loftily. He still used hair cream and we mocked him as we went on.

'A carafe, you mean. Oh quite, quite.' We passed the half-gallon of apple wine from one to another, regarding it quizzically and twisting our faces to suggest the features of the pale, bottle store man.

By twelve-thirty the cars were parked in rows along the beach frontages, and their occupants belched comfortably and waited for something to happen. Many people were down on the beach, impatient for the tidal wave to come. Peter's logical mind was outraged. 'My god, look at these people,' he said. 'If the tsunami does come it'll kill thousands, thousands of them.' He gave a shrill laugh of exasperation and incredulity. But Raf and I were delighted: it accorded with the youthful cynicism we cultivated at the university. We drove up the hill and parked in a children's play area, with swings, see-saws, and a humpty-dumpty amongst the grass. We took our apple wine and round pies, and sat with humpty-dumpty on his wall, looking down over the houses on to the crowds along the estuary and beach. Raf stuck out his corduroy legs in delight at the unsought demonstration of human nature acted out before him.

'Look at them, Peter,' he kept saying, and drew further joy from the resentment with which Peter watched the crowd press forward for the tsunami.

Another car drove on to the playground, and a couple got out and stood with their backs supported by the grill, looking down upon the sea. Then the man wandered closer, and I recognised Leslie Foster. He sat on a swing with his hands hanging between his knees. He had a thin, Spanish face, with a beard to suit it, and his shoulders were slightly hunched in that typical way that I recalled from the years we were at school together. At school at the same time would be a better description. He and I had mutual friends, but we never found ease in each other's company. I never trusted his sneering humour, and he considered me something of a milksop I think. Yet at university we gave each other greater recognition, for there our common background, always taken for granted, was something of a link.

I went over and sat on the bleached wooden seat of the other swing. I stretched my legs to pass the puddle in the rut beneath. 'How are things?' I said. He turned his head and gave his quirking Spanish smile. 'I don't think that tidal wave's coming,' I said.

'Bloody tidal wave. Who needs it?' he said.

We talked idly for a time, but every topic seemed to release the same bitterness, and he didn't even pretend to listen to anything I said. He would screw up his eyes impatiently, and rock back on the swing. 'She wanted to come out here today,' he broke in. 'It wasn't my idea.' We both looked over at the woman still standing at the front of the car and staring out to sea. As if she realised she was the topic of our conversation, she glanced back at us, then came over towards the swings. Les introduced her grudgingly as Mrs Elizabeth Reid, his landlady.

'Nice to meet friends of Les,' she said. I wouldn't guess at her age, but she wasn't a girl. She had a lot of flesh on her upper arms and shoulders, and her hips swept out like a harp. 'I like a run in the car,' she said. 'Blows the cobwebs out and that; don't you think?' Les screwed up his eyes, and gave his mocking, lop-sided smile. 'I wanted to go down by the beach with everyone else, but Les wouldn't.' She paused and then said, 'It's late,' as if the tidal wave were a train or bus delayed by departmental inefficiency. 'It's a run out, though, isn't it? A chance to have a breather.' She had an unpleasant voice: ingratiating, but with a metallic edge.

'Yes. Chance to have a breather,' repeated Les, mocking the idiom, but she didn't seem to realise it. She went off to sit in the car out of the breeze, and have a cigarette. Les and I were left swaying on the worn seats of the playground swings. 'Chance to have a breather,' said Les again, with morose emphasis. 'Well, I suppose that's fair enough. You'd laugh if I told you what she's sprung on me today.' I didn't ask; I wasn't really interested in any of his confidences, but I knew he was going to tell me anyway. It was something to do with his loneliness I suppose; picking on me just because I was there and we had been to the same school. 'She's pregnant, the lovely lady. She told me on the way out.' He rocked back and forth, setting loose a distorted image in the water beneath the swing.

'You could get something done, I suppose.'

'Not easy,' he said, with a sneer at my vagueness, and the ignorance of facts which it revealed. 'Anyway, she feels that marriage is the best answer. She's divorced, but thinks in terms of marriage.' I made a feeble reply about how nice she seemed, and how things had a habit of working out. Les ignored it completely.

'I'll have to leave varsity. I can't see myself getting by in full-time study with her and a kid.'

'I suppose so.' It did seem a waste. Les was a clever student. Even at school he'd been a clever bugger, and he'd had straight 'A's since then.

'I can't blame her for it happening.' I admired him for saying that. In his own crabbed way he'd always seen things as they were. He was honest with himself. 'She's rather a passive person, really,' he said. 'Likes to talk more than anything else. It started last year, when she went on a citrus fruit diet. I used to go into the bathroom and joke about it when she stood on the scales with a towel around herself. Sometimes I'd put a foot deliberately on the scales, and she would laugh and jab back with her elbows.' Les was going to say more, then he broke off with a barking laugh. 'Funny how these things get started,' he said, and he pushed out with his legs to get the swing going again as a sign he'd finished talking about the seduction of his landlady.

I hadn't wanted to hear about it, but personal revelations impose an obligation, and I asked him if he wanted some apple wine. 'Love it,' said Les, and he came with me back to the wall on which sat the patient humpty-dumpty, smiling in the face of his imminent fall and the tsunami. Les knew Raf, and I introduced him to Peter.

'I don't think the tsunami will persist across all that ocean,' said Peter.

'The what?' said Les.

'The tidal wave. He means the tidal wave,' put in Raf and me.

'That bloody thing,' said Les with belittling contempt, looking not out to sea, but towards the car and his landlady. He tipped the apple wine down his throat without appearing to swallow. We could hear its unimpeded gurgle as it went down, and we began to drink more rapidly to keep up. Les cast a malaise over our group, interrupting the established pattern of our relationship. He was interested only in his own problems, and our wine.

His impatience seemed to extend to the people along the foreshore below. The tsunami had not come; promises of something different had failed once again. Some people began to leave for the city, and only those with nothing they wished to return to remained. A few roared their cars across the asphalt frontage of the beach, while others stood in the sand dunes and pelted beer bottles with stones.

When the wine was finished, Les said he'd better take his landlady home. I walked part of the way towards the car with him to show a fitting sense of comradeship for a fellow old boy whose secret I shared. By now he wished he hadn't told me, of course, and not being able to say just that, he got in some remark about how heavy I was. I saw him cross the rough grass of the playground, walking in his round-shouldered, rather furtive way. I felt no loyalty whatsoever, and told Raf and Peter as soon as I rejoined them. We watched Les and Mrs Reid having a last look down to the beach. She was talking, and waved a hand dismissively towards the ocean. Her strong hips and jutting breasts seemed to accentuate Leslie's stooped concavity.

'Serve him right. Serve him damn right,' said Raf. It wasn't a moral judgement, rather a reference to all those nights on which Les had returned to his landlady, and Raf had fretted his time away with cards and bitter study.

Les and Mrs Reid drove quite close to regain the road. I could see her mouth opening and closing quickly as she talked to him, and Les glanced at me as they passed. It was his own smile though, inwardly directed and not for me; his tilted Spanish smile which he still wore as he turned the car again and began to drive down the hill. Elizabeth Reid had turned sideways somewhat in the seat, the better to watch him as she talked, and her mouth opened and closed effortlessly. It was a recollection which I found hard to shake off as we ourselves left. Peter was in a good humour because the tsunami had failed as he had predicted, but the unwarranted glimpse of Leslie Foster's life had chilled my mood, and Raf's too in a different way. He sat silently, holding the empty wine flask between his knees, and reflecting on his unwilling celibacy.

Before tea, as I prepared the vegetables, I listened to a government seismologist on the radio, explaining why the tidal wave hadn't come. I suppose he was a different seismologist from the one the papers had quoted the day before. I called out to the others to say it was on the news about the tidal wave not coming.

'Tsunami,' said Peter.

'Right.'

'The tsunami certainly came for old Les Foster though, didn't it. Talk about a shock wave,' said Raf. How we laughed at that. Raf and Peter came into the kitchen so we could see one another as we laughed, and better share the joke. All youth is pagan, and we believed that as the gods were satisfied with their sport, the rest of us were safe awhile. 'Came for old Les All right, the tsunami.' Even as I laughed I saw again Les and his landlady as they drove away, and that inward smile upon his face. As a drowning man might smile; for they say that at the very end the water is accepted, and that the past life spins out vividly. In Leslie's case it may well have been the future rather than the past he saw.

Holly

Tina Shaw

Every day of his holiday he had seen her out there in the deep water – even on the wet day, Tuesday, when the beach was deserted and everyone was mucking around inside their baches and caravans and tents, playing cards or toasting marshmallows or whatever they all did. Even then she still went out on her board, out into the seething water: he could hardly believe it.

He never knew when she'd be coming out onto the beach, or where she was staying either. Maybe she was even local. That might explain her skill and her lack of interest in the other kids. She had a proper surfboard, not a body board like the rest of them had, and she went out the deepest, stayed out the longest, and caught the most waves. He thought she was possibly the best surfer he'd ever seen. He had watched the way she got easily onto the board, was lifted up by the waves, then balanced, casually, until she coasted into shallow water. And the way she simply stepped off, taking the board under her arm again like it was a small whale or a friend, and guided it back out into the deep. If he hadn't tried surfing himself, that time last summer on his cousin's board, he'd think it was easy.

There were only two or three guys on real surfboards, yet she held herself apart from them and they didn't seem to know each other. He tried to guess how old she was: fifteen? Seventeen? He borrowed his Dad's binoculars one afternoon and studied her from beneath the shadowy pines that overlooked the dusty yellow bay, but he was still none the wiser.

There was also an old lady who watched her. A grumpy-looking old woman who would come out a while after the girl had been in the water, and set up her 'camp' on the sand. She had a faded orange umbrella, a camp chair, a chillybin and her knitting bag. Sometimes she just stood in the shallows with the water washing around her crinkly legs, and watch the girl. Mostly she'd be sitting in her chair knitting, or listening to the radio, though always watching. Some people said it was her mad aunt.

There was a lot of talk about the girl. That she had a baby, that her old man was filthy rich, that she couldn't speak English, that she was a mute, that she was a dyke, that she was up herself. He didn't believe any of it, and nobody seemed to have the guts to talk to her because of the old woman. Murray & co thought that the old lady had a house in the next bay because they had seen her driving past that way (in an elderly Triumph), but that was only guesswork. No one knew for sure. The only thing he believed was that her name was Holly, and that was because he'd heard the old lady say the name, one time when the girl had come out for a drink. *Have a scone too, Holly.* He had craned to hear her answering voice – she was saying something about the water, possibly, or about the day's form – but the breeze hushed away the words and he was left only with her name. *Holly.* That was enough: a name was knowledge, a gift.

Holly. He watched her covertly from his towel on the sand. His mates wanted to go rock-climbing down the other end of the bay and smoke cigarettes away from prying eyes, but he said he wanted to sunbathe. *Sunbathe,* they scoffed, and left him to it. There were other girls, bach girls mostly, who hung round in pairs and groups – he and Louie had met a group of them on his second day at the beach, four girls all wearing the same kind of bikini – but their incessant twittering reminded him of caged birds, and they only ever went into the water together. Safety in numbers, he thought. They didn't make him curious to find out more.

Holly. Often she was out there till dusk. Sitting on the board and waiting for the waves, like a spider, in her short-sleeved black wetsuit. Sometimes she would come down to the beach in just her togs and put on the wetsuit in front of the water. There was a sense of ritual about the meticulous way she pulled it on. Her swimsuit was shiny green, lurid green, the colour of sea lettuce. And then on went the dull wetsuit and it was like she was putting on another skin, a kind of shell, and away she walked into the sea. Invincible again. Maybe, he thought, there would be a day that was completely calm. She would just sit on the beach and he would go up and talk to her. But it never happened. There were always the waves and he remained at a disadvantage.

He wasn't swimming this summer. He had decided not to after last summer when a shark had touched his leg. It was on the last day of the holidays and he'd been out deep on his body board, just paddling about with his legs dangling, getting away from the noise and the smell of sun cream. The water had been oily greenstone, nearly black. He felt it first: a cool pressure like someone had pushed a plastic log against his leg, and then he looked back and saw the shark. It was pale, large, and sleek. It turned away from him, as if it might be swimming away, disinterested, but at the same time he knew it was coming back for him, for his leg. He panicked. You were supposed to be still, not thrash about, not attract their attention, but he immediately started paddling. Faster than he'd ever paddled before. Barely breathing, and then breathing too fast, like his heart might explode. Every minute, he expected the shark to grab his leg. But nothing happened. He made it back to the shore and collapsed onto the safety of the sand, unharmed. But he'd had a thing about the sea ever since. He had had nightmares about that shark, about lots of sharks circling in the water, wanting to get him. He wasn't worried about being called a chicken, let his mates go out there, he just wanted to stay on the beach this summer. *Sharks are territorial*, he told them, *it could still be out there. Yeah*, they said, *looking for your legs*. They probably didn't even believe him. Let them laugh, but he was staying on the beach. If it got too hot he would cool off in the estuary. He would watch Holly instead. Maybe that was what the old lady was doing: watching for sharks.

Wasn't Holly afraid of sharks? He wanted to know. It was as if she didn't recognise fear. As if she had the answer to *his* fear. He would've liked to have gone out deep in the sea with her. Her commonplace bravery astounded him. And because he couldn't face the water it seemed that even if he was brave at everything else it didn't matter because there was always the shark haunting him.

He had to talk to Holly somehow. But as he didn't want to approach her in front of the old lady – and she was always there waiting for the girl, even if it was nearly dark – he decided to write her a letter. *Dear Holly, my name is* – No. *Dear Holly, do you want a game of Monopoly?* No. He would've written her a song, but if she couldn't read music it would be indecipherable, like morse code.

> What grows in the sea, but is not seaweed? Once used as protective hedging, dark glossy green like Christmas. Brought over the oceans in tall ships, along with oak, pine, maple, roses, spices, pianos, guns. There is a sense of history between the islands – flax, kauri gum and timber. But none of these as precious as Holly.
> PS Meet me 9.30 tonight at Angle Rock.

He felt stupid, but he put it in an envelope and 'posted' it anyway. Left it in the folds of her towel while the old lady was taking one of her toilet breaks: hobbling up over the sand to the public loos under the pines. It gave him enough time to wait until the girl was paddling back out into the deep, her back to the beach.

Later, he watched from further along the beach as she got out of the water, peeled off her wetsuit and picked up her towel. The letter fell onto the sand, glittering white. She held the towel to her face like she always did, but then paused, as if she had smelt something foreign. The old lady pointed to the sand. The girl reached down and picked up the envelope, but although the old woman was looking at her expectantly, she simply tucked it straight into the chillybin without opening it.

As they walked up the beach to the road he looked the other way.

That night he waited by Angle Rock. It was only just getting dark around 9-30 and the sky and ocean were still edged with light; he could easily enough have seen someone coming along the beach. The roiling sea travelled harshly up and down the smooth incline of sand. The rocks loomed behind him, a black wall against the sky. He had purposefully worn dark clothing so that from a distance he wouldn't be readily seen. It gave him a feeling of security, but still he wondered if he'd done the right thing. Angle Rock had a ragged, gaping hole higher up, like an eye, though which you could see sky during the day. Now it was an oval of shimmering grey light.

He waited nervously. What would he say to her? Maybe she *was* a mute, maybe she *was* up herself. He faced the rock, cupped his hands and lit a cigarette, careful for the small orange ember not to be seen from the beach, but then what if she hated boys who smoked? He put the cigarette out in the sand, and chewed gum to hide the taste of tar in his mouth. She never came.

> This is not a blind date. You can walk away at any time. Have you ever seen a stingray out there? The ocean is teeming with life, and us on the skin of it.Like on the skin of a giant. The sea is full of secrets only because we live on the land. Just because I've never seen a mermaid, doesn't mean they don't exist.
> PS Meet me 9.30 at Angle Rock.

He wasn't going to be put off. No, he would bide his time, play it cool, not get paranoid. After all, she didn't know him – didn't know who it was that was leaving the notes. It wasn't her fault that he was shy in bright light. Yet that next day he watched her more carefully, from under cover of his parents' beach umbrella: a family group look, that was what he wanted to achieve, so he wouldn't stand out, so she wouldn't take one look at him and have him pegged for a dork. An unattractive person. *Dork, an idiot, an object of contempt – Chambers Dictionary. Dorp, a Dutch or SAfrican village or small town, a town considered provincial.* His mates were giving him funny looks, but they would have to stick it for a while. They were used to him acting weird sometimes anyway. *Where's the guitar,* Louie called. He could at least redeem himself by playing the guitar for them – Holly would be too far away to hear or to notice.

She never once looked down the beach. She concentrated on her technique, and the waves. Like it was the usual thing for her, to get letters left in her towel on the beach. Even when the second one fell out and the old lady was busy folding up her camp chair, still Holly just stuck it in the chillybin like it was nothing, a shell she'd found or a bit of driftwood washed up by the sea. He could've cried.

Lumpy, terrifying thoughts kicked against each other in his head: she hadn't read the other letter. She was in her twenties. Or, the old lady had read it and thrown it away. That she was kept locked up in her room all night. The old lady was a witch. Holly was bewitched. It would be the old lady who would meet him at Angle Rock.

Again he waited in the rapidly changing light. He drew a deep spiral in the cool sand with the knuckles of his fist, and paused, crouched over it like prehistoric man. Then he wiped hard at his face, forgetting he had sand on his fingers, and flapped frantically at his eyes to get it away. He had never felt like such a weed, such a weakling, in all his life. Well, not since he had run from the sea with an imaginary shark after him. Because he was doubting it now: what had he really seen? All this time it had been with him like a real event, but now, in the noisy dark, he wasn't so sure any more.

It was a relief when nobody came. After twenty minutes he stood up and walked away.

> There is a deaf woman who lives eight doors down from us in our street. She can call a cat by flicking her fingers. She can read a boy's lips and mind, and answer you back in a song. She eats fish and chips every night for tea but never drinks Coke. Her house is full of music boxes.
> PS Meet me 9.30 at Angle Rock.

It was raining again. Not bad for two weeks, only two days of rain. A nagging wind had turned the sea into froth, but still there was the distant speck in the water. He turned his back on the grey, pock-marked beach and climbed over the rocks all afternoon under a billowing grey sky with his little knot of mates. They smoked cigarettes sitting at the sea edge in oilskins, their faces wet like they were crying and their backs defended by the black spiky rocks. He considered telling Louie all about it. But then changed his mind. He felt feverish all over, and then broke into a cold sweat. The waves reminded him of only one thing.

> I believe in ghosts, but not in angels. I believe in having a good time but not in getting drunk. I believe in the orange of nasturtium flowers and the whiteness of lilies which glows in the dark, in playing cricket all day and the next and the next, in saying you're sorry only if you really mean it, in not eating meat, in the rhythm of a guitar, in camping under a pohutukawa then going to a café for cappuccino, in world peace and loads of other things – how about you?

PS 9.30, Angle Rock.

He decided to go back to town on the bus. The family had another week at the rented bach, but he thought it would be better back home. Louie might go back too. They could stay at Aunty Sherry's, and try out some new songs with his uncle's drum kit. Mum would understand, and after all, what was he doing at the beach except playing the guitar all day and developing a nicotine habit? Besides, there were gale force winds forecast. *Why don't you try the water again*, said his Dad. But that was no answer.

He made up his mind to catch the ten o'clock bus the next morning.

Please meet me. We are dead for millions of years. Angle Rock.

He timed it by his watch: he would give her ten minutes, then he would go. He would definitely go. He wasn't going to wait all night for a girl who wasn't going to come. Who probably hadn't even read his letters in the first place. Who was probably too old for him. Who was laughing at him from her surfboard.

Ten minutes came and went. He'd wait another ten, just in case she'd got stuck somehow. He counted waves and thought about whales. He had bare feet, and the sand was cold and damp beneath his soles. His feet, way down there in the dark, looked like Mexican walking fish. What stupid things he'd written – all those notes, they were really desperate. Thank Christ nobody would know how embarrassing he had been. And what it must do to your mind, he thought, disgusted now, being out in the sea like that for hours on end: she must be a vegetable, a retard, a socially neglected person. He turned his back on the water in despair.

'You don't know that.'

A voice rang down from above, the sound of it bright as sunflowers. Turning abruptly, he saw a figure perched on a rock ledge, way up behind him, dark against dark. It occurred to him that he had never thought about her voice, even the times when he'd seen her talking to the old woman, that all this time he had actually imagined her mute.

'Know what?'

'Dead for millions of years,' she said, jumping down beside him. 'You don't know that.' She was wearing a dark T-shirt and shorts, camouflaged just like himself. Her face was smooth and shining as if the last of the day's light was concentrated there, while her hair was pitch black and went in all directions like she had a collection of cowlicks. 'You're the boy who doesn't swim,' she said.

He shuffled in the sand, regretting everything. She was going to make fun of him. The sea was boiling in front of them like it was full of sharks.

'I swim,' he said quickly.

'Great.' She pulled off her tee-shirt and underneath were the sea-green togs. 'I'm glad you swim. Let's go for a dip now.' She was putting her gear carefully onto a dry rock.

'What?' His mouth was parched. 'Don't you ever get sick of the sea?'

She paused for a moment, her eyes shadowy grey. 'It's the best time, you know, at night. You'll see …'

He stood, lost, while she waited for him, in her glittering togs, in ankle-deep water. Everything inside him was rebelling: he wanted to shout, to make excuses, to bluff, to run back along the dark sand like a chicken, to just say no. And then he noticed that the sea had grown calm, as if before a storm, and the flattened surface was prickling with raindrops.

'Look,' she laughed, 'you may as well have a swim now, you're going to get wet anyway. Come on …'

The Seahorse and the Reef

Witi Ihimaera

Sometimes through the soft green water and drifting seaweed of my dreams I see the seahorse again. Delicate and fragile it comes to me, shimmering and luminous with light. And I remember the reef again, the way it was before the world began to change …

The reef was just outside the town where my family lived. That was a long time ago, when I was a boy, before I came to this southern city. It was where all our relations and friends went every weekend in summer to dive for kai moana – paua, pipi, kina, mussels, pupu and other shell fish. It was the home too of other fish like triplefins, butterfish, red mullet and octopus. It teemed with life and food. It gave its bounty to us. It was good to us.

And it was where the seahorse lived.

At that time our family lived in a small wooden house on the fringe of the industrial area. On a Sunday, my father would watch out the window and see our relations passing by on their old trucks and cars or bikes with their sugarbags and nets, their flippers and goggles, shouting and waving on their way to the reef. They came from the pa – in those days it was not surrounded by expanding suburbia – and they would sing out to Dad:

– Hey, Rongo! Come on! Good day for kai moana today!

Dad would sigh and start to moan and fidget. The lunch dishes had to be washed, the lawn had to be cut, my mother probably would want him to do other things round the house.

… Aue.

But after a while a gleam would come into his eyes.

– Hey, Huia! He would shout to Mum. Those kina are calling out to me today!

– So are these dishes, she would answer.

– Well, Mum! Dad would call again. Those paua are just waiting for me to come to them today!

– That lawn's been waiting even longer, Mum would answer.

Dad would pretend not to hear her.

– Pae kare, dear! How'd you like a feed of mussels today!

– I'd like it better if you fixed the fence, she would growl.

So Dad would just wiggle his toes and act sad for her.

– Okay, Huia. But those pipi are going to miss us today!

Dad was cunning. He knew Mum loved her feed of pipi. And sure enough she would answer him:

– What are we waiting for! Can't disappoint those pipi today!

Then she would shout to us to get into our bathing clothes, grab some sugarbags, don't forget some knives and take your time but *hurry up!* And off we would go to the reef on our truck.

If it was a sunny day the reef would already be crowded with other people searching for their kai moana. There they'd be, dotting the water with their sacks and flax kits. They would wave and shout to us and we would hurry to join them, pulling on our shoes, grabbing our sugarbags and running down to the sea.

– Don't you kids come too far out! Dad would yell.

He would already be way ahead of us, sack clutched in one hand and a knife in the other. He used the knife to prise the paua from the reef because if you weren't quick enough they held onto the rocks really tight.

Sometimes, Dad would put on a diving mask. It made it easier for him to see under water.

As for Mum, she liked nothing better than to wade out to where some of the women of the pa were gathered. Then she could korero with them while she was looking for seafood. All the long afternoon those women would bend to the task, their dresses ballooning above the water, and talk and talk and talk and *talk!*

For both Mum and Dad, much of the fun of going to the reef was because they could be with their friends and relations. It was a good time for being family again and for enjoying our tribal ways.

My sisters and me, we made straight for a special place on the reef that we liked to call 'ours'. It was where the pupu – or winkles as some people call them – crawled. We called the special place our pupu pool.

The pool was very long but not very deep. Just as well because Mere, my youngest sister then, would have been drowned, she was so short! As for me, the water came only waist high. The rock surrounding the pool was fringed with long waving seaweed. Small transparent fish swam among the waving leaves and little crabs scurried across the dark floor. The many pupu glided calmly along the sides of the pool. Once, a starfish inched its way into a dark crack.

It was in that pool we discovered the seahorse, magical and serene, shimmering among the red kelp and riding the swirls of the sea's current.

My sisters and I, we wanted to take it home.

– If you take it from the sea it will die, Dad told us. Leave it here in its own home for the sea gives it life and beauty.

Dad, he always told us that we must always treat the sea with love, with aroha.

– Kids, you must take from the sea only the kai you need and only the amount you need to please your bellies. If you take more, then it is waste. There is no need to waste the food of the sea. Best to leave it there for when you need it next time. The sea is good to us, it gives us kai moana to eat. It is a food basket. As long as we respect it, it will continue to feed us. If, in your search for shellfish, you lift a stone from its lap, return the stone to where it was. Try not to break pieces of the reef for it is the home of many kai moana. And do not leave litter behind you when you leave the sea.

Dad, he taught us to respect the sea and to have reverence for the life contained in its waters. As we collected the shellfish we would remember his words.

And whenever we saw the seahorse shimmering behind a curtain of kelp, we felt glad we'd left it in the pool to continue to delight us.

As soon as we filled our sugarbags we would return to the beach. We played together with other kids while waiting for our parents to return from the outer reef. One by one they would arrive: the women still talking, the men carrying their sacks over their shoulders. On the beach we would laugh and talk and share the kai moana among different families. With sharing there was little waste. We would be happy with each other unless a stranger intervened with his camera or curious amusement. Then we would say goodbye to one another while the sea whispered and gently surged into the coming of darkness.

– See you next weekend, we would say.

One weekend we went again to the reef. We were in a happy mood. The sun was shining and skipping its beams like bright stones across the water.

But when we arrived at the beach the sea was empty of the family. No people dotted the reef with their sacks. No calls of welcome drifted across the rippling waves.

Dad frowned. He looked ahead to where our friends and relations were clustered in a large lost group on the sand. All of them were looking to the reef, their faces etched by the sun with impassiveness.

– Something's wrong, Dad said.

He stopped the truck. We walked with him towards the others of our people. They were silent.

– The water too cold? Dad tried to joke.

Nobody answered him.

– Is there a shark out there? Dad asked again.

Again there was silence. Then someone pointed to a sign.

– It must have been put up last night, a man told Dad.

He elbowed his way through the crowd to read it.

– Dad, what does it say? I asked.

His fists were clenched and his eyes were angry. He said one word, explosive and shattering the silence, disturbing the gulls to scream and clatter about us.

– Rongo, Mum reproved him.

– First the land and now our food, Dad said to her.

– What does it say? I asked again.

His fists unclenched and his eyes became sad.

– It says that it is dangerous to take seafood from the reef, son.

– Why, Dad?

– The sea is polluted, son. If we eat the seafood, we may get sick.

My sisters and I were silent for a while.

– No more pupu, Dad?

– No more, kids.

I clutched his arm frantically.

– And the seahorse, Dad? The seahorse, will it be all right?

But he did not seem to hear me.

We walked back to the truck. Behind us, an old woman began to cry out a tangi to the reef. It was a very sad song for such a beautiful day.

– Aue … Aue …

With the rest of the people, we bowed our heads. While she was singing, the sea boiled yellow with effluent issuing from a pipe on the seabed. The stain curled like fingers around the reef.

Then the song was finished. Dad looked out to the reef and called to it in a clear voice.

– Sea, we have been unkind to you. We have poisoned the land and now we feed our poison into your waters. We have lost our aroha for you and our respect for your life. Forgive us. Haere, friend.

He started the truck. We turned homeward.

In my mind I caught a sudden vision of many pupu crawling among polluted rocks. I saw a starfish encrusted with ugliness.

And flashing through dead waving seaweed was a beautiful seahorse, fragile and dream-like, searching frantically for clean and crystal waters.

A Great Day

Frank Sargeson

It was beginning to get light when Ken knocked on the door of Fred's bach.

Are you up? he said.

Fred called out that he was, and in a moment he opened the door.

Just finished my breakfast, he said. We'd better get moving.

It didn't take long. The bach was right on the edge of the beach, and they got the dinghy on to Ken's back and he carried it down the beach, and Fred followed with the gear. Ken was big enough to make light work of the dinghy but it was all Fred could do to manage the gear. There wasn't much of him and he goddamned the gear every few yards he went.

The tide was well over half-way out, and the sea was absolutely flat without even a ripple breaking on the sand. Except for some seagulls that walked on the sand and made broad arrow marks where they walked there wasn't a single thing moving. It was so still it wasn't natural. Except for the seagulls you'd have thought the world had died in the night.

Ken eased the dinghy off his shoulders and turned it the right way up, and Fred dropped the anchor and the oars on the sand, and heaved the sugar bag of fishing gear into the dinghy.

I wouldn't mind if I was a hefty bloke like you, he said.

Well, Ken didn't say anything to that. He sat on the stern of the dinghy and rolled himself a cigarette, and Fred got busy and fixed the oars and rowlocks and tied on the anchor.

Come on, he said, we'll shove off. And with his trousers rolled up he went and tugged at the bow, and with Ken shoving at the stern the dinghy began to float, so Fred hopped in and took the oars, and then Ken hopped in and they were off.

It's going to be a great day, Fred said.

It certainly looked like it. The sun was coming up behind the island they were heading for, and there wasn't a cloud in the sky.

We'll make for the same place as last time, Fred said. You tell me if I don't keep straight. And for a time he rowed hard without sending the dinghy along very fast. The trouble was his short legs, he couldn't get them properly braced against the stern seat. And Ken, busy rolling a supply of cigarettes, didn't watch out where he was going, so when Fred took a look ahead he was heading for the wrong end of the island.

Hey, he said, you take a turn and I'll tell you where to head for.

So they changed places and Ken pulled wonderfully well. For a time it was more a mental shock you got with each jerk of the dinghy. You realised how strong he was. He had only a shirt and a pair of shorts on, and his big body, hard with muscle, must have been over six feet long.

Gee, I wish I had your body, Fred said. It's no wonder the girls chase you. But look at the sort of joker I am.

Well, he wasn't much to look at. There was so little of him. And the old clothes he wore had belonged to someone considerably bigger than he was. And he had on an old hat that came down too far, and would have come down further if it hadn't bent his ears over and sat on them as if they were brackets.

How about a smoke? Fred said.

Sure. Sorry.

And to save him from leaving off rowing Fred reached over and took the tin out of his shirt pocket.

That's the curse of this sustenance, Fred said. A man's liable to be out of smokes before pay-day.

Yes, I suppose he is, Ken said.

It's rotten being out of work, Fred said. Thank the Lord I've got this dinghy. D'you know last year I made over thirty pounds out of fishing?

And how've you done this year?

Not so good. You're the first bloke I've had go out with me this year that hasn't wanted me to go shares. Gee, you're lucky to be able to go fishing for fun.

It's about time I landed a position, Ken said. I've had over a month's holiday.

Yes I know. But you've got the money saved up, and it doesn't cost you anything to live when you can live with your auntie. How'd you like to live in that damn bach of mine and pay five bob a week rent? And another thing, you've got education.

It doesn't count for much these days. A man has to take any position he can get.

Yes, but if a man's been to one of those High Schools it makes him different. Not any better, mind you. I'm all for the working class because I'm a worker myself, but an educated bloke has the advantage of a bloke like me. The girls chase him just to mention one thing, specially if he happens to be a big he-man as well.

Ken didn't say anything to that. He just went on pulling, and he got Fred to stick a cigarette in his mouth and light it at the same time as he lit his own. And then Fred lolled back in his seat and watched him, and you could tell that about the only thing they had in common was that they both had cigarettes dangling out of their mouths.

Pull her round a bit with your left, Fred said. And there's no need to bust your boiler.

It's okay, Ken said.

You've got the strength, Fred said.

I'm certainly no infant.

What good's a man's strength anyway? Say he goes and works in an office?

I hadn't thought of that.

Another thing, he gets old. Fancy you getting old and losing your strength. Wouldn't it be a shame?

Sure, Ken said. Why talk about it?

It sort of fascinates me. You'll die someday, and where'll that big frame of yours be then?

That's an easy one. Pushing up daisies.

It might as well be now as anytime, mightn't it?

Good Lord, I don't see that.

A man'd forget for good. It'd just be the same as it is out here on a day like this. Only better.

Ken stopped rowing to throw away his cigarette.

My God, he said, you're a queer customer. Am I heading right?

Pull with your left, Fred said. But I'll give you a spell.

It's okay, Ken said.

And he went on rowing and after a bit Fred emptied the lines out of the sugar bag and began cutting up the bait. And after a bit longer when they were about half-way over to the island he said they'd gone far enough, so Ken shipped his oars and threw the anchor overboard, and they got their lines ready and began to fish.

And by that time it was certainly turning out a great day. The sun was getting hot but there still wasn't any wind, and as the tide had just about stopped running out down the Gulf the dinghy hardly knew which way to pull on the anchor rope. They'd pulled out less than two miles from the shore, but with the sea as it was it might have been anything from none at all up to an infinite number. You couldn't hear a sound or see anything moving. It was another world. The houses on the shore didn't belong. Nor did the people either.

Wouldn't you like to stay out here for good? Fred said.

Ring off, Ken said. I got a bite.

So did I, but it was only a nibble. Anyhow it's not a good day for fish. It wants to be cloudy.

So I've heard.

I've been thinking, Fred said, it's funny you never learnt to swim.

Oh I don't know. Up to now I've always lived in country towns.

Doesn't it make you feel a bit windy?

On a day like this! Anyhow, you couldn't swim that distance yourself.

Oh couldn't I! You'd be surprised ... get a bite?

Yes I did.

Same here ... you'll be settling down here, won't you Ken?

It depends if I can get a position.

I suppose you'll go on living with your auntie.

That depends too. If I got a good position I might be thinking of getting married.

Gee, that'd be great, wouldn't it?

I got another bite, Ken said.

Same here. I reckon our lines are crossed.

So they pulled in their lines and they were crossed sure enough, but Ken had hooked the smallest snapper you ever saw.

He's no good, Fred said. And he worked the fish off the hook and held it in his hand. They're pretty little chaps, aren't they? He said. Look at his colours.

Let him go, Ken said.

Poor little beggar, Fred said. I bet he wonders what's struck him. He's trying to get his breath. Funny, isn't it, when there's plenty of air about? It's like Douglas Credit.

Oh for God's sake, Ken said.

I bet in less than five minutes he forgets about how he was nearly suffocated, Fred said, and he threw the fish back. And it lay bewildered for a second on the surface, then it flipped its tail and was gone. It was comical in its way and they both laughed.

They always do that, Fred said. But don't you wish you could swim like him?

Ken didn't say anything to that and they put fresh bait on their hooks and tried again, but there were only nibbles. They could bring nothing to the surface.

I'll tell you what, Fred said, those nibbles might be old men snapper only they won't take a decent bite at bait like this.

And he explained that off the end of the island there was a reef where they could get plenty of big mussels. It would be just nice with the tide out as it was. The reef wouldn't be uncovered, it never was, but you could stand on it in water up to your knees and pull up the mussels. And if you cut the inside out of a big mussel you only had to hang it on your hook for an old man snapper to go for it with one big bite.

It's a fair way, Ken said.

It doesn't matter, Fred said. We've got oceans of time. And he climbed past Ken to pull up the anchor, and Ken pulled in the lines, and then Fred insisted on rowing and they started for the end of the island.

And by that time the tide had begun to run in up the Gulf and there was a light wind blowing up against the tide, so that the sea, almost without your noticing it, was showing signs of coming up a bit rough. And the queer thing was that with the movement the effect of another world was destroyed. You seemed a part of the real world of houses and people once more. Yet with the sea beginning to get choppy the land looked a long way off.

Going back, Ken said, we'll be pulling against the wind.

Yes, Fred said, but the tide'll be a help. Anyhow, what's it matter when a man's out with a big hefty bloke like you?

Nor did he seem to be in too much of a hurry to get to his reef. He kept resting on his oars to roll cigarettes, and when Ken said something about it he said they had oceans of time.

You're in no hurry to get back, he said, Mary'll keep.

Well, Ken didn't say anything to that.

Mary's a great kid, Fred said.

Sure, Ken said. Mary's one of the best.

I've known Mary for years, Fred said.

Yes, Ken said, so I've gathered.

I suppose you have. Up to a while ago Mary and I used to be great cobbers.

I'll give you a spell, Ken said.

But Fred said it was okay.

Mary's got a bit of education too, he said. Only when her old man died the family was hard up so she had to go into service. It was lucky she got a good place at your auntie's. Gee, I've been round there and had tea sometimes when your auntie's been out, and oh boy is the tucker any good!

Look here, Ken said, at this rate we'll never get to that reef.

Oh yes we will, Fred said, and he pulled a bit harder. If only a man hadn't lost his job, he said.

I admit it must be tough, Ken said.

And then Fred stood up and took a look back at the shore.

I thought there might be somebody else coming out, he said, but there isn't. So thank God for that. And he said that he couldn't stand anybody hanging around when he was fishing. By the way, he said, I forgot to do this before. And he stuffed pieces of cotton-wool into his ears. If the spray gets into my ears it gives me the earache, he said.

Then he really did settle down to his rowing, and with the sea more or less following them it wasn't long before they were off the end of the island.

Nobody lived on the island. There were a few holiday baches but they were empty now that it was well on into the autumn. Nor from this end could you see any landing places, and with the wind blowing up more and more it wasn't too pleasant to watch the sea running up the rocks. And Fred had to spend a bit of time manoeuvring around before he found his reef.

It was several hundred yards out with deep water all round, and it seemed to be quite flat. If the sea had been calm it might have been covered to a depth of about a foot with the tide as it was. But with the sea chopping across it wasn't exactly an easy matter to stand there. At one moment the water was down past your knees and the next moment you had to steady yourself while it came up round your thighs. And it was uncanny to stand there, because with the deep water all round you seemed to have discovered a way of standing up out in the sea.

Anyhow Fred took off his coat and rolled up his sleeves and his trousers as far as they'd go, and then he hopped out and got Ken to do the same and keep hold of the dinghy. Then he steadied himself and began dipping his hands down and pulling up mussels and throwing them back into the dinghy, and he worked at a mad pace as though he hadn't a moment to lose. It seemed only a minute or so before he was quite out of breath.

It's tough work, he said. You can see what a weak joker I am.

I'll give you a spell, Ken said, only keep hold of the boat.

Well, Fred held the dinghy, and by the way he was breathing and the look on his face you'd have thought he was going to die. But Ken had other matters to think about, he was steadying himself and dipping his hands down more than a yard away, and Fred managed to pull himself together and shove off the dinghy and hop in. And if you'd been sitting in the stern as he pulled away you'd have seen that he had his eyes shut. Nor did he open them except when he took a look ahead to see where he was going, and with the cotton-wool in his ears it was difficult for him to hear.

So for a long time he rowed like that against seas that were getting bigger and bigger, but about half-way back to the shore he took a spell. He changed over to the other side of the seat, so he didn't have to sit facing the island, and he just sat there keeping the dinghy straight on. Then when he felt that he had collected all his strength he stood up and capsized the dinghy. It took a bit of doing but he did it.

And after that, taking it easy, he started on his long swim for the shore.

self-catering

Emily Perkins

We have friends visiting from the UK and there is a lot riding on them having a good time. These are the first guests from our former lives in London and if they return to Blighty moaning, as *Herald* letter writers are often moved to do, about bad service, nobody else will come to see us. We must ensure a uniquely New Zealand fun time, complete with sand, silky waters and ideally dolphins. If we can get dolphins, the spare room will be booked solid for a year.

The obvious plan is to rent a place in the Coromandel. But which Coromandel? The 'Doctor No' style modernist palace, built of glass, with vertigo-commanding views and the risk of death by exposure? Or the hippie commune of my husband's youth, where the shelters are built from old spelt bread and clothes are a bourgeois conspiracy perpetrated by The Man? I have been to both (but never, as the song says, been to me) and would prefer something in the middle. Otherwise you come back from your holiday with either a squashed nose from pinballing into plate-glass windows, or six months' worth of hippie dog hair in your ears. It's itchy. The best protection is a woolly hat but then you become one of those people on communes who walk about naked except for woolly hats. And I never walk around naked anywhere; in fact there is no body under my clothes, only gleaming metal rods and pistons. This is why I can't go back to the modernist palace. Last time everyone mistook me for the cappuccino machine.

What are the other beach-side options? No hotels, we are control freaks about food and must be self-catering, even if over a gas burner. Campgrounds require minimum effort, only then there's the communal showers/nakedness issue again. Last time my friends and I stayed in a camping ground we spent most of our time trying to shake the short ruddy alcoholic who wouldn't leave us alone, even though I had told my boyfriend it was a weekend for the girls. A caravan is likely to make me want to neck myself. (The smell.) There's always real-life camping in a tent – I nurse a fantasy of being a rugged, tent-pitching type – but whenever I say to people 'Oh yes, let's go camping' the force of their laughter sends flocks of birds scattering with fright. In Stewart Island. You can, apparently, die of such laughter, so my mother should watch out.

Instead she comes through with the phone number of a friend who might let out her holiday house for a few days, after assuring me there is electricity and hot running water. We book it sight unseen, trusting to luck – how bad can the Coromandel be? – and days later find ourselves pulling up at the most beautiful beach I have ever seen. Our English friends are awestruck, used as they are to donkeys, deck chairs and nuclear power plants.

The Coromandel lives up to its lyrical, exotic name. Hushed days reading and walking melt into evenings of wine and conversation, gazing through blurred eyes at the rocks that sit moodily in the silver sea. On our last evening, joyously, dolphins from central casting arc across the bay. Best of all it is slightly too shivery to swim, so no semi-nakedness is required. The only thing that lets the holiday down is my cooking, which is rubbish. At least when I ruin the leg of lamb it is such a squitty undersized piece – more toe of lamb – that the loss is not too great. I'm usually never knowingly undercatered, so not sure what went wrong. But who cares, they can make toast if they're still hungry.

At the end of the holiday I sneak a look in the visitors' book to see what our friends have written. Gratifyingly, their entry begins, 'This place is exquisite…' Aha! I clench my fist with national pride – time to stock up on extra linen for the influx of English friends. Then I turn the page: 'But the food was appalling'. Oh, go back to London.

Broken Rhythms

Sarah Quigley

One two three. One two three. She is inside the car but really she is outside, a white horse cantering on a green verge. She keeps pace with the moving window, easy, smooth. One two. She is twelve years old and she is singing to herself and she is riding the wind, her mane is combed clean by the air and the air is singing in her head. Her long white legs see the water-race, soar, land, keep the beat. Two, three.

But she is spoken to and she is back on the vinyl seat, two pale legs not four sticking in the heat. And beside her is Annette, beautiful Annette who is staying in the next bach but one from theirs. Annette's legs are brown, browner than the vinyl on which they so lightly rest, and they are scattered with soft honey hairs that glint in the sun. She is three years older than Cam, who looks sideways at her new friend and is fiercely glad now to be human. She too will be fifteen one day, and beautiful.

Not far now, Cam's father, Mr Martin, says. His eyes meet Cam's in the mirror, slide away before she can smile.

Getting hungry? he asks.

Not really, Annette replies. Her dreamy smile elevates her to a place where bodily functions are of no importance.

Cam? Mr Martin says then. You okay?

Yes, I'm fine, she lies. Her stomach roars treacherously. She is hollow from galloping in the hot air, she is an empty shell scoured by the wind. She strokes the feathers of her mother's hair in front of her. Her mother's hair is blistered like a pizza, sizzled by sun. (Cam has Mrs Martin's skin.)

A rest area beckons with cool willowy fingers.

Why not stop there, Ed? Cam's mother suggests, swivelling in the seat.

No water, Cam's father snaps. His eyes (Cam's eyes) flick like dark lizards back to the road. We said we'd take the girls to the beach and that's what we're doing, he says.

If you're sure it's no bother Mr M, murmurs Annette. Her diffidence is mature, she accedes to both Mrs Martin's desire to stop and Mr Martin's desire to drive on.

Sure I'm sure, Mr M booms. The car leans confidently into a corner so that Cam is thrown against Annette and smells her coolness. Cam herself is bursting with heat; it expands dangerously within the tight walls of her skin and demands to be let out. She opens her mouth in little pants to let the red air escape from her lungs.

Her mother's head looks small and deflated, scrunched down behind the headrest. Cam feels sorry for her mother but she wants Annette to see their special beach, wants her friend to have such a fabulous day that their friendship will be officialised, forever. (She thinks of her father's secretary, of the silver stamp crashing quick as lightning down on official forms.) Later, years later, she will open Annette's letters and golden grainy words will sprinkle out – Remember that day we went to the beach?

Yabba dabba doo! her father shouts exuberantly. With a wave of his strong brown hand, he fills the windscreen with sparkling sea. How's that for a view? Worth a drive then? he boasts.

The bush falls away beneath their tyres, islands scattered before them like blobs of egg white from a wild whisk.

It always is, his wife agrees. Her starfish hand is pale on his leg. Sorry for doubting you, it says mutely.

Cam glances at Annette, sees a smile, smiles herself. Everything will be all right.

We discovered this beach three years ago, she explains. We come here every holiday.

The car lurches on the rough track. Glasses and knives clash stridently in the picnic box at Cam's feet. Anxious, her mother glances round, opens her mouth, closes it. Her eyes are faded from ten days of sun.

The picnic cloth is such a bright blue, it out-blues the ocean. Plastic plates bob on its square aqua surface.

A chair, madame? Cam's father is on his best form. Ceremoniously, he hands a cushion to Annette. Her laughter flutters up into the trees.

Lemonade, Annette? Mrs Martin, too, is trying her best to please their guest. Her moth hand hovers over the chilly-bin.

Lemonade! I think we can do better than that! Ed jokes. How'd you like a shandy?

Mmm, lovely, Annette says politely.

There are only three proper glasses; it is not often that the Martins have extras on their family picnics. One two three glasses. One two three plates. Willingly, eagerly, Cam claims the cup from the top of the thermos. Her lemonade tastes of warm white plastic but she doesn't mind. She eats her ham sandwich off a paper towel.

D'you like swimming then? she says. There's a great pool down past those rocks, she says, it's quite deep. She gazes about anxiously, responsibly. The sand is as golden as ever, the waves wiping it clean with lacy rags.

No swimming for at least half an hour, her mother says firmly, give those sausage rolls a chance to settle.

Annette glances away delicately, nibble her pastry, sips her brown drink. I wouldn't mind having a bit of a sunbathe first, she says.

Yeah, good idea, Cam enthuses. Her legs prickle hot and cold with remembered sunburn. Casually, she flips onto her stomach so her calves are in the shade.

*

They change behind open car doors. No one around to see, though, Ed calls from where he is lounging under a tree.

Cam strips off quickly, matter-of-factly. Annette changes underneath a

T-shirt. Her bikini is fuchsia pink, bright triangles cover her small pert breasts. Coming in? she calls to Ed, her toes turned inward like a little girl's.

I might be persuaded, he replies lazily. His feet are bare too, ridged by long strong tendons. His second toe is bigger than his big one, though this is the first time Cam has noticed.

Mrs Martin looks over in mild surprise. You don't usually swim, she says.

Well, it's time I was less predictable, her husband answers. His eyes are narrowed against the sun which spikes through the pohutukawa leaves. You should come in yourself, he says, do you good.

I think I'd better stay out of the sun, don't you? Mrs Martin seeks reassurance, but her wispy words are blown away by her husband's sudden energy. He strips off his shirt and springs to his feet.

What are you waiting for, girls? he cries. Last one to the rocks does the dishes tonight.

Squealing, the girls run ahead of him. The sand grasps the soles of Cam's feet but she easily leaves Annette behind. Down the beach she flies, legs gulping the distance in great chunks. Triumphant, she turns; disappointed, sees the others far behind. They're not even racing. They jog up to her, their pace perfectly matched.

Guess we dishwash together, eh? Ed complains to Annette. His pretend grimace pleases Cam. He's really making an effort with her friend.

The water streams through Cam's long pale hair. She lies like seaweed on the waves. When she shuts her eyes there are pink and gold blotches on the inside of her lids.

Ed swims way, way out to the red buoy. His arms carve the air and the water into perfect circles. When he comes back in, his black hair sticks close to his bullet head.

Annette still sits on the rocks. Her knee is hooked up, her chin is on her knee. Why isn't she swimming? Whenever Cam looks over, sideways across the sea, anxiety swamps her and she begins to sink. There is a curious look on Annette's face, almost sullen. Sour water floods Cam's mouth.

But now her father comes to the rescue. He flicks water at the fuchsia togs. Annie! he shouts. Annie, don't be a sook!

Cam's heart shrinks at his presumption. But it's all right – Annette is looking livelier. Suddenly Ed shoots out an octopus arm, grabs a tanned ankle. There is a struggle, a scream, and then Annette is in the water. You pig! she laughs, and splashes Mr M back.

Cam can relax again, everything is all right.

*

It is much later. Cam lies on a cliff, idly peering through clover flowers as big as marshmallows. She squints into the earth with one eye, trying to keep the other eye on the horizon. Sun and grass merge in an aching blur. She lets her eyeballs roll straight again, swivels both in the same direction to see if the others are still swimming. She can never stay in long, she is too skinny.

Far below, she can see two dark seals lying on the rocks. Their tiny seal heads are sleek, they turn to each other and turn back again. Her father's is the bigger, darker one; Annette's is a smaller dot, her legs curled underneath like a question mark. They lie daringly in full sun, with identical defiant tans. Slip slop slap, hums Cam unconsciously. If her mother were there she'd be telling them to put on sunscreen and hats.

And there she is, her mother, a pale driftwood figure wending her way down the long beach. Her mother cannot see round the headland of rocks, the others cannot see her approaching. Omnipotent Cam holds all three in her sight. From her eyrie, she spies on her kingdom.

Now the eagle turns her gaze to her father, to her friend. They are fooling again, she sees indulgently. Their bodies roll against each other, tumble like empty bottles before breakers. Now they lie still, locked together. The high gaze sharpens; something is not right.

The eagle's breath gasps inwards, stabbing her throat. She sees her tiny white mother toiling over the rocks. Closer, closer. If Cam could fly now she would, she would fly down and swoop up her mother and soar her away, away from the treacherous pointy rocks.

But she cannot fly. She is marooned on her cliff top, hampered by her inadequate human form. She lays her face against the earth. Her fingernails claw, find damp soil beneath the scratchy grass. Her heart beats in her ears and her body lurches with the motion of her blood. When she raises her head she looks out to sea and the horizon swings sickeningly and the ground beneath her shakes with her breath.

*

Grey shadows are stalking across the sand on long legs when Cam returns to the others. Creeping towards the rug she is a reptile, she has been made hideous and she is old, old.

Only her parents are there. One. Two. Her mother is packing away the debris swiftly, clumsily. She looks up at her lizard daughter and tries to smile. Her eyes are watery like the sea.

Legs apart, Mr Martin is a pyramid of fury, a volcano of emotion. Where the hell have you been? he erupts. His voice hurts like sandpaper.

Where's Annette? asks Cam. The name sticks, then glugs past her swollen tongue. This is all she can say to her father. She sees a tawny pink figure prowling at the water's edge. The bikini is the colour of guilt, it burns Cam's eyes.

That little schemer, her father says contemptuously. That's the last you'll see of that little whore, he spits.

Ed, Edward, leave Cam alone, whispers her mother. Her voice is only a sigh of sand against cutty grass. She is hurrying, hurrying with the packing. Into the box she crams a glass which snaps. There is scarlet on Cam's mother's hand, scarlet to match her raw face, but she does not cry. Perhaps she will never cry again. She is stony still, has locked herself into round rock walls and cannot be reached.

It is Cam who is weeping.

I'm sorry, she says to her parents. I'm sorry.

(from) The Lonely Margins of the Sea

Shonagh Koea

During the afternoon of the following day they went down to the sea, skimming through the houses at the bottom of the road, through the outskirts of the shopping area, the car like a dark shark.

There had been the usual muffled telephone conversations early that morning, half heard through the gloom of the hallway and, when Stephanie had looked out through the kitchen door, Louise was sitting at the foot of the stairs, on the final and widest step, like a child unable to decide whether to go up or down. A little brass chair with a velvet seat had always been placed by the shelf that held the telephone, yet Louise had chosen to sit on the stairs as she had done years ago, when the enticements of the dolls' pram lay on the middle landing, looming above them all like a crown.

Yes, everything was going along well. The measured voice cut through the faint sound the wooden spoon made as Stephanie stirred Louise's porridge. Yes, they seemed to have slept well. It was all very quiet. Today they might go down to the coast, to the sea. What for? Nothing, really. She just had a yen to walk along beside the sea. Yes, even though it was too cold to swim yet. They still – and she made it plural this time – had this yen to go down to the sea. No, they wouldn't be going shopping because Stephanie had bought anything they needed for a day or so when she went over the road to the shops yesterday and no, she wasn't frightened. Money? Well, she had given Stephanie the purse to get the meat and things and then Stephanie had brought it back and given it to her. And, yes, she had given her the dockets, and yes, it all tallied. Everything was very quiet. Goodbye. The voice became cold and reedy then, a snub that would be incomprehensible to anyone else. Would it really be necessary to talk to them tomorrow? Perhaps they could ring the day after tomorrow as things were so quiet. Might that be a good idea? It wouldn't. All right then, tomorrow it is. Goodbye. The final word was as eloquent as the snap of the receiver back on to its cradle.

'I think you slept better last night.' Louise had come back into the kitchen now, filtering through the doorway almost like a visitor in her own house, slightly apologetic. Behind her lay the locked dark door to the little sitting room where once the chocolate box had been proffered so gently, where a pound note sometimes slipped into a small hand.

Tell your mother, Stephanie, that I want you both to go into town and buy something nice, something you might need, and here's something extra – the flush of a ten shilling note would crush into her hand – to get a nice afternoon tea for the two of you. Just tell her quietly, Stephanie, when you get home, when there's no one else about. It can be our little secret, you and me. Don't let him know you've got it, now will you, there's a good girl. But he could always smell money, her father. He had a nose for money. I'll toss you for it, Steph – double or quits. It was difficult to know exactly what that phrase meant – double or quits. Heads I win, tails you lose, okay? He would say that, a big man flushed from a day out somewhere, always with a ready smile, a canary yellow waistcoat and cold eyes. Are you ready? Are you watching? Okay, off we go. There you are Stephanie – heads, so I win. Now give me what you've got in your pocket. Give it to me, Stephanie. Fair's fair, if you won't give it to me I'll have to take it off you.

'I woke up just after midnight by my clock and your light was off. I looked out my window over the trees and there was no sign of light from your room. I think,' said Louise, 'that you're sleeping better.' Calmly satisfied and almost benign, she began to eat the porridge. 'Mother,' she said, 'always made porridge for me.' So they both sat there, in the sunny kitchen, like old children, somehow resisting the marks and the passions of the years. It seemed suitable and inevitable after that to climb in the car, leaving the dishes in the sink, and to skim lightly down through the town to the beach like girls on holiday and, once there, to breast the top of the sand dunes with a sort of ancient triumph as they had done when they were children. They even made some pretence of sliding down the other side, Louise's good arm clutched carefully in Stephanie's two hands, the slidings small and manageable so that if they tripped the little strappings across Louise's chest and up under the other arm would not tear away from that sliced and shrinking flesh. Behind them the car sat amid burgeoning tussock and sea grasses in a parking area that might not have been mowed all winter and all about them was the sound of the sea and the gulls and the waves breaking upon that untouched and deserted shore.

'Let's walk as far as the house.' That was Louise, already setting off along the sands towards where the old beach house had been, nestled behind the first row of dunes, only its red roof showing then above the rank growth of the shore. 'It mightn't even be there any more. Hurry up Stephanie, let's go and see. What do you think it might be like?'

In the evenings they had sometimes sat and looked at one of the old photograph albums, the pictures often faded to sepia on the black pages, the writing beneath each view, each face, done in silver ink, like the wandering trail of snails. The old beach house, hidden in the dunes, had had a row of wide windows in front, jutting like teeth on to a rough rolling lawn and, in front of this architectural grin, in various poses, they had all appeared like people in a play. All slightly self-conscious, those who were better-dressed and might perhaps have done better for themselves pert and slightly aloof, the invisible lines between cousins who married well and those who did not marked by the pointed toe of a silently eloquent Spanish espadrille of the more expensive sort, the turn of a ringed hand. Her mother had always been at the back, if she were there at all, and wore a frazzled air, her hair slightly untidy and falling down in wisps from a bun at the nape of her neck, her expression fraught as if there might be, at that very moment, something burning inside the cottage, in the little kitchen. She wore no rings at all.

Your mother was a very pretty girl, Stephanie. When she was young, people used to turn to look at her in the street. Now I want you to take her into town one day, perhaps when you're on holiday from school, and I want you to get a really nice lunch for the two of you. There would be the familiar feel of a pound note in her hand.

The sparse population of children – they were not great breeders – hung about on the edges, scowled from behind bushes made ragged by the sea wind or lolled, plump and satisfied with themselves, in the very front row. These were the offspring of cousins who had married well and they wore swimming togs with exclusive labels and had gold fillings in their teeth, their mothers loitering with beach towels slung over slim, handsome shoulders, the hands brilliant with rings. They liked things, liked to display their things to each other, particularly if what they had might be larger and better.

'Show them your new ring, Elizabeth.' That was the dry voice of some husband or another, and the hand would be outstretched for admiration. 'It's a Brazilian diamond, that's why it's so yellow. And the other ring's a sapphire – well, a sapphire in the middle with diamonds all around. I always think it's nice to have a really large cluster, don't you. Children, don't push and shove like that to see your auntie's hand. You can all have a turn to see in due course. She might even, if you're very good girls, let you have a little try-on, just for a moment. Who wants to have first turn? Hands up for first. You must be very, very careful because it's very valuable and your auntie might cry all day if you lost it.'

There would be a pause then, time enough for someone to notice their withdrawal. 'Margaret? Where are you off to? Have you seen Elizabeth's new ring? And what did you get for Christmas, my dear? Doesn't the little girl want a turn too? No?' Embarrassment turned them into hangers-on. They would hurry away to the kitchen, to hide their lack of gifts, their absence of ornamentation, her mother's hand gentler now and hot with embarrassment or the summer heat or distress, or all three. No one ever asked why they came alone, just the two of them with no father, no husband, no rings, no new dresses to show off, requiring a ride in someone else's car because no one drove them himself. Sometime or another he got two names. He was called he and no one. *Margaret and Stephanie have got no one. Did he come with them? No? So they had no one again, did they?*

'I must see to the scones,' her mother would call over one shoulder. 'I must just put the kettle on. I must put the salad in the refrigerator. I must whip the cream.' So they would escape from the tangible displays of affection, respect and status to sit by themselves in the kitchen for a moment or two, till lunchtime, till after the box Brownie was taken out for the holiday snaps in which neither of them wished to appear, the shabbiness eternally caught by the camera, their isolation held forever in the albums. *Margaret and her little girl Stephanie – he wasn't there, of course. He never is. They say he's even taken her engagement ring away and sold it.*

'I found this for you.' Her mother would fish around in her apron pocket to find a battered treat – perhaps one chocolate biscuit only slightly chipped and not entirely unfresh, or a segment of orange, a little sandwich made of hundreds of thousands, or sugar, anything that no one else had noticed. 'It was the last one,' she would say. 'I saved it for you. Just sit quietly on the step and eat it – don't let the others see. Let them have their rings. See if we care.' Sometimes it might be the last uneven wedge of cream sponge, the jam bleeding slightly into the cake. 'Eat it up quickly dear, before the others see.'

Today I teach you how to make sponge. I teach you how to make Victoria Sponge, very special. But, Tony, I don't really want to know how to make a sponge cake. What use would I have for a sponge cake? Here? You'd be better off teaching me how to make a mutton pie. So, you want to learn a good way to make mutton pie, next week we learn a good way to make mutton pie. This week, Victoria Sponge. Now take a nice piece of butter, like so. Please pay attention and I don't want to see faces pulled like that, thank you Stephanie. Today we do Victoria Sponge. Think of it like this – it's a way of passing the day. What other way would you pass the day? Exactly, so we make Victoria Sponge, Stephanie. In the evening, when she went along the corridor to see the man with the notebook, he said, how many marks would you give yourself for today, Stephanie? None? Why none? Because I was rude to Tony, she had said. I was rude to him about his cake and it wasn't his fault. I was offhand. I was rude in my own way, which is not the same way as other people are rude, but I was still rude by my standards. I might as well learn to make a nice sponge cake as do anything else. And he had looked at her for a long time. The difficulty with you is that you won't mix, he said. They're just trying to occupy you, to give you some reason to – and he stopped there. To live? To breathe? To show some interest? To stop lying on the bed with your face turned to the wall and your eyes shut? To refuse to speak or eat? But he had stopped before he said any of that. I know, and I'm sorry, she said. He's a kind man. I know he comes all the way out here from town just as a sort of thing he does to help. And it's not just me, you know, it's some of the others as well, I suppose. I think he'd like other people to go, other people to be interested in his cooking lessons. It's not just me that's a pain in the arse, it's the others as well. If some of the others would come to the lessons he'd be happier, even just one person. Ah, he said, the man who always wrote gently in the notebook, there's just a slight problem with that and I know it's ridiculous and you know it's ridiculous.

They're frightened of me, she had said. I know that. I know they're frightened of me. I'm the only one here – and again she stopped – the only one who stabbed someone. She stopped once more. There was that woman who shot a man but it was kind of an accident. She didn't mean to do it. I seem worse somehow, carving someone up. Quite so, he said. I know that. You know that. What should we do about it? he had said and seemed genuinely puzzled, had stopped writing and sat there with the pen in his idle hand. Nothing, she said. That's why I've given myself none out of ten for today and also overall. I've given myself none out of ten forever in a universal kind of way as well. And as for what can be done about it. Nothing. I can't do anything. You can't do anything. She almost felt as if she should snatch the notebook and write in it herself, about him. He is a kind man and does his best, but some of the cases are hopeless, all written in a firm, strong, official hand like that of a doctor. All I can suggest, she had said, is that next week when Tony comes here you let me into the kitchen early and I'll make him a Victoria Sponge as a surprise so he can see I really was listening and I did kind of learn how to do it even if today it was a disaster, and then he can teach me the mutton pie he mentioned and everything'll be all right again. Is there anything else you've got to say? he said. I haven't heard you talk so fluently for a long time.

I dunno, she said, just give me a minute or two and I might think of something. Only joking. I might go back to my room now, thanks.

'Tonight,' she said, as they breasted the last dune, 'I'm definitely going to make you a Victoria Sponge for your dessert. It wouldn't take long, half an hour at the most. You've got butter in the refrigerator, haven't you? And eggs and sugar and stuff? Okay then, it's a bargain.'

'Whatever made you think of that?' Louise was regarding the old cottage with care. 'The windows are all different,' she said. Behind them the beach stretched back to the carpark, their footsteps still clearly marked on the damp sand. 'They've taken out those old windows that went all along the front, those ones with the little panes, and they've put in those doors. I'm not sure I like it.' She stood with her head slightly tilted, as if she might be contemplating buying the place. The old gypsy look of crooked chimneys was gone and had been replaced by the straight finger of a gas flue. 'Did you ever come here? I can't remember seeing you. Are you in any of the photos?'

'I was usually in the kitchen. I must just be in the back of some of the pictures, kind of peeping round the corner or something like that.'

'Why were you usually in the kitchen?'

'I don't know,' she said. Another lie.

Have you been skiing? The cousins who had gold in their teeth specialised in expensive questions. Do you have tennis lessons? What school do you go to? Where is it? I've never heard of it. Where did you get that dress? I've never seen a funny dress like that before. Is it home-made? Why is the hem like that? My mother bought my dress. All my dresses are bought. Can you swim? We can all do breaststroke – we have lessons every Tuesday and we have French lessons on Wednesdays. Parlez-vous francais, mademoiselle? Vous n'etes pas tres belle, ha ha. *If you want a job you could top and tail those beans for me, her mother would say when she slipped into the kitchen. Don't you want to play with the others? They're all out there having a lovely time. Why don't you want to go and play? You're an odd child, aren't you? Fancy wanting to be hidden away in this funny old kitchen with me when you could be outside playing lovely games with the others.*

'I've got a lot of photographs back home of those old summers. I must get more of them out tonight and have a look.' Louise was turning away now, looking back towards the car. 'Did we walk that far? But the time seemed to go so quickly, Stephanie.'

'It's not so very far.' She was taking Louise's arm now, leading her down from the sandhills, to the flat beach again, where their footprints showed them the way back past the rock pools. The cousins in new togs every summer found sea anemones and shells undamaged by the tide there.

Look what Henry's found. Isn't he a clever boy? It's such a pretty shell, Henry. It looks most unusual, as if it could be in a museum. Aren't you clever? If Stephanie wasn't so silly and would go out and play with you other children she might find something nice, too, mightn't she?

'I think we'd better go, Louise. When we get home I want to make you that Victoria Sponge for your dessert,' she said, enticing Louise forward with the idea of a treat as if she might truly be a child again., 'and it takes at least half an hour to get the mixture in the oven and that's not counting cooking time. We'd better hurry.'

In some places, on the way to the cottage, she had idly trailed a piece of driftwood behind her, drawing loops and whirls on the clean damp sand, half-circles like the rope of a hangman's noose. Now, on the return journey, she scuffed these scars with her feet, obliterating the patterns, tearing up the sand so that, when she looked back finally, the mark of her passage looked like the backbone of a mythical creature, huge and marvellous, marked on the lonely margins of the sea.

'Do you remember,' said Louise as they climbed in the car again, 'all those games you children used to play? Do you remember the big red beach ball? And the quoits? And the beach races you used to have? And how someone always had an old box Brownie and took photographs of everyone?'

'No,' she said. 'I don't remember any of that. I don't think I was there.'

The Outsider

Graeme Lay

The girl in Kaimara's chemist shop stood behind the counter, staring through the plate glass window to the street beyond. Tuesday morning, and even less happening than usual. Not many people came to town on a Tuesday, but especially not today, with a bitter southerly raking the main street from end to end.

It was only April, but it was like winter already. The girl heaved a sigh. All there was to look forward to was spring, and that seemed a lot of southerlies away. She was pretty, with a clear pale skin which was well suited to showing off the pharmacy's beauty products. She had a slender figure, a long narrow face to match, and large green eyes. Her name was Justine, and she had been seventeen for three months.

A kilometre away, on the cliff-top above Kaimara beach, someone else was casting his eyes over the town. But unlike Justine, who had been born and raised in Kaimara, he had never seen the place before. He was not tall, but his back was broad, his hair was straw-coloured and untidy, and his blue eyes squinted from a deeply tanned face. He wore a faded green duffel coat, jeans and battered sneakers. His gaze was concentrated on the headland at the northern end of the bay, from which, he had already deduced, a submarine reef extended, because at a point some distance from the headland, the big swells sweeping in from the open sea reared abruptly then half-broke, and their crests were ripped to spindrift by the off-shore wind, pluming them back towards the horizon.

Still frowning with concentration, the man, who was twenty-three, followed another wave during its journey from the open sea to the beach, watching it rear, half-break, rear again, then re-form twice more before it finally dumped itself down on the bay's black sand. The young man had seen a lot of waves over the past few years. California, Hawaii, Mexico, Peru.

He studied the sea for a little longer, then got back into the brown Austin van beside him and drove the short distance from the cliff top to the town's main street. He parked outside the Criterion, Kaimara's two-storeyed wooden hotel, and entered the public bar. Two male drinkers and a heavy-bellied barman studied him curiously.

'Yes mate?' asked the barman. The newcomer scanned the bar, nodded at the pie-warmer beside the till.

'I'll have one of those, and a can of beer.' The curious looks of the other men intensified. American visitors to Kaimara were rare.

'What part of the States're you from?' said the barman.

'San Diego,' the young man replied, starting to devour the pie keenly.

'Passing through?' asked one of the other drinkers.

The American swallowed. 'No, I'll stay a bit. Is there any accommodation round here?'

The barman nodded keenly. 'Plenty of rooms upstairs.'

The visitor shook his head. 'I was thinking more in terms of renting some place. I saw some cottages down at the beach. Any of them for rental?'

The barman nodded. 'Yeah, could be. Beach's pretty dead now it's past Easter.' He thought for a moment. 'Tell you what, I'll give Doug Dawson a ring, he rents his bach sometimes.' He moved to the phone on the wall behind the bar, then paused, turned back. 'What name shall I tell 'im?'

'Carl. Carl Sikowsky.'

'And what do you do, Carl?'

'I surf.'

Doug Dawson turned the big key in a lock corroded by sea spray. 'Course it's a bit sandy,' he said apologetically. 'Hasn't been used since Easter.'

They went in.

The one main room had a row of windows along its seaward side, a coal range recessed into one end wall, a sink and a small fridge at the other. There were two plump old lounge chairs, a dark oak table in the centre, rattan matting over the board floor. The room smelt of stale fried food. The American drew back a tatty curtain, peered into the small bedroom, went to the windows. The sea was a hundred metres away, and foamy remnants of the great waves slid back and forth across the sand. He turned back to the owner.

'It's great, I'll take it.'

He bought a carton of groceries, some steak and a bag of tomatoes in the main street. As he was loading them into the van he noticed the chemist's shop. The girl behind the counter looked up as he entered.

'Hi,' he said. 'I'd like some wax please.'

His accent flustered her. She smiled nervously, felt herself colouring.

'What kind of wax?'

'Paraffin wax.' He measured a short distance with his hands. 'It comes in blocks about this long. Drugstores usually have some.'

'Oh yes.'

She turned to the shelves, located the packet, passed it to him. He had a wry, bemused expression on his face.

'It's to put on my board. I'm Carl. Do you live around here?'

He put the paperback aside, got up and walked to the windows. He studied the little cloth tell-tale he had erected in front of the bach. Nor-westerly. The waves would hold up well today. Above the bay the sky was pewter-coloured, and spray thrown up by the breakers blurred the horizon. The beach was deserted, as it always was. The locals had told him that in summer people came from all over to swim here, but looking at it now that was hard to imagine. He had never found such a place before, that he had to share with no one else. What did it matter that the town was Hicksville, when he could have all this to himself? He went out onto the little back porch to put on his wetsuit.

They gathered on the cliff top to watch him, small groups of people from the town. One man had a camera with a telephoto lens, another a movie camera on a tripod. They watched the small black figure carry his board across the beach to the line of boulders at the foot of the cliff, then leap from rock to rock until he had reached a spot three-quarters of the way to the headland. There he waited for a lull between the swells. The sky was still overcast and a cold wind was blowing across the bay, but he didn't care about the coldness because the offshore wind was smoothing the water further out. He attached the board's leash to his ankle, then when a lull came, waded out into the water, his feet feeling their way from stone to stone until it reached his thighs. Then, gripping his board in both hands, he launched himself forward.

In seconds he was clear of the rocks and kneeling on the board, his hands making swift dipping strokes, his head bobbing like a Moslem at prayer as he moved out into deep water. Half a kilometre out in the bay he veered right, towards the area beyond the headland, where the ocean swells were steepened by the reef. As he did so he began to feel the sea surging and roiling beneath him, and feeling its power caused his heart to pump. Glancing to his left he could see, now just a hundred metres away, the tube forming, and the roar of the breaking water filled his head like the noise from an approaching tornado. Only once before had he been among waves as big as these, and that was off the north coast of Oahu. But in Hawaii he had had to share the waves with dozens of others. Here he was alone.

By the time he reached the reef the people on the cliff-top were straining their eyes to still see him, and at times he vanished altogether in the troughs between the swells.

Then he sat up, his board protruding from the water like a taunting tongue, steadying himself with one hand, watching, waiting, paddling patiently. Turning and facing beachward, rising and falling steadily from the swells passing beneath him, he studied the breaking waves, trying to calculate the distance he could ride before they closed out. Earlier, from the cliff-top, he had studied the wave patterns, had seen the violence with which the waves broke as they eventually reached the shallow water. Whatever happened he must not stay with the waves for that long. If he did the dumping would be as dangerous as going over Niagara Falls, as bad as hitting Hawaii's coral. He remembered his friend Amos Leakaha, who – crowded out by other board riders – hadn't been able to spin out soon enough and had been dumped straight down on the coral reef. Amos, paralysed from the waist down, now watched the other surfers from his wheelchair on a hill above the beach, a bottle of Coruba always in his hand. At the age of twenty-one, an alcoholic as well as a paraplegic.

Carl spent several minutes lying on his board at the edge of the break, paddling gently, watching closely, waiting to make his move. Glancing down into the cold, crystal-clear water, he could see the reef several metres below him. The rocks were black and mottled with pink growths. Brown seaweed moved slowly back and forth in the current like a girl's long hair. He stared down for some minutes, fascinated by the sight, before he looked up again and out to sea where the water mountains were forming. Then he began to paddle forward, urgently, cutting a track across the surface of the water and into the path of the swells.

Instinct as much as experience told him which wave to choose. Pointing his board landward, he began to dig into the water, deep and hard. And as the huge wall began to build up behind and below him, he thrust himself forward with all his strength.

And on the cliff-top above the beach the cameras began to click and whirr, and Justine's eyes tracked him, her throat tight with fear and love.

As the swell became a wave and the surge caught him, he felt the board achieve its own momentum. It overtook the wave and began to slide diagonally downward, the water beneath him moving like an avalanche. He sprang to his feet and planted them firmly on the waxed part of his board, his right foot in front of his left. Crouching, he glanced left and right, keeping just ahead of the break at his shoulder, trying to estimate the height of the wave. Five metres, at least. Maybe even six. Now the moving wall of water was carrying him in three dimensions – forward, downward and across – at scintillating speed. As always he felt a multitude of sensations – exhilaration, anticipation, fear – which in just a moment came, went and returned, a constantly shifting series of impressions, all-powerful, all-thrilling.

Crouching like a skier, he reached the foot of the wave, where he again glimpsed the shadowy, pink-mottled reef rocks before swerving and rising swiftly to the wave's crest. Just a metre behind him, the roar of the white water sounded like a cataract in his ears. Ahead of him the glass wall was steepening. Twice more he plunged and rose, getting the maximum speed from his friend and enemy the wave, always keeping just ahead of the break, knowing that if he misjudged, slipped and was taken down he would in that instant be fighting for his life but knowing too that if it happened he would regret nothing, for nowhere else had he known waves like these. Glancing back once more, he saw that the wave was coiling, was about to close out. He powered up its face, but this time instead of swerving he kept going, powering through its crest and out the other side, launching himself into space for a few seconds like a ski jumper before coming down on calm water.

He lay still for a few seconds, regaining his breath, then, looking around, saw the breaking wave seethe, bulge and collapse in a deadly cauldron. As he stared he saw the churning water turn black with volcanic sand from the bottom of the bay before the wave surged on towards the beach. Then, triumphant, chest heaving, he pointed his board seaward again.

And at the end, when he was so tired that he could paddle no more, he would allow a wave to collapse beneath him, ride the white water straight into the beach. And Justine would already be at the bach, and the fire in the coal range would be alight, the tin bath running hot, ready to bring colour back into his hands, feet and face, which were bleached by the cold.

'Warm now?' She set the mug of tea on the edge of the bath.

'Aaaah…yes.' He tipped his head back, closed his eyes.

The room was suffused with the warm air and the smell of the simmering stew on the coal range. A Tchaikovsky symphony came from the record player on the sideboard. The only music he played was classical, and although she thought it was, well, a bit gloomy, she accepted it in the way she accepted everything else about him. He was different to anyone she had ever known, different in the way he spoke, and what he said, and what he did and knew and had done. He had no need of a job, money came to the local bank for him in some way from southern California, where his father sub-divided orchard land for housing. His parents were divorced, he was an only child. Carl knew about places she had hardly ever heard of – Costa Rica, Colombia, Peru. He spoke Spanish, he could cook Mexican food and he drank mainly red wine. Around the walls of the bach he had pinned up enlargements of the photographs of himself board riding that Mr Leslie, her boss from the chemist's shop, had taken from the cliff top. They showed Carl glissading down the face of a huge wave, crouching under a break so that only his head and one shoulder were visible, and the one she liked best, he with one arm around her, walking along the beach, his board under his other arm.

'Another cup?' She picked up the empty mug. He sat up and began to rinse the soap from his neck, screwing up his eyes as if in pain.

'No, just open a bottle of wine and bring me a glassful will you? A big glass.' And as she poured it and brought it to him, settling the glass on the edge of the bath, she thought, yes, it is because he is so different that he means so much. And to him I am different, and that is why we are so good for each other.

Half the winter passed. The beach and the little house beside it became their entire world. With the club rugby season at its most feverish, the town concentrated its passions on the rugby ground at the far end of Kaimara, but Carl showed not the slightest interest in that game. Neither did the seasons have any meaning for him. Only when the wind turned to the west, and the waves were whipped to a gigantic, unrideable size, did he not take his board out into the bay. Then they would collect driftwood from the beach for the fire, light it, then lie on the sagging bed and listen to the records and the sea spray being driven against the windows. Justine knew how the town was talking, knew by the sniggers of the youths and the matrons' stares, as frosty as the paddocks that surrounded Kaimara, but he taught her not to care. He would laugh and say, 'They're hill-billies, Justy, those people. Shit-kickers. They belong in the Appalachians.' And after he had explained what that meant, they laughed about it, and he mimicked a mountain man accent. Once, after a day when the sea had been like glass and the waves perfect, translucent tubes, he said to her,

'Why don't they surf?'

'Who?'

'Anyone in this place.'

'They body-surf, in the summer.'

He grunted, derisively, went on staring up at the sagging pinex ceiling.

'Think how many years those fantastic waves out there have been rolling into this bay, and no one ever rode them. Hundreds, thousands of years maybe…'

She propped herself up one on elbow and studied him. He had grown a beard, and to her fascination his whiskers were a pale auburn shade, and there were two completely bald patches on either side of the centre of his chin. Justine said:

'I'll bet other people will try to surf, next summer, now that they've seen you do it.'

He frowned, hard, as if that hadn't occurred to him before.

'That'll spoil it. It'll make this place like all the others. Over-crowded.'

She felt a tremor of fear. For a moment she did not know why she felt it, then she realised why. It was the only time he had ever mentioned the future, the what-could-happen, and the way he said it gave her the feeling that if he could not have the beach and the bay all to himself, then he might leave, and the thought of that was unbearable to her. She knew that for him, riding the giant waves was not sport, it was a life force that could not be considered separately from breathing or eating or making love.

It was September, and they had known each other for five months, when she learned what could be, was true. She went directly to the beach. There had been another frost, and vestiges of mist hung over the bay as she walked down the track, her coat collar turned up against the still, chilly air. Half way down the track she stopped. Today there was not a whisper of wind, and the sea was as shiny and smooth as shot silk. From the track she watched him moving among the waves, gleaming like a seal in his wetsuit. Selecting the right wave, cutting a narrow furrow down its face. She went on down to the bach and lit the range. He came in just after midday, grimacing with the cold, teeth clicking like an abacus. But he was ecstatic as he squatted in front of the range, a blanket wrapped around him. 'They're incredible Justy, incredible. They're holding up for a kilometre out there. And the shape. *The shape.*' Then, as he subsided into silence and sipped his tea, she knelt beside him, put her arm around his shoulders and told him the news that would keep them together always.

He sat staring into the grate, nodding as she spoke, as if he had known all along. His hair was stiff and shiny, like wet straw, and the skin beneath his stubbly beard was ice-white. When he turned to look at her his eyes were brightly amused, as though she had told him a long and very entertaining story. Then he turned back to the fire, and as she told him the plans that she had made, of the bigger bach that would become available for the three of them, he nodded again, approvingly, and said with the same amused expression on his face, 'So there's going to be a Kaimara branch of the Sikowsky family, eh?' And he laughed, and hugged her, and opened a bottle of red wine, and they drank most of it, joking about what people in the town would say. 'Those old women on the … what do call the switchboard?

'The telephone exchange.'

'Right. They'll have the news all over Kaimara by Monday. They're like those town criers, in the Middle Ages.'

And they both laughed, and drank, and made love in front of the fire, and when she made her way home later that day she was happier than she ever believed a person could be.

Next morning the sky was overcast, and there was a soft off-shore wind. When she reached the cliff-top she saw that the waves were even better than the day before, because now the breeze was holding them up, preventing them breaking for several minutes, and when they did finally collapse the spray hung above them like lace. She looked for the sleek black figure among the waves, but he was not yet out. She walked on down the track and through the long kikuyu grass to the bach. The van was not there, and neither were his boards. The back door was ajar. She pushed it open. There were unwashed dishes on the table, an empty wine bottle, ashes in the grate. The windows that faced the sea were all open. She went to the door of the bedroom. No clothes, no bags, just a heap of sheets and blankets. She went back into the main room. The photos had been taken from the walls. All except one, of two people, walking on the beach. There was no fire, no food, no note. She stood very still, staring towards the open windows, her mind frozen too, her ears filled with the sound of the waves, breaking violently against the distant reef.

The Picnic Virgin

Victoria McHalick

Some of our friends get to go away as soon as school breaks up, but we stay at home until after Christmas so that we can go to church. Mum's always told us that Christmas is not just about presents. She says we are part of the Sunday school so we have a duty to be in the Christmas pageant.

When they first worked out the parts, I wanted to be Mary. She is the prettiest. She gets to wear a blue dress and it's all bright and shiny. And she has a veil too. But there's another girl who is older and Mum says it's only right that the older one gets to be Mary. She said I might have a turn next year when I'm eleven.

I didn't want to be an angel but they needed someone who could speak clearly to be Gabriel. Mrs Green said I'd be wonderful as Gabriel and you can't say no to a Sunday school teacher because it would be a bit like saying no to God. Also I was afraid of being in trouble with Mum and Dad if I made a fuss about Mary.

This morning my sister Josephine woke up and said she wanted to be a sheep. They said she could be an angel but she wanted to be a sheep or else she wouldn't be in it. Mum said, 'It's all right, you can be a sheep,' but she wouldn't let me be Mary.

After we open our presents, we put on our costumes. My hair has been freshly washed and I have a piece of tinsel twisted in a circle attached to a wire around my head. Mum tells me I look beautiful but I know Mary is the most beautiful and Mum just has to say that because she is my mother.

We walk to church in the sunshine and even Dad comes, with his suit and tie on. All the people in the play are still outside. The vicar's dog, Jerry, is going to be the donkey. Brian, who is Joseph, is leading him along by his collar. Jerry is barking and the vicar is telling him to siddown in a voice you don't expect from a vicar who talks about caring for even God's smallest creatures.

Mrs Green is calling all the animals and the angels together. We are allowed to go in first because we have speaking parts. I say my words looking at Mary. She is so lovely that I forget how much I wanted to be like her and only think about how I want to help her understand this amazing thing that is going to happen. She looks so frightened and I tell her in my most gentle, clear voice, 'Don't be afraid, Mary, God has been gracious to you. You will have a baby named Jesus. He will be great and will be called the Son of the Most High God …'

Then Mary, Joseph and Jerry walk around the choir stalls until they get to the stable. The animals are coming up the aisle now. Josephine is crawling on her hands and knees. She's got an old sheepskin rug tied to her back. She makes sure she is at the front and I can see her looking up at Mary. She is the only other person who understands how wonderful Mary is and she's there just gazing at her with her mouth open. She doesn't even notice Jerry behind her, sniffing at the sheepskin, trying to get at it with his teeth and doing this funny hunched thing until the vicar races up and drags him out by the collar.

Later we read prayers from a little green book. It must be an old book because the words sound like they are from the olden days. Things you can't really understand like 'thee' and 'thou', 'born of the Virgin Mary', made incarnate' and 'bless-ed be'.

Outside the church the vicar tells Mum and Dad how much he enjoyed the play but sorry about the dog. 'That's the last time we'll use a German shepherd as a donkey,' he says.

Mum tells us afterwards that she was really proud of us being in the pageant, 'especially you, Margaret, because I know how much you wanted to be Mary'. I don't say anything but I smile at her because she's telling me she knows I've been good.

We are all in the car and driving to our grandparents' house. They live further up the coast where the weather is warmer. All our cousins are much younger than Josephine and me. They're already there when we arrive, running about and playing with their tricycles. Grandma is telling them to be careful of the furniture and to keep outside with the bikes. She tells them to be careful of her flowers. Then Mum says Grandma is getting worked up and it would be a great help if we'd just keep all the kids outside.

Grandpa comes out and asks Josephine and me if we'd like a drink.

'Got any whisky?' asks Josephine and Grandpa roars with laughter and tweaks her nose, saying, 'We've got a right one here.'

I wish I could make Grandpa laugh too but when he asks me what I want it is impossible to think of anything funny like Josephine.

'What's the matter? Cat got your tongue?' he says to me. I feel my face getting hot but I laugh as if he's said a good joke.

'Well?' he says. 'What do you want?'

'Oh. Lemonade please. Or just a glass of water would be fine. Thank you.'

'So it's whisky for Josie and just a glass of water thank you for Miss Margaret,' he says, imitating my voice. I can't think of anything to say so I look ahead and pretend it doesn't matter. I wish he would just go inside but he's swinging the littlies around. They're all yelling at him, 'my turn, my turn', and Josephine's the loudest of them all even though she's bigger. I want to tell her to come over here with me but I don't know what Grandpa might say.

I sit by myself on the patio between the house where all the adults are talking and the garden where the children are romping with Grandpa. Why was Mary so afraid when everything Gabriel told her seemed so good?

Grandma calls out the window, 'Come on, you old goat. This turkey's not going to carve itself.'

'God, love a duck,' mutters Grandpa as he goes back inside.

At lunch we have to sit in the kitchen at the children's table because there's not enough room at the dining table. Grandpa brings two glasses of lemonade in special glasses for Josephine and me. He tells us that we are the only ones allowed to have his best crystal. I say, 'Thank you very much.' Josephine picks up hers and says, 'Cheers, Big Ears.' Grandpa winks at her and shakes his head, laughing, saying she's a little monkey but they wouldn't swap her for anyone.

We stay all afternoon playing with the little ones, trying to keep them outside. It's strange that Christmas is meant to be such a great day but for us it's always so slow. Finally Dad says we'll have to go because he wants to get to the bach before it gets dark. We drive over the bridge, past the wooden stand where we buy brown paper bags of plums and put the money in the tin. Then Mum says, 'Look, there she is. It's Mary on the hill. And the lights are all lit around her head.'

We look out and see the huge white statue of Mary. It's always like that. We watch in silence as she looks down on us. Sometime you can almost see her face. Eyes downwards and a sad smile as if she could start crying at any moment, but that she would never allow herself to do it. It's never the same during the day. It's just a piece of painted concrete. But at night the white looks so white. And the lights around her head glow golden on her face.

As we drive past the hill I whisper, 'Don't be afraid, Mary. God has been gracious to you,' and I am sure I can see her mouth quiver as she disappears out of my view.

Soon we arrive at the bach. It's painted bright pink because Grandma said she'd like it to be pink. 'I didn't mean *that* pink, she'd said once Grandpa started slapping on the paint but he wouldn't stop once he'd started and so that was the colour it remained.

I share the room at the front with Josephine. The bunks go across the window and when I'm on the top bunk I can see people walking along the street. It is great to lie there just as it's getting dark, with the sliding windows open. You can hear the sea. The brushing of the waves onto the sand. Sometimes when people walk past you can even hear them talking and they don't know you can hear. Once I heard a man say to a lady that he'd like to give her one but she was giggling and I couldn't hear the rest. Mostly they talk about the weather or the houses on the street. One night

I'm going to sneak out the window with Josephine and we're going to run down the street in the dark without anyone knowing. But we'd have to get the timing right because Mum always comes in and shuts the window later so the mosquitos don't get us.

She closes the curtains and they jangle along their metal runners. I can hear her closing the curtains on the other side of the wall where our parents are sleeping. I can hear Mum and Dad murmuring and then Mum laughs and says sshhhh over the creak. They think we are asleep. Josephine is, but I stay awake thinking about Mary and wondering what it would be like to be told your baby was going to be a king.

The next morning, even though we've been up for ages, we are still in our pyjamas with the pink rosebuds. We are practising doing forward rolls off the top bunk. I stand at the bottom to catch Josephine in case she falls and then I show her how to do it again. When I land my pyjama top is open. Josephine laughs and says, 'You're getting bosoms. I can see your bosoms.'

She wasn't allowed to say that, especially when I was just trying to help her. My face is hot and I tell her to stop it but she's laughing. I am crying now and Mum comes in to find out what's going on. I don't want to tell her.

'Something must be wrong or else you wouldn't be so upset. Tell me now or else I'm going to get really cross with both of you.'

So in the end I tell her. She laughs but she tries not to. She tells Josephine to stop being silly and she tells me not to worry about it.

I get dressed and we go outside to play in the back garden. It stretches right up to the hill behind and there are fruit trees and a big wire cage with kiwifruit growing over it but they're always too hard and sour for us to eat. I like it under there. No matter how hot the sun is, it is always cool and dark under the kiwifruit. I lean against the pole and smell the fragrance of the leaves and fruit and sand. I tell Josephine that this is the castle where the princess lives and there's an evil prince who wants to have her as his wife even though she is already married to another nice prince. Josephine says we have to both be princesses and we should be tied to the poles waiting for the bad prince to kiss us. I tell her not to be so silly. That this is our test. We have to fight the evil prince off and stay faithful. She says she wants to play cowboys instead.

Then Dad comes in and asks us if we want to go for a swim. We put on our togs and jandals and walk down the tarsealed road with him. Once I tried to go in bare feet along the grass but there were too many prickles.

Dad jumps Josephine over the waves and I try to race the bigger waves up the beach. They always seem to be winning and then at the shore they suddenly slow down and disappear into nothing but a thin strip of popping foam. It's funny too how you always hold your breath and gasp as you jump under that first wave which is so freezing. But then the water seems warmer after that.

Sometimes we walk down to the corner dairy to buy raspberry buns with Mum. Today Mum is reading something on a notice board about a holiday programme she thinks we should go to. I am happy just being in the garden or on the beach but she says she wants us to try this at least for a day. I don't like the sound of it.

'Margaret, you mustn't do this. Being negative about everything until you've given it a try.' The words sting. I wasn't 'negative'. What about Gabriel? I'd been good about that. I bite my lip and don't say anything else.

We go along to a big tent on a grassy section next to the local church. Mum says it is supposed to be great fun for boys and girls. There are lots of us there. I am one of the oldest. Up the front are five people with guitars. They are grown-ups but not like Mum and Dad. They are much younger than that. And they aren't wearing suits and dresses. They have on T-shirts and jeans. One woman has long blond hair and she is wearing a wonderful skirt with lots of layers and all different colours. They say things like, 'Hi gang, great to have you all here. Now let's clap our hands for Jesus and tell Him how much we love Him.' They sing songs that are fun to sing, like they could be off the radio, and we get to clap and even put our arms in the air if we want to but I don't quite feel like it.

Then they put us into groups. I stand in the corner with the ten-to-twelve-year-olds. When we are all herded to another corner, the woman in the lovely skirt comes over. She has bare feet too. 'Hi guys, I'm Angela. Hey, we're the oldest group apart from the teenagers, which makes us pretty special. Let's all sit down and tell each other our names.'

We go around the circle. There is one girl who seems older than the rest of us. When it is her turn she says 'Catherine' in a quiet voice and looks down. She has soft reddy-gold hair and her eyes look as if she might even have a tiny bit of mascara on. And her lips are glossy like in the magazines. When we stand up to get our books she is taller than the rest of us, too. She is beautiful. I can't help watching her because she looks like something from a film and I even wonder if she might be famous. When she shakes her head her hair moves behind her shoulders. Then, as she lowers her eyes, slowly her hair falls forward until she shakes it back again.

We are given books about Bible stories with blank bits to draw pictures in. I'm not very good at faces and in fact at school everyone said I was really good at drawing cats. I decide I will illustrate all the stories with cats rather than people. Today I draw a cat giving out loaves and fishes. It looks really fantastic. I am quite proud of it. As the days go by, Angela always wants to see what I've done and she shows all the other leaders. Especially Mark. He has blond hair too and he often seems to be looking at Angela and when they play their guitars it almost seems like they are playing and singing for each other. I'm not completely certain but I am pretty sure that one day Angela and Mark might actually get married. I can tell. I don't talk about it to Josephine because she is too young and I don't think she'd understand. But I like to watch them and imagine them together. Once I even let myself think about what they would do when the vicar said, 'You may kiss the bride.' She would still have bare feet and he would put his arms around her and kiss her very lightly on her lips.

I lie in bed thinking about them. I can't sleep. I think about Catherine too and try to work out how I could be like her even just a little bit but I don't know how. I can feel the sand in my bed. No matter how much you wipe your feet, the sand always creeps in with you. Then it works its way all over your body without your knowing until days after you get home again it's still between your toes and in your ears and hair.

In the morning I am so tired I don't want to get out of bed but that is partly because I want to keep thinking. I have an aching head later that day. It's the first time I've ever had that. I am allowed to go back to bed and Josephine has to stay out. Mum comes in and says that Dad and she thought that I might want to talk. I get up straightaway and tell her it's just a sore head. Josephine wants to come with me but Mum holds her arm.

'Margaret just needs a bit of time by herself,' she says in a way that Josephine listens to.

I sit under the kiwifruit and hold my head. I feel mean because Josephine and I do everything together and I don't want her to feel left out. I don't know how to tell her that I just don't feel like myself any more. I call out and she comes running out immediately. She'd been waiting by the door.

'Do you want to play cowboys over by the woodpile?' I ask.

'Yeah,' she says. 'You can be the girl.' It's her way of saying, 'Are you OK?' It's always best to be the girl in our games. If you were the boy, you were only there for the girl.

We go along to an afternoon activity. It's the sandcastle competition on the beach. The wind is blowing in the toetoe and the long sea-grass cuts our legs as we all run down to the waves with dirty white foam everywhere. Catherine is wearing shorts and a little shirt cut off above her waist. She has a fine gold chain around her neck. I hope one day I could have a chain like that. Our group is making a castle and she is hunting for shells to put around it. One of the boys from the teenage group gives her his cap so she has something to put her shells in. She smiles at him and then looks down again. Then they all play cricket but I don't really know how to play and I don't want to look stupid so I just watch. Catherine hits the ball and runs. The little gold chain bounces from side to side and the hair blows across her face. The boy who chased the ball could have got her out but he pretends to drop it. She smiles and he winks at her. She laughs and tosses her hair back.

'We're having visitors over for a barbecue tonight. It's the Thompsons from across the road,' says Mum when we get back.

'Oh no. Do they have to?' I ask. There are two boys a bit older than me and one girl about Josephine's age. Mum sighs and Dad looks up.

'I don't know what you're complaining about when you'll be the one with two boyfriends,' he says to me.

Mum and Josephine laugh and Josephine's saying, 'You've got a boyfriend, you've got a boyfriend,' and I feel like I could die.

Dad is out lighting the barbecue. It's burning too hard so Dad and Mr Thompson are having a beer while they wait for it to calm down. The boys are climbing up the bank at the back and then running down through the bushes as fast as they can, shouting like they're Tarzan or something. Their father calls them over to say hello. They look at their feet and grunt. I wish they weren't here. Josephine is already playing with their sister and I have no one. Mr Thompson is asking me how I like school and what I want to be when I'm older. He keeps saying he can't believe how much I've grown up and I feel uncomfortable with those boys there and him saying that.

I go inside to our room.

'Are you all right? What are you doing?' asks Mum as she comes in.

'Nothing. I'm just getting changed,' I answer with my back to her, taking off my brown skivvy.

'Margaret, I hope you're not embarrassed about your …'

'No, it's just I'm too hot and I'm sweating and this shirt shows it under my arms.'

It is the first lie I tell my mother. She leaves and I change into a cotton shirt.

As the night moves on we finally get our sausages and chops with tomato sauce. There's also the lettuce salad that I put the slices of hard-boiled egg on, and there's buttered white bread. I pick the black bits off my sausage and watch the parents. They're drinking wine out of a cardboard box with a tap on it and laughing with each other. All these jokes that don't make sense but Mum is shrieking with laughter as if it's really funny and saying to Mr Thompson, 'Oh Barry, you're so outrageous.'

The boys ask me what sports I like and I shrug. I ask them and they talk for ages about it. They ask if I'd like to see their bikes. We walk back over the road. They're flash boys' bikes, not the old rickety things Josephine and I ride on that used to belong to Mum and her sisters. They ask if I want to try. I climb on and pedal around their garden. We have a few races taking turns up the road in the dark. It's quite fun. I think they let me have a head start at first but then they are really trying and sometimes I still win. One of them skids and falls off in the gravel. The other one is laughing and it does look pretty funny. I laugh too and he gets back on his bike and starts to chase me to push me off for laughing. He says he's going to get me and I think he might like me and I almost feel special.

I leap down from the bike to get away but forget there is a bar across on boys' bikes and I nearly pass out with the pain. I manage to walk and not to cry in front of them. I pretend I hurt my leg and they let me be. They follow me across the road back to our place. Josephine is singing in her loud voice and the parents are clapping and cheering for more. I sit down and watch. The boys sit with me and we talk about people in our classes at school. The one who fell off his bike asks if I'd like to go for a ride with them tomorrow but I tell them I'm doing something else. I couldn't stand it if Mum and Dad found out and teased me.

The next day in the tent they are talking about Christ dying for us. I draw a picture of a cat being crucified and Angela takes it to show the other leaders. They are singing their songs again and we are clapping. They tell us just ask the Lord Jesus into our hearts and He will come in. They tell is that He is just waiting for us to ask and that He loves us. They tell us you can't just say it, you've got to really mean it and then it will set you free. They say that once you have Him, He will protect you forever. I want to ask Him in but I'm not sure if I'd really mean it and then I don't know what would happen.

In the afternoon we go on a bus for a picnic to a park further down the coast. All the way on the ride I am thinking about asking Christ in but I don't think I can do it with all these people sitting around me. Also I'm trying to sing with them at the same time.

When we get there we divide into our groups to eat our lunches. Afterwards we are allowed to go for a swim in the river. There are changing rooms and we all go in to put on our swimming togs.

Catherine is wearing a bright shiny blue bikini and she looks like she should be in a beauty contest. She has real breasts, not these little things I've got, and she still has on her gold chain about her neck. I can't help wishing I could be like her. We all go together to the river and swim and splash about. I can see Josephine and she waves back at me. She is with her group further down.

It gets colder and I'm starting to shiver. I get out to go back and change. There are a few of us. As we get towards the changing rooms, I can see there are some older boys, almost men in fact. They don't belong with us. They're sitting on the ground with their legs across the path, holding cans and smoking. They're wearing jeans and heavy jackets even though it's a really sunny day. They're laughing but not like the parents at the barbecue. It's sort of deeper and slower and you can't really hear them saying anything except mumbling.

We walk past trying not to trip over their legs. I can't help flinching. Catherine is behind us and one of them says to her,

'Hey you. Are you a virgin?'

Then they all laugh. I look at her. She's wearing that look. Like she's afraid. And suddenly I understand what it is. They think she is the Virgin Mary because she is so beautiful. And Mary had that frightened look too. Maybe she's scared because she doesn't want anyone else to know but her and God. They're all standing around her now. One of them reaches out to touch her on the blue and she pulls herself away. They are laughing and pushing her between them. Then she runs into the changing room with her hands over her chest like a cross.

I want to tell her not to be afraid but it doesn't seem right now. We are all getting dressed and she leaves with her bag over her shoulder. I can't see her on the bus home and someone says she got a lift with one of the leaders in their car.

That night Mum and Dad are asking how our day went. I tell them what the men outside the changing rooms said. Dad doesn't say anything but his face almost crumples. I'm lying in my bunk and Mum comes in after Josephine has gone to sleep.

'Do you understand what that meant, what those boys said?'

'They thought she was Mary. They must have know we are Christians.' I'm quite pleased with myself for knowing so much.

'Darling. That wasn't very nice what they said to her.' And she tells me what it means.

I'm so glad it is dark and Mum can't see my face. I can't believe what she's saying because it seems so embarrassing that they'd keep calling Mary 'the Virgin Mary' in a place like church.

Mum asks me what happened next. I tell her nothing happened. And when I think of Catherine's face now, I'm sure she wouldn't want me to say anything else. Mum asked me where our leaders were when it happened but

I don't know.

She kisses me goodnight. I lie in bed and think about Catherine and why she was so frightened and how I did nothing. I remember them trying to touch her and how she groaned and wrenched her arm free to hold her top as it started to fall. I can't stop myself thinking about what they might have done if it was all dark, even though I don't want to think about it, I can't help it, to imagine them so big and dirty and Catherine like she is, so perfect. I think about what the leaders said and I want to ask Jesus into my heart so I can ask Him where He was today when Catherine needed protecting. But it's sort of ruined for me now.

It's the last day and Angela says she forgot to bring my book. I was going to give it to Catherine but she isn't there either. We all sing and clap and then they announce that Angela and Mark are going to get married. Everyone cheers and whistles when Mark puts his arm around Angela and kisses her right in front of us for ages.

That night, after Mum has closed them, I open the windows again. I open them slowly so that they make no noise, inch by inch. It's important for me to see the sky even though it is so dark. I want to run down the road in my pyjamas with bare feet just to see if God would protect me. But I can't because I am too afraid.

I listen to the distant waves and the wind in the lupins along the fence. A dog is barking but it seems so far away now. And I know that next year it really doesn't matter if someone else gets to be Mary.

My Late Father

Kevin Ireland

The evening before he remarried, my father went fishing. For several days there had been easterlies, which blew in hard in our part of the harbour, and that meant it was too rough to take out our ten-foot dinghy. Then suddenly the wind dropped and the sky cleared. As always, after a storm from that quarter, lines of long slow rollers would swell then thump with a booming echo against the beach.

My brother and I discussed the matter seriously and decided that going fishing was a funny item for someone to put at the top of a list of things to do before getting married. We agreed we couldn't work Dad out, but I was thirteen and Athol, my brother, was ten, so we had only just begun to dwell on the mysterious ways of grown men.

Normally, we would have been invited to go along too, so Dad's strange fishing expedition became even more peculiar when he asked us just to give him a hand to carry the oars and the anchor and the fishing gear down to the beach, and to help drag out the dinghy.

He said he was only going out for an hour and wanted to be alone. He would be back at half past six, just as it would be getting dark, so he told us to be waiting when he came in, to grab the boat and clean the fish, if he caught any, because he had to be at Catherine's parents' place for tea at seven. Catherine was to be our new mother and the wedding ceremony would be on their front lawn.

We recited the instructions we'd been given as soon as we got home, for Catherine had dropped by to make sure that all her arrangements were not going to get mucked up at the last minute. She was only too well aware that the man she was going to marry had two serious problems. The first wasn't too difficult to put up with – it was just a common enough obsession with fishing – but the other was the kind of kink that could drive anyone crazy. My father was late for almost everything he ever did. He regularly missed buses and ferries, and he usually failed to turn up on time for appointments. If, by accident, he happened to be early, he would find something to do to make himself late. He didn't just apply himself to being late, he was a genius at it.

Which is why, when Athol and I went down to the beach at half past six, we knew with absolute certainty that there wouldn't be a single dinghy in sight. For a while we didn't bother much, but just hung about and waited. Then we got a bit bored, so we walked up and down the beach, peering out to sea in the dim evening light, and listening, in between the rhythmic crunch of the rollers, for a call or the squeal of oars in the rowlocks.

It got dark quickly. There was no moon, but the stars were as hard and sharp as broken glass, as they always seemed to be after a storm. The sea turned black, and soon only the foam of the waves picked up the silver glitter of the night sky.

Then, possibly a bit after seven o'clock, Catherine appeared out of the darkness. She had a torch, which she shone up and down the beach, as though she expected to summon our father out of the darkness. 'Where is he?' she demanded.

'He's late,' Athol said bluntly. He hadn't yet acquired any useful conversational frills.

'As per usual,' I added, trying to sound as though this was a sufficient explanation.

'Well, he was supposed to be back half an hour ago,' Catherine said. 'He knows we've got to go out.'

Athol and I kicked at the sand with our bare feet. 'He'll be in any minute,'

I said. 'He'll have to come in. It's pitch black out there and he hasn't got a light.'

As soon as I'd finished, I knew that I'd come out with the wrong thing, so it didn't surprise me when Catherine snapped, 'Why didn't he take a light? That's stupid. He shouldn't have gone out without one.'

'You've got the only torch that works,' Athol said.

Catherine switched the torch off, as if she'd been doing something wrong, and that cast us into deeper gloom. For a minute or so we couldn't even see the foam of the waves.

None of us spoke, until eventually she said quietly and steadily, 'It makes you wonder of you're doing the right thing, doesn't it? It calls everything into question. It forces you to consider whether some people actually believe fishing is more important than anything else in the world. More important even than getting married.'

There was a second pause, then she went on, 'Anyway, I'm not waiting around here and getting upset. I'm going back to the house. It's simply not fair.'

The moment she went, Athol and I decided to walk the full length of the beach. We didn't discuss what Catherine had just said, because we needed a bit more time to come to terms with it, so instead we talked about the darkness and how Dad might have made a mistake and come in somewhere else along the coast – though neither of us really believed what we were saying, and Athol closed the whole topic by telling me he didn't like the idea that it was so black out there that Dad might have lost his bearings.

It must have taken us at least half an hour to cover the whole beach, and while we did so, we discovered a strange thing about the light. Because the stars reflected directly on the sea, if you were actually in the water as you strolled along, you could make things out a lot clearer. You could observe how the rollers rose in low black walls against the night horizon, and then you could pick out a hollow curve as they came in towards you, before toppling over in a cascade of foam. It was quite different from standing up on the beach and trying to gaze into the void until your eyes ached.

'Of course he can bloody well see out there,' Athol decided. 'So he couldn't have got lost, could he? He's just decided to keep on fishing and to hell with going around to the old bastards' place.'

'Don't swear and don't be stupid,' I said. Some of the things my younger brother came out with made me really angry. 'They're throwing the wedding tomorrow. You know that. It's on their front lawn. He's got to go and see them.'

'Why?'

'You know why,' I tried to explain. 'It's the done thing.'

'Huh,' Athol said in disgust. 'If it was me, I wouldn't bloody turn up either. They don't want him in their family. Not really. I'd go fishing and stay out all night, too.'

'You know it's not like that,' I said. 'He's just late – he's always been the same.'

'Not like this,' Athol announced. 'It must be bloody midnight.'

'You're a nutcase. It can't be more than about eight,' I told him. Athol had no sense of time, as well as all the other things that irritated me about him. He didn't seem to realise that by exaggerating he was making everything seem much worse. There and then I decided I'd punish him.

'Do you want to know something really weird?' I asked, in what I hoped was a hoarse and spooky whisper.

'What?'

I couldn't see the expression on Athol's face, but I knew from the sound of his answer that he was expecting something he mightn't want to hear.

'When someone's *late*, it can mean they've croaked it. Late means they're dead.'

'I know that,' Athol said uncertainly.

'Well think about it,' I told him. 'When you're dead you're called the late Mr So-and-so. It's like this – suppose your name was Mr Early, and you were dead, they'd have to call you the late Mr Early. Get the idea?'

'Dad's name isn't Early. It's Green. Same as you and me,' Athol replied. Sometimes he was distinctly lacking in savvy and imagination. 'Anyway, he's not dead, he's out fishing.'

'All I'm trying to tell you is, he mightn't be Early, but he's certainly late. I'm not suggesting anything else. So just pay attention, okay?'

It was a pretty nasty game I was playing, and all I can think of all these decades later, as I look back, is that my own nerves must have been pretty frayed. Catherine had just been having second thoughts out loud about the wedding that was supposed to take place the very next day, and I was becoming increasingly apprehensive about how, whatever happened, our lives were certain to be changed. And all the time, nagging away at the back of my mind, was a terrible awareness that Dad was late on a dark night, and there were only our voices to keep us company as the rollers drummed against the beach.

I began to wish that I hadn't said the stupid things I'd just come out with, when we were spared the possibility of Athol's tears by the light of a torch coming towards us. It was Catherine again, and she'd brought us a piece of cake and a pullover each. We hadn't realised we'd got quite so cold till we began to feel warm again.

'Are you feeling okay?' I asked her after she'd finished cross-questioning us about whether we'd been paying attention and keeping a proper lookout, and if we'd heard anything.

'Of course I'm not,' she said – and she sounded it. 'I'm worried sick. He's two hours late. What could have gone wrong? There's no wind. It's not rough. And the breakers aren't very big.'

'I wish it was daytime,' Athol replied. He was trying to be a big help and making things worse as usual, and he'd completely missed the fact that Catherine wasn't wondering any more about whether she'd made a mistake in wanting to marry our father. She was temporarily past all that.

'Perhaps we ought to phone the police,' I proposed.

'A policeman on a bicycle?' Catherine said. 'What could he do?'

This was long before the days of helicopters and fast police launches and cell phones. In those days the only telephone we had access to was a public callbox at the top of our road, and our local constable lived more than a mile away.

I shut up, but a couple of minutes later Catherine made me feel important by saying, 'I think you've got something, Rob. I ought to drive around to the station and tell him. He might come up with something.'

'What about collecting a pile of driftwood first, and lighting a fire?' Athol suggested, and made me wish I'd thought up the idea.

'We could get a good blaze going,' I added straight away. 'You'd see it right around the harbour. It'd be like a beacon.'

'Good boys,' Catherine said. 'I knew there was something practical we could do.' And she shone the torch, while Athol and I dashed around and gathered a heap of wood from just above the high-water mark. I found some old papers and a magazine, which we tore up, and – just as I expected – Athol magically produced a box of wax matches that he was banned from carrying around. Dad had called him a young pyromaniac and had warned that if he ever found another wax match in his pockets, after the last patch of gorse he'd set fire to, there would be hell to pay.

The tide was going out, so we set the fire well down the beach and soon we had flames shooting up into the air, lighting the whole place up. We chucked a few large broken branches on top to keep it going steadily. For a few minutes the sight even cheered us up.

'He'll see the fire,' I told Catherine. 'He couldn't miss it from miles away.'

'*Miles* away?' she repeated. 'What are you trying to tell me? He went out just off the beach. He wasn't going miles away.'

'I didn't mean that,' I explained. 'What I meant was …'

I stopped in confusion, but Athol got in quickly. 'Rob never knows what he means,' he explained. 'He talks without thinking. Like all that stuff about the late Mr Early. Ask him.'

'What's the time?' Catherine asked, cutting through our nonsense before I could retaliate by raising the subject of Athol's box of matches.

'It must be nine,' I told her.

'Then that's it. I'm going for the police. Even if it's just to give me something to do.'

She stayed long enough to help us stack more wood on the fire and to tell us to keep a sharp lookout, and she had just begun to walk away, when Athol suddenly jumped up and down, and shouted, 'I heard something. I tell you, I heard something.'

Catherine turned, then ran over to Athol and clutched hold of him, as if he had some sort of secret possession.

'I heard something again,' he yelled.

Together, we all walked quietly away from the fire and stepped out into the water, careful not to make splashing noises. Then we all heard the sound. It was a voice calling very faintly, just before a wave broke and obliterated the sounds. But we definitely picked up a 'Coo-ee', followed by an 'Oy'.

We all began yelling, until Catherine ordered us to stop. 'He won't hear us,' she said. 'Wait until the next wave has broken, then I'll count to three and we'll all shout 'Oy' together.'

We did and we got another 'Oy' in reply. This time it was a little louder.

'Can you see him? Is he swimming?' Catherine asked frantically. She was up to her knees in the water by now.

'He's in the dinghy. Over there,' Athol shouted, pointing frantically. 'I saw him first.'

On the crest of a roller, outlined darkly against the stars, then glowing as it caught a faint light from the fire, I could make out the white shape of the dinghy. For some strange reason, it didn't come on in, but sank out of sight again, as if the sea had swallowed it.

We all began to shout again, and we heard another 'Oy'. Then the dinghy rose on another wave. It hadn't come much closer. It seemed to be glued out there.

'What's wrong with the boat?' Catherine yelled. 'Has it hit a rock? It's not moving.'

'There's no rocks out there,' Athol said, and as he spoke the dinghy rose on another wave and moved forward slowly, with Dad rowing like crazy. Then mysteriously, instead of surfing in towards us, the dinghy disappeared again as the wave broke.

'He's towing something,' Athol said. 'It's holding him back.'

Once more the boat rose, and the same thing happened. Athol and I were soaked as we tried to get out through the waves and take hold of the bow or the anchor warp. Then, as a second roller rose behind the one on which the dinghy seemed for a moment to be perched, we saw the dark shape of a sea monster.

Suddenly Dad shipped the oars, stood up and leapt into the water, clutching a handline. 'Grab the boat,' he yelled, as the next wave picked the dinghy up and sent it careering towards us. It spun sideways and nearly capsized, but we grabbed it and dragged it to the beach.

'You should see the bloody monster,' Athol yelled, and for once Catherine didn't tell him off for swearing. 'He's hooked a bloody whale.'

Catherine said something, but neither of us heard, for we both dashed back into the sea and caught hold of Dad. He was easing the fish in, wave by wave, so that the weight of the back-surge wouldn't break the line, and each time the fish rose with a new roller we could make out its huge shape.

'It's a shark,' Athol decided. 'It's got to be a shark.'

'Take the line. Both of you,' Dad told us. 'And don't pull too hard. I'm going to grab it by the gills, or I'll lose it in the surf.'

It seemed a wildly dangerous thing to do, but it was his fish and there was no stopping him. He went out into the waves and lunged at the huge black shape. For a moment he seemed to be wrestling with it, then he moved towards us, waist deep in water, dragging his catch with him.

Athol and I kept hold of the line and walked backwards to the beach. Then suddenly Dad half-lifted the monster and brought it up onto the sand by the fire. It was longer than the dinghy – except that it wasn't a fish at all. It seemed to be just a gigantic straggly heap of seaweed.

'Biggest kingie I've ever seen,' Dad said. Then he parted the huge bundle of seaweed, and suddenly we saw the long and lovely bulk of a giant kingfish. 'It's towed me up and down the harbour for three hours. I just managed to hang onto it with one hand while I pulled in the anchor with the other. It took me wherever it wanted. It was like an outboard motor. It went crazy.'

'I though you were drowned,' Catherine said. 'We've missed dinner. I don't even know if we ought to …'

She didn't finish the sentence, for Dad put a wet arm around her and gave her a kiss. 'I've always wanted one of these, and the gods have given me one for a wedding present,' he said.

She didn't complain about his wet arm, but began to tell him, 'Well, at one stage I had to think I'd made a mistake and there wasn't going to be a wedding at all …' Then she stopped and her voice changed completely. She said, 'All three of you will catch your death of cold. Bring that fish up and have a hot shower, and get changed. I'm going back to get some cocoa on.'

We hauled the dinghy to the tree where we always chained it, then Dad slit the fish open and ripped out the gut and gills. Even standing by the fire, Athol and I were shivering, so we were glad to head back again. Dad picked up the oars and the anchor and the fishing gear, and set off. We had become part of the glory of it all, just by being there and helping. The only thing we were sorry about was that it was so dark that none of the neighbours could look from their doors or windows and witness our triumph.

That night, when we had washed and got into our pyjamas – and the next morning too – we ate giant kingfish steaks. But we had to give away most of the fish to friends. Dad and Catherine went off on their honeymoon, and Athol and I had too many sausage rolls and cakes at the wedding to bother about eating again that night.

The extraordinary thing, it now seems to me, is that no one thought of taking a photograph or of trying to weigh the fish. So my father's giant trophy exists only in memory, in the shape that first amazed me, when it rose on the rollers, twice its real size, in a cowl of dark seaweed.

It will always be the biggest fish I have ever seen, and often when, for no particular reason at all, I remember my late father, I see him bending to a dark massive raggedly bundle and parting it to reveal that beautiful silver shape inside.

It's a gift to have moments like that to hold on to. Yet a couple of weeks ago, I was taken over to Athol's place for his fortieth wedding anniversary and we got talking about funny things that happen at weddings. I asked him how much he thought Dad's kingfish weighed and he looked at me with a frown and said, 'What kingfish?'

I told him, 'The one he caught the night before he married Catherine. The kingie the gods gave him for a wedding present. The one we thought was a sea monster.'

'Oh yes,' he said, with a chuckle. 'That just about summed up the old man. Always late. And to prove it, he went fishing that night, didn't he? When he should've been going out somewhere. Catherine damned near called the whole thing off. It was a case of no fish, and almost no wife too.'

'What do you mean, 'No fish'? It was the biggest kingfish I've ever seen,' I said.

'No. That was another time,' Athol insisted. 'He came back empty-handed the night before he got married.'

'We ate the steaks that night and the next morning. And we gave a whole lot away,' I said. 'You can't have forgotten.'

'Yes, but that was a year or so later. We had to go down to the beach and help him land it. He was all in and he wouldn't have managed without us. I'll never forget our fire and the soaking we got.'

There was no point in discussing the matter any further. I was only too well aware that we had avoided chewing over the events of that night, and I had always thought the fault was mine. It had never occurred to me that for some problematical reason Athol might have managed to transpose his memories to a different, safer time.

But I knew I was right. Every detail and every word had been carved into my whole being. So perhaps the only way of looking at Athol's version of what happened is to accept that there is no absolute truth to fishing. Its moments of perfection are all in the mind. If he had chosen to lose the gift of that experience, there was no way of restoring it to him.

Yet it's a pity in a way, because I'm an old man and I had an itch to tell someone at last how that fish had changed my life. Without being able to give my fears a name and deal with them, as Catherine had managed to do the night before she got married, I'd been secretly scared witless by those hours of waiting at the beach. I used to wake up with nightmares about the whole horror for years after. I couldn't come to terms with it. The memory tormented me.

And the experience made an early bird out of me. I've never been able to be late for anything important in my whole life. My children and my grandchildren often call me 'Mr Early'. It's a family joke, with a special private meaning for me.

Everyone seems to laugh at my genius for always being ahead of time. But it isn't the result of strength of mind or self-discipline; it's fear that has made me the way I am. Without closing my eyes, I can still see that little clinker-built kauri dinghy rising on the crest of a roller. Helplessly, I watch it hurtle towards me, then my late father, with his oars working frantically, is clutched backwards, to disappear forever into an invisible trough. I couldn't force myself not to be early even if I wanted to.

The Line

Rhonda Bartle

Charlie woke and for a moment could not remember exactly where he was. Then he did. God, yes. Mokau. The middle of nowhere.

Three young boys lay curled up in the bed opposite, legs and breath tangled with the blankets. Charlie put his hands up behind his head and made a higher pillow. He stared at the ceiling with its buckled and peeled paint. He wondered if his mother in London would have a fit if she could see it. She'd more than likely take him to one side and say, in her infuriatingly, calm way: 'Charlie, you're making a mistake.'

He could hear his heartbeat in the stillness of the morning, telling him the same thing. Mis-take, mis-take, mis-take.

Carefully, so as not to disturb the children, Charlie sat up and pulled back the ragged bach curtains to let an inch of daylight in. The sun was not properly up, but even in this light he could see the sea below. He'd never seen sea like this before. He wasn't used to beaches, except those where small waves pulled in, parked up briefly and pulled out again. But here, the waves thundered in with such ferocity, the foam fled before them. Here the foam was not white but a slimy, sickly yellow. It piled up on the jet-black, almost-blue, sand. The kids yesterday had run for miles in it, coming back looking like unkempt laundry workers. And when it dried, it left marks on their clothes and skin.

Lisa had only laughed. 'This is the west coast, Charlie.'

But to Charlie, it had seemed an entirely different planet.

And Lisa, a different girl. Lisa, from the city, who worked in a city bank, had somehow turned into Leese of Mokau overnight. *Leese, catch the ball. Leese, come and see!* Her name had turned into a nasally whine which caught in the throat. In the short time he'd been at the bach, he had had to watch her slit the throats of a dozen flounder before dumping them into hot fat like some short order diner cook. Fat.In Auckland, she wouldn't eat butter. Here she mixed a dozen eggs with whitebait so fresh they flipped out of the pan as they were cooking. Here she wore borrowed jerseys and black rubber boots.

Here she laughed at him and said, 'Oh, Charlie,' often.

They slept in different beds, in different rooms, full of foreign bodies. She wouldn't sit on his knee, but she'd sit on her father's, and hold hands with her mother like a six-year-old. At Mokau, she treated Charlie in the same kind but careless manner she did all her nephews and nieces. 'You hungry, Charlie? You warm enough?'

Charlie put his feet to the cold lino. Perhaps, he thought, if I go out now, catch her by herself, she might turn back into Lisa. But as he arrived in the kitchen, he saw her parents, Joe and Maia, had got there before him.

'Sleep well?'

'Sure,' he said. And a little begrudgingly added, 'thanks'.

'Them boys didn't keep you up awake too long? What did you do to shut them up? Smother 'em with a pillow?'

'No,' Charlie said. Instead, he'd chosen to ignore them. In the middle of their endless chorus – Charlie, barley, oats and rye – he'd rolled over and gone to sleep. Really, he'd felt tired out since he'd first arrived.

'The beach can bugger a bloke,' Joe said, as though it was a compliment to nature. Charlie nodded.

It had been Lisa's idea. 'Time to meet the whanau,' she'd said. Lying beside her in her futon bed, with one hand on her breast, it had been easy to agree.

'Whanau?'

'Family, you immigrant. My family.'

Lisa had said she was a thirty-second Maori. 'You know, half a sixteenth. Enough to stop a racist joke dead in its tracks at parties.' She told Charlie he was three-quarters English and a quarter Pom, but she kissed him long and hard. 'I've never had blue blood in me before,' she laughed as they made love.

Perhaps, Charlie thought, if she came through the door now in her red silk kimono, he would remember exactly who she was, who they were, but Lisa padded into the room in bare feet and someone's red t-shirt.

'Morning, Miss Mokau,' Joe said. Charlie watched Lisa ruffle her father's hair as she wandered past, rubbing sleep from her eyes. 'Seen the sea this morning?'

Like Joe, Charlie obligingly peered out the window. The sea had amazed him yesterday, and it amazed him again. There was that line that ran parallel to the shore about a kilometre out. The water on the far side shone a perfect marine blue, while the water closer to the shore ran a thick, soupy brown. When it rained, dirt swept down from the hills into the Mokau River, over the sand bar and out to sea, so Lisa had told him. A few miles north, the Awakino River competed and managed a tie. The stretch between them ran dark and choppy until it hit the open water, then the colours met, so distinct, so certain, so straight, a person could swim out there and cut them apart with a knife.

'Dad calls it billy-tea and ink,' Lisa had said. 'But I call it Bailey's and Aqua Vitae.' Charlie had watched her lips turn up in a smile. 'It's amazing,' he'd said.

'Let's walk the beach before breakfast.' It seemed a good idea, to be together, alone. Charlie found his shoes while Lisa threw on old pants and dragged a jacket over the top. But by the time they reached the sand, the beach was alive with kids. The boys from Charlie's room and the two girls who had slept in the room with Lisa had beaten them down. He couldn't remember their names, though Lisa called out to them all, one after another, laughing as she struggled to catch up with them. 'The mokopunas,' Maia called them.

They belonged to Lisa's absent sister.

It was impossible for Charlie to see them as anything other than a team. They were all feet and noise.

'Come on!' Lisa called. He squeezed her hand hard when he came alongside, and stamped on a row of shells until they broke.

'Don't,' she said.

'Why not?'

Lisa bent and retrieved a single whole shell and slipped it over his finger. 'Look. It's a ring.' She smiled so sweetly at him that Charlie suddenly felt as fragile as the shell. 'You shouldn't wreck things just for the sake of it,' she scolded.

It was on the tip of Charlie's tongue to say, 'They're only shells. They'll go out with the next tide anyway,' but Lisa dashed away to capture a child. He watched her round a renegade up, hold it while it wriggled, and draw up pants legs that were dripping with water. Wrecking things for the sake of it, how dare she tell him that.

Yesterday, he'd watched the kids gouge craters in the dirt and uncover the roots of several coastal trees. They'd poked holes in the bank. They'd pulled small flax plants growing along the track.

Charlie eased the shell ring from his finger and tossed it as far as it could go. He thought of the one still hidden in his soap bag with his shaving gear. Still waiting for him to find the right time to bring it out.

'Hell, I'm hungry,' Lisa shouted. 'I want breakfast!'

Lisa of Auckland never ate breakfast and never raised her voice.

As they came back up the dunes, she plucked a bright pink flower on a fat juicy stem out of the sand. 'This is called an ice-plant,' she said, 'because it likes a lot of heat.' She smiled at the lunacy of it, and passed it to him to hold.

Charlie held it out like a bloodied knife, until Lisa wrenched the flower back, planted it into her hair where sticky fluid snaked towards her ear. Then she ran so fast from him, sand flicked into his face. Alone, he walked back to the cottage and washed his hands under the rusting tap. Then he sat on a step at the back door, hoping she'd come and find him. His heart was thumping again. Mis-take, mis-stake, mis-take.

Maia called him into the house for breakfast that was late enough to be lunch. Lisa was quiet but charitable. 'More bread, Charlie?'

In the afternoon, he was enlisted in a game of cricket, which at least gave him something to do. He helped divide the kids into batsmen and fielders and kept a note of the runs. But Lisa insisted he adjust the tally, deducting points from the adults and adding them to the smallest players, and he gave the game away.

In the shade of a twisted pohutukawa, he leaned against the trunk and wished Lisa would come. But it was Joe who delivered a beer.

'Well, done, old chap,' he said. 'An Englishman loves his cricket, wot?'

Charlie picked at the bottle label. Waikato Ale, not even in a glass.

'I've never played cricket before in my life,' he lied.

'Well, neither have this lot,' Joe said. 'Which makes us all even. We're putting down a hangi so we need a hand. Best way to feed a pile of kids. You look like you need a decent feed, too. Doesn't that girl of mine feed you?'

Charlie wondered what Joe would think if he told him that it was usually he, Charlie, who did the cooking. Italian. He was very good with pasta, but he liked French as well. Lots of wine and lots of herbs. The only rule he followed was quality and class.

He watched the slabs of pumpkin laid out next to the kumara in their skins, while Maia top-dressed everything with a fistful of salt. He didn't expect anyone here would know parsley if it bit them on the arse. They were going to bury the food in a mound of dirt and cook it over coals.

Baskets of mutton and fish fell together into the hole.

'This is how everyone cooked in the old days,' Joe said. 'Damn good kai.'

Lisa joined them now, cold despite the fire. She took his hand and tucked it up under her bushman's shirt. 'We used to cook the whiteman up like this.'

She smiled, and for a second, he almost knew her again, as she leaned her head into his shoulder and let her body fall against him. But the sun went down fast and Charlie went down behind it. He stared at the steam that hissed from the pit, as wet sacks were thrown across its mouth. The mokopunas ran around in bare feet. He lifted his eyes to the horizon and there it was, that line, where brown met blue. You could swim out there and wrench them apart with your bare hands.

Charlie watched Joe shovel dirt and close the hole. He took his hand from Lisa's shirt and let it fall.

'I'm going tomorrow,' Charlie said.

Bitten Tongue

Norman Bilbrough

Each morning in summer Martin would wake at six-thirty, slip into togs that had dried to the texture of parchment from the previous day's bathing, and cross the empty street to the beach.

The sea would be waiting for him, neutral, and smelling as clean as fresh fish. His body was neither hot nor cold, it had not taken on any of the temperature of the day, it was neutral too.

He would slip into the deep quiet coolness without exclamation. Sometimes he gently swam, but more often he lay on his back with his feet sticking out of the water.

In the evening he would bathe again, and then he would walk the length of the sand with a plastic bag, picking up the detritus of the day: food containers, stray shoes, an occasional disposable nappy. And there were the forgotten towels and t-shirts. Martin would drape these over the sea wall or the benches beyond, for their owners to claim the next day.

Always he looked forward to the dignified emptiness of the morning beach when the occasional dog walker greeted him, and the dignified exhaustion of the evening beach, when strolling couples also greeted him. But mostly he looked forward to the languid embrace of the sea.

Some days he would visit at midday when it was the domain of many: the beautiful and the lithe, the overweight, the old, the children digging strenuously to reach the other side of the world; all divesting themselves of their everyday lives. And since there was generally more wind, the sea was fractious; it was energetically sociable.

Then Martin swam rather than wallowed, cursing when the waves smacked his face.

He was not a man who believed in uninterrupted happiness: that seemed too ambitious a state to strive for. But he was content .... Content with the state of his brain, and his body, a thing that had never been beautiful only serviceable; an assemblage that, as a 53-year-old man, he was some days proud of. He was not noticed of course; he knew the beautiful beach people saw him as just another inhabitant of a middle-aged hinterland, patrolling the sand and existing apart from them.

Martin had lived near another beach in a nearby suburb thirty years previously when he was newly married; a beach that was a pebbly stretch beside a yacht club. There he had struggled against the water, shouted in it, complained about it, but he had never *bathed* in it.

And back then, his wife Ruth had been one of the beautiful people.

The pebbly beach had captured her. She had attended it religiously in summer, clad in the merest strips of material, veritable strings over her thighs, and acquiring a deep tan and the admiration of men. Their child Daniel had not inherited his mother's glamour and was happy to be an undemanding beach kid, a suitable accessory for the woman who needed any attention that came her way.

Ruth was a painter who was unable to paint enough. Martin worked in the city that was a short walk then a ferry ride across the harbour, and Ruth could only work at evenings or weekends, or when Daniel slept.

She complained, Martin pacified and felt guilty, but privately he thought her a poor painter. She had the personality, the beautiful exterior, but lacked talent. Indeed the first painting she exhibited seemed only complete when it acquired a frame. And Martin suspected that Angus Stubbs, the gallery owner, only accepted the painting because Ruth flirted quite openly with him.

'Do you find him attractive?' he had enquired. Angus Stokes was fleshy, verging on the overweight.

'He's not unattractive,' Ruth had replied. Then she had said, 'He looks cuddly. I can imagine women wanting to sit on his lap.'

'Do you want to sit on his lap?'

But Ruth had only laughed.

Then one day Martin was given the afternoon off to finish work at home and he walked from the ferry to the beach where he knew Ruth and Daniel would be.

He saw her sun-filled blonde hair and delectable shoulders from a distance. She was laughing with a young man: one with the kind of torso and shoulders that Martin would never attain, indeed did not aspire to.

Daniel was curled asleep in the shade.

'Hullo?' he called, and when Ruth looked up, startled, he said, 'Are you all right?' Which was silly, for what was the worry? She was laughing with the guy wasn't she?

'Of course I'm all right!' And she introduced the bronzed youth.

Martin instantly forgot his name, but the stranger became lodged in his mind as 'the beautiful boy', a boy who was polite to Martin, no matter that he was obviously beguiled by Ruth's slender and half-naked figure.

And when he had departed, Ruth told Martin he was a funny boy who lived nearby. Ha ha funny? Or simply quaint funny? Both it seemed. Martin was not impressed.

Yet he was not jealous, not even when he discovered the beautiful boy in their kitchen drinking orange juice one afternoon; not even when Ruth divulged – with a giggle – that he had tried to kiss her.

'You didn't let him?'

'Oh yes. It was very pleasant.'

'And you kissed him back?'

'Of course! It would have been churlish not to.'

And Martin was still not jealous when he returned to the flat early another day and heard Ruth's orgasm as he entered the front door. He was startled, shocked even, then noted with disappointment that her orgasm was considerably more expressive than those she had with him.

The beautiful boy came into the kitchen some minutes later, evincing further politeness to Martin, but no real surprise at his presence.

Although Martin was a caring person, he was essentially distant. This worried him. Maybe he was unnaturally objective? Maybe he should order the beautiful boy from the house?

He didn't.

Then, after Angus Stubbs had sold Ruth's second painting – a mediocre version of the beach and adjoining yacht club, done after the style of Paul Klee – she casually admitted she *had* found the idea of sitting in the art dealer's lap, attractive.

'So you have sat on it then?' Martin had asked.

'Yes,' she said abruptly. 'He wants me to go away with him this weekend. In his new car.'

Angus Stubbs owned a MG hardtop that Ruth had expressed a desire to ride in: possibly a very long ride.

'But hasn't he got a wife?'

'Of course! You've met Felicity, the sculptor.' Ruth had smiled and kissed Martin on the cheek. 'You'll look after Daniel won't you. You can have a boy's weekend together.'

While you sit on Angus Stubbs's lap, Martin thought. He wished he could get properly jealous.

Maybe he was just a fool…

But he also knew that if Ruth had free range the household assumed a kind of a peace. His frenetically dramatic wife was diverted from the humdrum and frustrating aspects of motherhood, and even her life as a sun goddess of the scruffy beach. It was important he accept her lovers, and even, for the sake of general harmony, be friends with them.

Friendship had not had the chance to occur between him and the beautiful boy because Ruth had discovered he was too young, and he only wanted continual boring sex. As well, he stopped making jokes, and his ignorance of the world of finer artistic things was abysmal. He thought Henri Matisse was a French soccer player.

But now Martin was expected to befriend Angus and to appreciate him as a person – and not as a plump art dealer whose lap, inexplicably, attracted women.

On his evening walks Martin often discovered odd garments that seemed to have no relevance to the life of the beach: an expensive shoe, a fine silk dress, a pair of rugby socks... And then he found a sand-filled garment in the rocks at the northern end.

He shook it out and laid it over the rocks. It was a man's cardigan that, although abused by the water, was of good quality.

Martin puzzled as to how it had arrived: perhaps lost from a heaving pleasure launch; maybe even thrown overboard, the victim of a passionate argument between a man and a woman.

This last thought made him laugh, a hollow laugh, for once he had owned a similar garment.

He was not a cardigan man, believing that they were essentially feminine garments: his mother had owned drawers of them. But Ruth had bought him a grey one from the payment she received from that first sale of her painting. She vowed that it suited him.

Despite his reservations, he was pleased with the gift, touched by her generosity. It seemed to show she cared for him. Certainly it felt soft and comfortable, and even looked stylish and casual in the mirror.

He wore it the evening Angus and Felicity Stubbs came for dinner.

'Although Felicity is charming,' Ruth had warned, 'she's steel underneath. And I don't like her sculptures. They're derivative of Barbara Hepworth.'

Martin made no comment on the tendency to be derivative, and was not drawn to the idea of a steel-like woman. But he decided to focus on her charm: he would get enough mileage out of that to get through the evening.

Felicity was a tall woman with a full figure, a woman who seemed anatomically unsuited to sitting on laps. And she was more watchful than charming. She watched Ruth holding the floor after they had eaten dinner, and she watched her husband being beguiled.

Did she know Ruth and Angus were lovers?

Martin could not be sure.

Predictably the talk was about art, and Ruth started arguing good-naturedly with Angus on the mediocrity of certain artists who exhibited in his gallery. Angus was not affronted, and he laughed and verbally jostled with Ruth, showing himself to be a tolerant and even intelligent guest.

But Martin found he did not want to be his friend.

There was a noise from down the hall. 'Not so loud,' he cautioned the arguing lovers, and he went out of the room. Daniel was standing bleary-eyed and crotchety beside the bed in his small room.

Martin tucked him up again, and sang his way through a list of favourite nursery rhymes. He stopped singing when the boy started breathing deeply.

Felicity said quietly from the door, 'You are a nice father.'

Martin stood up, surprised. 'I do my best,' he said.

They paused in the hallway and a squirt of flirtatious laughter, then more bantering argument, issued from the lounge.

'You're not interested in art?' Felicity said.

'Not art ad nauseam.' It was true: Martin was bored with the talk. 'I think I'll go for a walk.'

'I'll go with you.' She touched his arm through his cardigan.

Martin was surprised again, and pleased.

He told Ruth of their intentions, and they went out into the street.

It was a cool night, and as they walked down toward the pebbly beach Felicity said with a trace of bitterness, 'They don't care what we do.'

She slipped her arm through Martin's.

Even though he liked smaller women and did not like her kind of watchful toughness, the intimacy of the gesture excited Martin. And when he felt the insistent weight of her breast against his arm, he felt a sudden electric tension. The pressure of her breast, along with her succinct statement, seemed like permission.

'Let's sit on the beach,' he suggested, then led her down the steps and along the pebbles towards the buildings of the yacht club, to a place where they could not be seen from the street.

They sat down, and Felicity kissed his cheek.

Martin kissed her neck.

It was the first time he had touched another woman since he had married Ruth. He felt tentative, and yet excited. Felicity's skin was fresh, and of course she smelt different...

He liked the difference.

'Would you like to see my breasts?' And without waiting for a response

Felicity pulled up her top and undid her bra.

They were full and smooth with desirable nipples: a wonderful possession. Martin could understand why she wanted to show them off so readily.

She pushed herself towards him. 'Kiss them!' And after he had done so, but tentatively because now his excitement had been replaced by confusion at the abrupt and hasty progression of events, she commanded, 'Kiss me.'

He raised his head and kissed her shyly on the lips – and she abruptly pushed her tongue into his mouth.

It was not exciting; it was too much like a forced entry. And yet Martin felt it should be exciting, he felt he should be aroused, and he pushed his own tongue back into her mouth.

She bit down hard.

He could not protest: his tongue could not move to form any sound; he made a strangled noise in his throat – and somehow managed to pull his tongue out.

If she had tried by the brutish gesture to ignite a possibly violent and passionate reaction in him, she had failed. Martin slumped back on the pebbles, distressed, nursing a tongue that felt half amputated, a tongue that might not ever work again.

He could not believe what she had done to him.

Felicity looked at him, her face unreadable, then she shivered, and tucked her breasts back into her bra. 'I'm cold!' But when her top was pulled down once again, she still shivered.

For a moment Martin forgot his wounded tongue: he took off his cardigan, the cardigan Ruth had especially bought for him, and gave it to Felicity. She slipped it on gratefully.

'It's so warm!'

But now that the passion had not eventuated there seemed no point in sitting further. And, even if he had been able to use his tongue coherently, little left to say. Indeed Martin feared that presently his tongue might totally fill his mouth, and being a man who was often a mouth breather, he was alarmed.

He stood, and although he did not wish to, gave Felicity his hand. She pulled herself up.

But as they walked back toward the flat she put her arm once more through his. She was friendly again – although Martin considered she might've only been grateful for the warmth of the cardigan.

They walked into the lounge. Angus was sitting on the floor holding Ruth's feet. He did not stop holding them, obviously he felt no need to be guilty of the intimacy; but Ruth's eyes went immediately to the cardigan: her husband's garment pulled lovingly over the other woman's breasts.

Her face flushed with rage.

Later when the guests had departed, Ruth picked up the cardigan and flung it at Martin. 'You had sex with her didn't you! I could tell by the way she was wearing that!' And despite how much he tried to protest around his grossly distorted tongue that they had not had sex, she did not believe it.

She wept.

She would not let Martin comfort her that night, and he slept on a mattress on the floor of Daniel's room. And in the morning when he could only drink warm milk and barely swallow, Ruth burned the cardigan in their small garden.

It made an awful, and tragic, smell.

*

'Mum is having a retrospective here in March,' Daniel said when he visited his father in the New Year.

Daniel was now an energetic young man who lived in Sydney with another man. He seemed barely connected to the introverted child who had fitted into Ruth's life all those years previously.

He had joined Martin for the early morning swim and stopped to catch his breath after swimming vigorously up and down the bay. Martin was glad; his son's thrashing spoiled the quiet emptiness of the morning.

'She hopes you might have a drink together. And that you might come to the exhibition.'

Ruth had remarried, had a daughter, divorced, and had success with her paintings. Martin wondered if they had improved; if she had got beyond creating poor imitations of Klee.

He had never seen Felicity or Angus Stubbs again, and even though he lived barely thirty minutes walk away from the beach where his tongue had been bitten, he never returned to it.

Daniel did not know the story of his parent's marriage, of their unhappiness, and Martin was not about to tell him, to let the jagged painful details break into the calm of this place he had found for himself.

'No, I won't see her,' he said, surprising himself.

Daniel did not seem put out. 'Okay,' he said.

Martin turned and swam thoughtfully away through the still water.

He had tolerated a marriage of selfishness, of deceptions and insensitivity, and the attraction of other men's laps. Of course he had an illicit kiss on a beach, and he could be accused of being a man severely cut off from his emotions.

But this last fact was not true. His emotions simply arrived late. He did not want to see Ruth, ever. Only now did it occur to him that he had not forgiven her.

Only Waving

Sue Emms

This is the beach we've been coming to for years.

Generations of Macmillan feet have pounded, run, tip-toed and leapt across the sparkling white sand; from the soft and eager soles of my son, to the calloused, yellowed monsters that belonged to my grandfather, to generations back that I've never known.

We're all swimmers in this family, we're known for it. But my grandfather was the best. It was his big feet, everyone said. When he swam, his feet were flat slabs of muscle and bone churning behind him like fleshy motors, taking him through wave and foam at a steady pace. He died out there, in the rolling blue waters. I saw him from the headland, heading toward the horizon. Terrible tragedy, the family whispered, but I knew better. I have my grandfather's feet. It used to be a joke, a 'standing' joke, as my father once said, slapping his thigh and roaring with laughter.

Hot sun, warm beer. Goes to a man's head, that does.

This holiday the family sprawls, a human wriggling octopus, across the best patch of sand: a nicely sloping dune with a view of Rabbit Rock, and the curve of the bay where a miniature lagoon puddles warm water for the kiddies. We always claim this spot, consider it ours for no other reason than we always have.

Just a short way behind us is our bach; an alarming structure of fibrolite and second-hand weatherboards. A corrugated iron water tank staggers behind it on unsteady legs and the boundary is massed with flax and toi toi and red-fuzzed pohutukawa. The place is a relic of the old days, a quarter acre mess surrounded by mini-palaces in shades of apricot and slate blue. The new houses crowd our boundaries and look down with blank, uncomprehending eyes.

We've been offered more than a million dollars for our little patch and most of the family are in favour of selling. I am the one holding back. I watch Uncle Martin carrying Great Aunt Ada, 90 and venerable and mad, down to a deckchair and place her in a patch of blue shade. I think of my grandfather and wonder, how can I sell my history?

My sister Helen and her husband are just arriving, late as usual, and shout greetings as they unload their car. Their kids spill eagerly down the slope to join us.

'Aunty Karen, Aunty Karen!'

Jemmy, the youngest, throws her arms around my legs and gives me a joyful hug before hurtling off after her brothers, shouting 'Wait for me!' I watch her little feet flying across the sand and I wonder: how can I sell our future? How do I do that? I dig my toe into the sandy soil and draw a wobbly line.

The kids scamper and somersault their way along the tide line, dancing with impatience. 'Can we swim now?'

I take pity on them. 'Justin,' I say, 'do you mind?' And my son, one of those pretty young men with golden skin and bleached hair, a mouth that is too full and eyelashes the girls envy, the kind of boy that looks vulnerable, pulls himself to his big, 16-year-old feet and lets himself get dragged by a swarming crowd of kids down to where the ocean skitters and froths. Except for his Macmillan feet, Justin is the living image of his father. He has told me that he hates me.

Louise, my oldest sister, says, 'Go and get the other umbrella, Kar.'

I don't argue or ask Lou, for the thousandth time, not to call me Kar. Instead, I trudge back up the dune and wrestle with garage doors that shriek on their rollers.

*

Grandad had a black 1939 Alvis that he kept parked in the sagging garage, out of the salt. He never let anyone drive it but him, but I remembered sitting on his knee, his big rough hands over mine as he let me steer. 'Good to be in the driving seat,' he'd said. I like my hands on the wheel, too. *Bit of a control freak*, according to my mother, but I understand it differently. Why let the waves toss you about if you can help it?

I have my grandfather's will. Hitler in a skirt, my father once sneered.

This is how it always is: by midday the umbrellas are up and the canopies in place. The children have been dragged into the shade and the boys, all bony knees and salt-stained skin, are flicking sand at the girls. The oldies, shouting at each other over the noise of the kids, sit in a row of canvas chairs. Great Aunt Ada snores in the middle of them. Grandad courted her once, but she was voted Queen of the Beach and he could never forgive the adoration her beauty brought her. She married his brother instead. He never forgave her that, either.

Thirty holidays ago, Grandad had offended half the family with one short statement. Eyeing Ada's time-scoured face and a body bent by hard work on the farm, he'd swallowed another whisky and said, 'Close call that one.'

I've always wondered if she felt the same.

Grandad had sat on the beach, as the sun disappeared and the moonlight beat a hard path across the ocean. Staring outward, he'd said, I never stopped, never.

And I have always wondered – did she feel the same? Looking at her now, her ninety-year-old body nothing but a husk, it's hard to imagine she feels anything at all.

Up at the bach the uncles, John, Cec, Malcolm and Martin. hover over the barbeque. There's a male missing from around the cookout. Not Grandad, he's been gone a long time. It's my male who is missing. James, my son's father, the man I've loved since I was fifteen, who has told me with great compassion that he can no longer bear to live with us. He cried, as if that were supposed to make me feel better about him finding another woman. A younger woman, of course, and childless. I saw her waiting in the car for him, with dark hair and a firm chin, eyes downcast demurely as she waited. Serene, almost, as if there were no blame attached to her. As if it were just me, the first white strands in my hair and the beginnings of round cheeks slurring into sagginess that were to blame.

Don't come crying back to me when you realise your mistake, I'd said, and seen Justin, his face stricken, look at me as if it were all my fault.

Perhaps it is. I'm told I have my grandfather's unforgiving streak. I get a lot from my grandfather, a lot from my family. I look around at them now, sprawled beneath the canopy, or turning red in the sun, and I know that whoever's fault it was that my marriage failed, it is only these people who have stopped me from falling apart. Only this bach and this stretch of shimmering sand that has give me a sense of self.

How do I sell myself?

This is the last plate of blackened chops, the last bowl of salad to be brought to the beach. The table – an old door on a couple of beer crates – is jammed with plastic containers of food, drinks, plastic cutlery and paper plates. The children attack like a pack of starving dogs while the older folk look on and smile indulgently. There's enough here for an army – no one will go hungry today. Not for food, anyway. Overhead, the canopy makes strange music with the wind as it flaps and snaps and creaks against a sky faded to white by the heat. Beneath my feet the sand glitters in the sun, and just a short distance away the ocean hisses like a snarling cat. It'll be cool out there. Here, beneath the canopy, the air is solid with heat and the strain of being nice. Shannon, 13 and old enough to know better, turns to me with a smirk and says, 'Isn't Uncle James coming today?' Helen shushes her and turns to me with an apologetic shrug.

I don't care so much. Some hurts can't get any worse. Betrayals can't be made greater than they are. Besides, Helen too wants to sell the bach and there are all sorts of jagged edges between us.

'Kar,' Louise eyeballs me as I fill a plate with rubbery round eggs. 'Don't you think you're being totally selfish, refusing to sell?'

As her voice cuts through the heat, other conversations still and faces swivel toward us. Everyone is interested in the outcome of this battle. But whatever I decide, things will change. Half the family will stay away next year – a protest, they say, at being unable to release their capital. 'Why should we be forced to holiday here because we haven't got the money to go elsewhere?' Helen has said.

Don't they know that if I had the money I would buy them out? But where do I get a half a million dollars from?

'We all know how much you love it here,' says Helen, 'but things end, you of all people should know that, Karen. Things end.'

'And sometimes that's good, you know? Endings mean new beginnings,' says Louise.

I'm suddenly tired. Tired of the sand dragging at my legs, the pressure from my sisters to sell, tired of being alone, of feeling the tides in my body receding. Once she hits fifty a woman's useless, my father always said.

I am 49. Old. Useless. Broke and alone, with a son that hates me.

This is where I came to look for treasure, where I gathered stones sparkling for mica, where I saw the tiny shape of my grandfather's head and the flash of his arms slicing through the blue water. The white speck of foam churned up by his big, paddling feet.

All those years ago and here I am again, standing at the same ocean's edge, staring out at the same horizon. The sun prickles hot needles into my shoulders, burns along the parting in my hair, razzles and dazzles off the water so my eyeballs ache. A wave rushes in and swirls around my ankles, scours beneath my feet; I sink into the sand and a shell slithers beneath my toes. It's easy to wade out, to feel the chill of the water ease to something balmy around my calves, my knees, my thighs. Past Rabbit Rock and through the breakers that surge against my hips, my waist, my breast, out to where the waves roll beneath my chin and lift my feet so I'm suspended between sky and sand. All about me the ocean hisses and thrashes towards the shore in trillions of tiny, exploding bubbles and I feel the surge of it bending my body, swaying my arms and tugging me along. All I can see is deep blue troughs, the rippling backs of wave after wave rearing beyond me; a pale, uninterested sky and there, not so far away, the rocky slope of the headland.

I catch a glimpse of the bach, crouching beneath the glare of the sun and the mini-palaces that surround it. I see me, clutching my pretty stones and standing still. Watching, as I begin to kick with my big, grandfather's feet.

Things end, I think, and my arm flashes across the blue back of a wave. It lifts me, and I see Justin, standing where the water swirls into white froth, his hand shading his eyes. Yes, things end.

Justin wades out, begins to kick with his big, grandfather's feet. The water churns behind him, and his arm flashes through the blue.

Yes, I think, things end. But things begin. I lift my arm and wave to my son.

Storms

Charlotte Grimshaw

I was sitting in the car; the radio was playing a song. I was looking at where a lane runs off the main road. The lane lay ahead of me, a long narrow stretch, with a high bank overgrown with agapanthus on one side and houses on the other. The song played loud. There was no other sound. An old woman came out of a driveway, carrying a shopping bag. She started to walk away from me down the lane. There was a yellow line painted on the lane. She walked along it. I watched her going steadily away. The lane, the yellow line, the old woman's bent shoulders. A girl came out of the bushes on the bank and jumped down onto the lane, landing in a crouch, righting herself in a quick athletic whirl of limbs; the old woman, startled, still walking, turned her whole body, shoulders hunched, head sideways, to look at the girl, then kept walking away. The music played. The girl went into a house. There was a bend in the lane. The old woman reached the bend and was gone.

Sun on the asphalt. Figures in the distance. The absence of words. The old woman making her way, the whirling girl. The empty lane, the yellow line, the song.

Rob came out of the house, loaded up with bags. 'What's wrong? What? Why don't you help me? See what I've got here. Everything we need. Everything.'

He opened the boot and packed in the gear, tossing a couple of bags on the back seat.

'You relax. Enjoy the drive. This is going to be good. It won't take long to get there. What a beautiful day. Look at the sky.'

We never had children. I always thought there would be time.

'All set?'

Rob got in. He rubbed my shoulder, shook the hair out of his eyes, glanced in the back seat, briskly checking. He saw the newspaper in my lap. The black headline: *Released to Attack Again.*

His expression changed. He went solemn. He put his arms around me.

'Don't read it. Don't think about it. Look there's dear old Osama at the window waving goodbye.'

My dog's name was Robbie, but Rob called him Osama bin Laden because he was such a villain of an animal, and because he said I couldn't possibly have a dog with his name. Robbie was barking at the window. My housekeeper would feed and walk him while we were away. I didn't feel bad about leaving him. He was really Raymond's dog.

Rob took the newspaper off my lap and folded it. 'Don't think about anything. No work, no sorrows, just holiday.'

I smiled. 'OK.'

Everyone said Rob was a lovely man. I met him after a Francis family meeting in Wellington. He was a barrister, a QC. He was divorced, the father of three boys. It was six months since Raymond had left me.

I had been staying at work until late, coming home to the dog and the empty house, sleeping in the study on the top floor because I felt afraid, waking in the night, listening to the whirr of the pool pump and the dog snoring on the floor, and feeling stunned with loneliness. Grief started to feel like fear. I was jumpy. There was an odd side effect to my rawness: I felt as if every part of me was reaching out for sex. I was washed out, nervous, tired, but I felt I was radiating *need* and that people – men – were responding. The world was suddenly full of sexual currents, looks, glances.

I was glad to go to the Francis meeting because it meant I could stay in a good hotel and forget myself a bit. The meeting was routine, the usual thrashing out of issues to do with distribution of the family wealth. I went back to the hotel on the second night and Rob was in the bar. He'd been appearing in the Court of Appeal. He was tall, shabbily dressed, with alert, humorous eyes and messy, wavy hair that fell across his forehead. We started talking. He knew who I was, and that I worked in an arm of the Francis Group of companies. He told me a lot about himself. He was humble and funny. His wife had left him. Had 'despaired' of him, he confessed, with a rueful laugh. 'She was terribly respectable. She didn't approve of my cigars or my old car or my messy clothes – or anything really. She stuck it out for decades. Then she went off with a chap, a hugely wealthy *corpse*. She met him at tennis.'

We laughed. We drank a fair bit and I told him I lived alone. At the end of the evening he took my hand and held it hard, and I said something, some cliché, about not wanting to spend the night alone.

Afterwards I lay in the hotel dark looking out at the city lights with the feeling that I was utterly lost and that Rob – this stranger beside me – was the only point of reference I had.

We parted casually, but when we were both back in Auckland he started ringing me, and it wasn't long before we were going out together.

I looked at the dog scrabbling along the window. 'You can't have a dog and a boyfriend with the same name,' Rob had said. Recently I was a wife – newspapers called us a 'high-achieving couple.' Now I had a *boyfriend.* I turned the word over in my mind, neutralising the protest that rose, some convulsion of the old self that I would not regain.

Now we were driving up the Harbour Bridge in Rob's elegant, battered old car, heading to Gulf Harbour on the Whangaparaoa peninsula. It was summer. We had both taken a week off work. He had borrowed his brother's yacht. We were to set sail, just the two of us. 'Nothing fancy,' he said, winking. 'We'll be at one with the elements.' He joked about my lifestyle – my family wealth, my job. He wasn't materialistic. He liked things to be natural, honest, down-to-earth. He loved the outdoors and sailing. I wasn't so sure about boats. But I was willing.

'Look at the sky.' I pointed.

There was an intense turquoise haze on the horizon. The sea was navy blue and broken up by choppy waves. Over Rangitoto Island there was a strange configuration of clouds, like great rags hanging in the pearly-blue glare. Below it the colour of the sea had intensified, as if there was a disturbance spreading across the water.

Sudden changes in the light. The wind buffeting the car on the bridge.

'Good sailing weather,' he said.

I smoothed out the paper. *Released to Attack Again.* I looked at the picture of Chase Ihaka, the man who had ruined my marriage.

Rob shook his head. He put his hand over the page. I took it off, gently.

Chase Ihaka was awaiting sentence. He had been convicted of murder. There was an old picture of him, a school photo perhaps – a round-faced, gap-toothed Maori youth with a shock of messy hair, smiling.

The wind hit the side of the car with a roar.

Ihaka, now aged 20, has a substantial list of criminal convictions, having first been arrested for theft when aged just ten. In January last year, the career burglar broke into the substantial Remuera home of prominent businesswoman Jenny Francis and her husband, the filmmaker Raymond Wright. Surprised on the premises by Mr Wright, Ihaka subjected him to a beating that left Mr Wright permanently scarred. Ihaka received a light custodial sentence and…

'All right?' Rob said. 'I'll put some music on.'

'Released into the community only five months after his conviction for attacking Mr Wright, Ihaka lived on the streets. He had significant drug and alcohol issues, and acquired numerous further convictions for theft, before the night when he broke into the home of Mr Eric Crombie, owner of the Firebrand chain of clothes shops. Mr Crombie was found beaten to death in his kitchen. Ihaka was arrested driving Mr Crombie's car and wearing items of Mr Crombie's clothing. He had bragged to associates about beating Mr Crombie, and admitted the assault when spoken to by police. During his trial, Ihaka claimed that Mr Crombie had made sexual advances to him, and that he had 'lashed out' in reaction to this 'provocation'. The jury rejected this claim, finding him guilty of murder.

Following his conviction, questions are being asked about why this youth was released to attack again*, only months after being convicted of the serious assault on Raymond Wright.*

Rob looked sideways, shook his head.

I said, 'Journalists keep ringing. They say, "The man who attacked your husband went on to commit murder. How do you feel about that?"' They can't understand why I don't want to comment. But it's done. There's nothing to say.'

'Keep your answerphone on. Screen your calls.'

I remembered going to the hospital. Raymond's face. He was badly hurt; his nose was broken. But it was his expression that struck me most. The bewilderment, vulnerability.

It made it worse for him – my pity. His spirit was damaged. He'd been so frightened. The youth could easily have killed him. He became depressed. A doctor recommended we have counselling together – a mistake, I know that now. It made Raymond shy away from me. I was a witness to his hurt, his shameful tears. To his fall.

I said, 'We'd done all that charity work for street kids. The Francis Foundation, the fundraisers. Raymond did his free film school in South Auckland. All that "reaching out".' I laughed bitterly. 'What rubbish it was.' I looked for a handkerchief. 'Ridiculous … Sorry.'

'*I'm* sorry,' Rob said. 'Told you not to read it.'

He reached over for the paper and threw it hard into the back seat. I stared at him. We drove in silence for a while.

Rob looked at me. He said in a softer voice, cautiously, 'Just because your husband was attacked doesn't mean the charity wasn't worth it. The Francis Foundation does good things.'

I wound my handkerchief round my fingers. I looked out, white houses against a blue-black sky. 'It was all bullshit,' I said.

I stood at the Gulf Harbour marina looking at the boats. The wind blew hard and constant, jinking and clinking the lines and struts; there was the sound of straining ropes, the whine of the wind in the masts. The light was bright, and the sea was pale, turquoise, stained with patches of darker blue.

I helped Rob to load up the gear. The yacht was small and compact, well-kept, with a neat little cabin and a scrubbed wooden deck.

'Snug eh?' Rob said. He busied himself with ropes. I had been on yachts but had never had anything to do with the actual sailing. Rob sailed every year. He knew what he was doing.

He started the motor and we chugged out of the harbour. As soon as we hit the open water we felt the force of the wind. Rob shouted instructions. I did what I was told. We raised the sail. We were tacking up the channel. Boats passed us, racing for the harbour. We were the only ones making for open sea. I looked ahead and saw great clouds hanging ahead of us, and then the nose of the boat dipped and I was looking at the churning water. I felt the jolt in my stomach as we ploughed into the wave, then, rearing ahead were the clouds again, like a robed phantom with its cloak stretched out to catch us, and I thought I could see matter whirling in the depths of the cloud mass, a fury of agitated air, and then I was looking down again, into the green water, and felt the plunge in my stomach, as if I had fallen off a cliff, and the sickening pull as we rose.

I held the rail with both hands. I shot out a burning stream of puke, saw it whisked away on the surface. Spray hit me, stinging drops. I retched again, although there was nothing to bring up but miserable strings of bile. Above me the sky loomed like a cathedral, all points and buttresses, ragged banners, a monstrous edifice into which we battled, up and down, rising and plunging. We were well into the channel, heading past the islands. The waves were getting bigger, and the sky ahead had got much darker. The wind was ferocious. Behind me Rob was all action, but I was so overwhelmed by my physical crisis that I couldn't speak. I assumed he was trying to turn back, and that we would probably die.

I lay on my side along the rail. A green bush-covered island rose and fell. Ropes of sunlight broke though and shone hurtingly bright on the sea around it, a jumbled, foaming mass of pale green. Water came over the side as we hit each wave, showering spray. Rob had edged over to me. He was shouting above the scream of the wind.

'Bit rougher than I thought!' He said something about the weather forecast.

I moaned.

'Feel better?'

'Can we get back?' I said.

'We'll make for Kawau Island. No problem.'

'Let's go back,' I said, but he had gone. I felt angry at the hyperactivity of males, why they needed to complicate everything, drag one on elaborate adventures. But another wave of nausea carried me away from thought, and I was leaning over the side again, crying my complaints into the sea.

I don't know how long it took to make it to Kawau Island. The wind screamed so hard that it whipped the words out of our mouths. Rob fell over once. There was a trickle of blood on his temple. 'It's nothing,' he shouted. His eyes were screwed up, his hair was blown wild by the wind. His jacket billowed behind him. I wondered how much strain the small boat could take.

I mouthed, 'Sorry.' I meant sorry to have been so useless.

He shook his head and pointed. 'Nearly there,' he shouted. 'Hang on.'

We were passing the coast of the island, heading for the mouth of the harbour. I looked at waves crashing onto rocks, at the dark slopes covered with bush and pine forest. Rob pointed out the harbour mouth, a swirl of silver water with the light shining on it, and above it a sky that was growing intensely black. It looked as if every cloud was hurrying towards that place, the sky gathering energy into itself. Rain was sheeting down, and soon great squalls of it were blowing over us. We made for the harbour, and it was like riding into the end of the world. I did cry then, with fear. Just before we got inside the sheltering edge the sky unleashed itself, and we were blinded with rain, ripped by wind, jerked and tossed and thrown about, both of us shouting, every rope straining and the mast groaning. At the moment when I thought the boat would be ripped to pieces we came about, the sail filled with a jolt and we skimmed sickeningly over the crest of a huge swell. I looked into the green trough and saw fish streaming through the wave. Water slapped into my face, the boat heaved and Rob yelled. The wind slackened, the water became calmer and the rain, although it kept pouring down, stopped lashing our faces. We had entered the bay. I looked back at the jumble of silver and foam and sunlight and rain, and couldn't believe we'd come through it.

Rob made me a gin and tonic. I lay on the deck in the strange, hot light. The sun was shining, yet directly above us the sky was swollen with purple-black clouds. I was light-headed, smiling with relief, with the joy of no longer feeling sick.

'That was the most inadequate weather forecast in history,' Rob repeated.

We listened to the radio. The rough weather wasn't a storm any more; it was a cyclone. There were severe gale warnings in all parts of the country. Rob insisted that it hadn't been predicted at all. I watched him from my invalid's position on the sunny deck. I had an intense feeling of well-being that made me sanguine, careless. I turned over in my mind, detached, the fact that I didn't believe him. I'd lately been avoiding all news except business and finance, and the paper I'd had that morning was the first I'd looked at for days. I thought a cyclone must have been mentioned at least, in marine forecasts, which he said he'd listened to. Perhaps he'd dismissed it as only a possibility, or thought we could outrun it. We had outrun it, and now we were trapped in the harbour at Kawau, a perfect shelter, deep inside the encircling hills of the island. We were protected from the wind, and the sun, when it broke through the vast black clouds, was extraordinarily hot and intense. In the distance on the hills the trees were being lashed by the wind but down here at the jetty we were floating in calm water, the light dancing on the wall of the cabin, clothes hanging on the railings to dry, Rob propping another cushion under my head…

I watched him. Everybody said, 'Rob Farnham. What a nice man.' He bustled cheerfully about on the deck, making things ship-shape. I closed my eyes and felt slightly drunk. I was helpless, weak. It was a sensual feeling. 'I've lost control,' I thought. I remembered that first night in the hotel, where I'd thought that everything in my old life was gone, and that he was the only point of reference I had.

Had he wanted the trip so much that he'd turned a blind eye to an approaching storm?

We swam and lazed on the beach. In the evening we made ourselves a meal and ate it on the deck. We drank a lot of wine. We could hear the wind tearing the trees on the hills, a roar that died as the sun was going down but began to rise much higher as it got dark. In the brief stillness at sunset the sky was a jumbled black mass, cloud piling on cloud, and the air was heavy, humid, full of whirling drops. We were drunk. It got very dark, and there were only the few lights from other boats shining on the water. The roar of the wind deepened and intensified. Rob took a torch and we walked up a track into the pine forest, shining the light on the branches, hearing the whole forest shifting and creaking above us. We walked a long way, towards the top of the hill. Up there the storm was battering the tops, and when Rob shone the torch up the trees were crashing and lurching together. He walked away from me. There was blackness all around him; he walked in a pool of light. A branch fell near me, then another. I went towards him; through the dark. The crashing of the trees was exciting, agitating. Lightning lit up the forest, followed by a boom and crack of thunder. Rob started to sing. Lightning flashed again. We linked arms and marched down the hill, falling about in the deep pine needles, hauling each other up, ignoring the falling branches, laughing, singing drunkenly at the tops of our voices.

Back at the jetty the rain came, great sheets of it, drumming on the deck, hissing into the water. We went into the cabin and dried off. Rob poured some more wine. We sat at the little table, laughing at each other. One of his shoes had disintegrated in the wet. The toe had burst open. 'I've got another pair somewhere,' he said, tugging off the sodden relic.

I had a sudden vision of Raymond's wardrobe. The sharp suits. The lines and lines of fashionable shoes. Raymond loved shopping for clothes. He liked to look good because he had a strong visual sense. Our house was full of good art because we had the money to buy it, and Raymond had good taste. Not that I didn't, but he was the one with the real eye. He had left his paintings, just as he left his dog. Soon we would divide them up, through our lawyers, in a settlement. After Chase Ihaka beat him, his face was no longer symmetrical. He was still handsome. Is. Was. I don't live with Raymond any more. Raymond is not dead but he is gone. He was gone.

When he told me he was leaving I begged him not to go. I said that we could live through this. I said that a burglar, a nobody, should not be allowed to destroy our marriage. I shouted. 'Fuck Chase Ihaka! He's nothing to us!'

I remember Raymond's expression. He despised me. For begging. For wanting our lives to carry on as before, even though everything – words, promises, memories, shared ideas – all the things that had held us together had been spoiled and broken.

By Chase Ihaka.

Those words. I hear them sometimes when I've been asleep and I'm just at the point of waking. I hear them as if it's my own voice, whispering in my head. The smiling brown boy in the photo, gap-toothed, head on one side, the crooked collar of his school uniform resting on his smooth cheek, long eyelashes, the narrow brown eyes. Little man, his mother's lost boy. Little destroyer.

I was in the narrow bunk, squashed up against Rob. I lay with my eyes closed. These days I struggled with that point, between sleeping and waking. I often woke with a feeling of dread.

There was something all around me, an unpleasant, alien presence. I realised it was a smell.

Rob sat up.

'Oh, Christ. Oh my God.'

I rolled over. I grabbed his arm. 'What is it?'

The floor of the boat was covered with something dark and pungent. I felt sick. My head reeled.

'The engine's leaking. Bloody hell.'

I pulled on some clothes. He said, 'You'd better get out. Get some air, love.'

The morning air whirled with rain. All the trees were tossing and roaring now, even those near the harbour. The sky was heavy with intense black clouds. There were flashes of purple sheet lightning and cracks of thunder: sharp after one another, like a series of gunshots. It was hot. I breathed in, deeply, to get rid of the taste of the fumes.

After a long time Rob came up. He sat down heavily. 'It's terrible. I can't get at the leak. What a mess.'

'We'd better get the food out,' I said.

He looked blank.

'We can't get back in this weather. We'll need it.'

'Right.' He leaned his face against the rail. 'I've got a blinding headache,' he said.

'It's the fumes.' I laughed. Horrified.

'What a disaster,' he said. He looked bleakly at the hillside.

We worked to pack the supplies into boxes and bring them out onto the deck. We covered them as best we could from the rain. Everything was drenched. Clothes hung dripping from the railings. Cardboard boxes were sodden. One box broke up and cans crashed onto the deck. Some rolled off into the water.

The cabin was uninhabitable. The floor was soaked with fuel, and Rob couldn't figure out how to drain it, or to stop the leak. Some of the bedding had fallen onto the floor and was wet and stained. Packets of food that we'd opened were spoiled.

We got everything out onto the deck. Rain splattered across our faces. Rob got up, grim-faced. He stood with his back to me, staring at the tossing trees. My wet clothes clung to me. My skin hurt, pinched by the shrinking material. There was rain in my eyes. I'd been inclined to laugh, but the discomfort was increasing. I couldn't think how, or where, we were going to spend the days until the storm had passed. Then there was the question of how we were going to get back. If we couldn't fix the engine we would have to steer back into Gulf Harbour under sail, and I knew that wouldn't be easy.

Rob said, 'I know what we'll do. Load up the dinghy.'

'Where are we going?'

'You'll see.' He didn't confer. He wanted to be in charge. He would *provide.* I thought about this.

He rowed around the point and out across the bay. The wind hit us. I stopped talking and leaned forward, resting my elbows on my knees. It was rough out from the shelter of the trees – not as bad as the open sea, but choppy enough to bring the nausea swirling back. Spray broke over us. There were sticks and branches floating in the water. Rob rowed, grunting with effort, muttering to himself, 'There? There? Where's it gone now?'

We were passing a stretch of pine forest that had been cleared for sections. Small houses showed among the trees.

'Here we are,' he said, steering the boat towards the shore. We landed on a tiny jetty. He fastened the rope and pulled me up onto the wooden boards.

'Right. You wait here.'

'Where are you going?' I was concentrating on not being sick.

'I'm going to reconnoitre.'

I sat down with my arms around my knees. I looked through the wooden planks to the green water sluicing below. Nausea broke my thoughts into odd patterns. I thought: children think adults are a different species. But adults sometimes feel as if they are only ten years old. I sat there, hugging my bare legs. Once I'd stopped feeling sick, I decided, I would go behind a tree and relieve myself. I had been reduced to very simple things. I was soaking. I was sick. I was even hungry. My legs looked skinny, ridiculous, in their baggy shorts. My shoes were full of water. How had I let this happen? I could have been in an expensive hotel anywhere in the world. I had a moment of dismay, almost fear. I was letting everything fall away. I was lost. I didn't know the man I was with. Who was he?

Rob came back, crashing down through the pine needles and scrub, bullish, jolly and commanding, in control once more.

'I've got this client…' He looked sideways. I waited.

We were standing on the deck of a small house. There was a covered barbecue, a spa pool draped in canvas sheeting. The blinds and curtains were drawn. As he spoke Rob was looking under plant pots, shifting a doormat, running his hand along the top of ledges.

'He says to me, if you ever need it, the house is here. He knows I come sailing round Kawau all the time.'

We had hauled our belongings up from the jetty and piled them on the deck.

I said, 'Are you sure this is the right place?'

'Definitely.'

He went around the back of the house. I sat down. I looked at the orange pine needles, the tossing trees. I heard a tearing, wrenching sound, like old iron being ripped. There was a loud bang.

Rob appeared inside the French doors, unlocked them and stepped beaming out onto the deck.

'Madam. Your palace awaits.'

It was really very cosy. There was a double bed with a striped cover. There was linen in the cupboard. Everything worked, once Rob had figured out how to turn on the pump. The water came from a rainwater tank at the back of the house. We unloaded our food in the kitchen and I set about making breakfast. The cooking utensils were expensive, elaborate. Rob took the cover off the barbecue and fiddled with it. I had a sense of relief at the space. I hadn't liked being cramped into the yacht. I was glad to be off the water too. To stop feeling sick.

The wind shifted the trees, rain drummed on the iron roof.

'So who's this client?'

'Longstanding one. A good guy. Obviously he's not going to turn up, what with the storm.'

'No.'

'But I'll tell him we've been here,' he said innocently.

I'd looked at the bathroom window where Rob had got in. The metal catch was broken off. The frame had been wrenched out.

I thought, with a kind of hilarity, a QC breaking in? There was a mirror over the kitchen sink. I looked at myself. I'd had a feeling, ever since Raymond had gone, that some outer layer had been peeled away. I was raw, open. I had attracted men – Rob. I had allowed him to take me away. I felt like a kid, limping and snivelling one minute, hilarious the next. And when Rob took over, when he finished his breakfast and grinned at me merrily and pulled me onto the bed, I had the sensual feeling of surrender, of allowing everything to fall away.

Rob went out. He said he was going to check on the dinghy. When the storm had died down, he said, we could go back to the wharf and work out what to do about the yacht.

Before he left he'd said, 'There's a shower.'

I lay on the bed. 'Let's not wash,' I said.

He looked shocked. 'Not wash?'

'Oh all right.' I laughed.

He left. I had a short chilly shower – the water hadn't yet heated up. I lay on the bed. There was a shelf of old detective novels. I pulled up the duvet and lay luxuriously reading. The rain was loud on the roof. Out the window the forest swayed and heaved with the squalls. Sticks clattered onto the deck.

Later we put on the oilskins that were hanging in the laundry and went down to the jetty.

'There's no one in the houses round about,' he said. He held my hand. Our feet sank deep in the pine needles. The bay was wild, grey-green and running with currents. We walked along a path, past the other houses. Their windows were blank, curtained. We came to a point and looked out at the churning water. The trees were thrashing across on the far shore. It occurred to me that a branch might fall on us.

We went back and spread out our clothes to dry. We lay on the striped duvet, listening to the gale.

I woke in the night. It was pitch black. The darkness was unnerving, so absolute that nothing showed. The wind was howling, lifting the iron on the roof. I moved closer to Rob.

A dream had woken me. It was about Raymond.

We got married when we were both twenty-eight. He was handsome. He was a filmmaker. He had directed successful New Zealand films. After we'd been married a couple of years he was invited to make his first film in America. He would go on making films. That wouldn't change.

In the last months of our marriage I'd thought about trying to get pregnant. I needed to get on with it, if I was ever going to. I stopped taking the Pill. I didn't tell him. I wondered if he knew. What with working so much we barely had time for each other. I didn't get pregnant.

I thought about sex. I forced myself to look back. Was I just thinking this way because of what had happened? What was I getting at? When we'd been in bed together and I was happy, had I sensed, once or twice, a kind of distance, almost malice, in his tone, as if he had performed a task, performed it well, and now could be released?

He was a polished performer. He kept some part of himself separate. It was that distance that made me yearn after him, as well as the moments when his vulnerability showed, and I was all the more smitten with him because he tried to keep his dignity, and to hide it. He was the fourth son of a solo mother. He knew what it was like to be talented and poor. That was why he did free film workshops for street kids. There were parts of himself over which he had grown a shell, in order to get on in the world. Old hurts, things he was ashamed of.

Chase Ihaka took away his dignity, and afterwards he couldn't face me, couldn't stand that I had seen him reduced.

He despised me for begging, for not being able to face the fact that everything had changed.

A voice came out of the blackness. 'What are you thinking about?'

'About Raymond,' I said.

He sat up. I couldn't see anything. He got off the bed.

'Where are you going?' I asked.

He didn't say anything.

'Where are you?'

There was no answer. There was only blackness. I heard a sound. He was standing in the room, near me.

'Where are you?'

Silence.

'Oh, turn on the light! Turn on the light! Turn on the light!'

He jumped and snapped it on. He leaned over me, gripping my wrists. 'What's the matter? What's wrong?'

I pulled away. 'You didn't answer. You didn't speak.'

'I was asleep,' he said, wondering. He held me tight. 'You've been dreaming. Just dreams.'

'There's no one I can trust.'

'I'm here. You can trust me. I'll turn off the light, shall I?'

The blackness came down. I was shaking. I couldn't get warm.

We stayed in the bach for three days. On the fourth day the wind dropped. There was stillness, quiet. The sky was low and black, shot through with sudden, surprising beams of sunlight. Rob went to the yacht, and came back with the news that a man who had been sheltering at the wharf in his own boat had helped him with the engine, that they had drained the boat as best they could. The man had given him a bit of fuel. If the engine failed we would have to get into Gulf Harbour under sail. He thought we would make it. The storm had passed. People were leaving the island.

We packed up and tidied the house. I didn't want to leave it. I had grown fond of it. Rob went into the laundry and hammered the window frame back into place. I pretended not to hear.

'It's been an adventure,' he said.

'It's been great,' I said.

At the wharf the yachts were leaving. The beach was strewn with branches; the trees hung with broken sticks, paper, plastic bags. The water was brown and churned up. I looked at the yacht. It was stained with oil, sodden, smelly. I was dreading the sail back. I felt nauseated already.

The engine started, and we headed towards the harbour mouth. Rob waved to other boats, whistled. Looking ahead anxiously I saw that the sea was still rough. When we hit the open water I was immediately doubled up with nausea, and the waves seemed to me terrifyingly high, although the wind was moderate. Soon I was lying along the rail, watching the green shoreline rise and fall. Sunbeams shone down on the sea. Rob shouted to point out dolphins. I watched them leaping through the waves. Foam blew in the air. I rested my cheek on the rail. Beyond Kawau the wind strengthened. The boat rose and plunged, hitting the water hard. I felt the sickness rising and rising. I leaned, heaved, and my breakfast hit the water and was carried away, a curl of matter on the bubbled surface, like a question mark.

I imagined my own body, falling, hitting the surface, whirled away in the current. I looked across at waves, jumbled cloud, grey water lit up silver in the beams of light, birds riding on currents of air. To lie here like a limp rag, weak, sick, drenched, watching the currents, to yearn only to get from this moment to the next, to be *reduced to simple things*. Was this the way to confront what I shied away from most?

Raymond told me the truth just before he left me. He told me as a final, savage assertion of himself, as if I had forced him into a lie all these years. Afterwards, he despised me for pleading with him. For wanting to carry on as before, despite what he'd told me. It was our secret now. He told me what Chase Ihaka had done, and what he had done to him. The brown young man with the gap-toothed smile. His eager face, his shining eyes. The sort of youth the Francis Foundation wanted to help. He was poor. He may have been talented. It didn't matter now. Living on the streets, a thief and an alcoholic, he had started selling himself for sex. He had not broken into our house. Raymond had invited him in.

Had arranged to meet him secretly, at home, while I was at work. Had heard the knock, opened the door, ushered him inside. Made small talk, poured out wine. Drawn him down onto the couch. At what point the youth went crazy – before or after the sex – I do not know. Raymond wouldn't say. I don't know why he exploded in such violence. I know that he did it again, not long after coming out of jail for attacking Raymond, and that the second time, instead of clamming up, he told the police a version of the truth. He said the victim had made sexual advances to him. That he had recoiled and lashed out. He didn't say he went to men's houses all the time. That it was the way he made money, because he was drunk and drugged-out and poor.

Raymond was right. We couldn't really have stayed married. In the end I would have had to face up to things.

It was when Chase Ihaka was arrested for murder that I came home to find Raymond waiting for me, drinking, a strange, heightened expression in his eyes.

He told me. In my distress I tried to make bargains. I thought it was something we could solve.

He looked at me with contempt.

'I thought you would guess,' he said.

I never would have guessed. I had faith in our marriage. I wanted children. I wanted to believe.

'You married me for my money,' I said.

I saw him flinch. He laughed scornfully. I looked at his pale, scarred face and saw it was true. I felt a wave of pure sorrow for him, as well as for myself.

'What about the Foundation? The sheer hypocrisy of you…'

But I didn't go on. I had done my begging. He left the house. I watched him walk unsteadily away up the drive.

Perhaps he didn't think he and Chase Ihaka were all that different, in the end.

*

Rob shouted. He pointed at the land. We were on a tack, heading for the entrance to Gulf Harbour. He was going to lower the sail and hope the engine would restart. If it didn't I couldn't see how we were going to get back in.

At the harbour mouth he tried the engine. It wouldn't start. He tried again. The boat was tossing badly. I staggered against the rail. He shouted some instructions. I didn't understand. The current was pushing us towards the shoreline, where there were rocks. The engine made a moaning sound. It coughed. I could see the edge of the marina, the tops of the clinking masts. The boat turned and was hit side-on by a wave. I crouched down by the railing. Rob swore and leaned down again, and the engine spluttered and turned over and started, and then he was steering the boat, heading us in through the channel, and as the sun broke out, casting a livid light through the black clouds, we sailed into the calm lanes of the marina.

I was sitting in the car. I was looking along the lane that runs off the main road. It was strewn with leaves, broken branches, bits of paper. The gutters were running with rain. Leaves swirled in the blocked drain. The footpath was flooded.

The dog, Robbie, was at the window, scrabbling, barking.

Rob got out and started unloading my things. He leaned in. 'Getting out?'

We carried my bags to the door.

'The bach. Did you really know who owned it?'

Rob tossed his keys from one hand to the other. 'Sure. He's a client of mine. Lovely bloke.'

There was a silence.

'Shall I come in?' he asked.

I looked at him. A sudden squall blew through the garden, flipping the leaves, driving rain onto the tiles. I looked up at the white sky.

'Yes.'

I unlocked the door. Whistling, he picked up my bags and followed me inside.

The History Of

Jenah Shaw

After it all, he drove for a day to the edge of the world. There was a place he knew where a sea stretched into an opaque sky and where gulls wheeled in the still after the rain. Wind dipped low over the water. Surf curled white. Clouds blew away and out of view. Each day the sun rose then fell to leave the beach and sea and lonely road lit by a sailing moon.

It had been some time, but he remembered the path that turned up from the headlands to the bach. Weeds now obscured the path and the grass grew so long that the pohutukawas seemed to be wading through them, knee-deep. It was a small bach, two rooms and a dunny out back with a creaking door and damp, dark smell. There was a bed, a small kitchen, a window that looked to the turn of the sea. Most importantly, there was a desk crowded next to the bed and a row of bookshelves – empty.

It's quiet, that far out on the edge of the world. The first week the silence of the place – the utter, desolate, completeness of the silence – ached in his bones. It cramped his legs during the night, pounded his head with the too-bright day. But then, he thought as he stared dimly at the wrinkles of his reflection, maybe it wasn't the silence. Maybe it was something else entirely.

He had no telephone out this far. When his daughter wanted to speak to him she had to drive as far as the beach and struggle across the unseen path to the bach. She didn't know the place like he did – she stumbled over the hidden steps and uneven ground. He was sitting outside when she arrived, having a smoke and watching the sky turn a deep purple over the sea. He'd washed a few of his shirts that morning, they flapped from the line like save-me signals billowing from the mast of an abandoned ship. (*save my soul, save my soul, save my soul*).

– Afternoon, he said when he saw her. – You arrived before the rain.

He nodded out to the sea. – Just look at those clouds.

She stood a few feet away from him, shrugging deeper into her over-sized jacket, hair whipping around her face.

– Dad, she said. Behind her the purple-grey of clouds were stretching higher from the horizon, reaching closer, closer towards him.

– Dad, please come home.

He exhaled the last of his cigarette, watched the smoke dissipate in the waiting air and stamped out the butt.

– Why don't you come inside, he said. – I'll put the kettle on.

They'd bought the bach the year after they married, because his wife had loved the sea as much as he had. It wasn't much, even then, but with a teacher's salary you couldn't expect something too fancy now, could you? They came out whenever they needed to escape. They walked among discards of driftwood and talked about a world that rested somewhere across the vast blue of the ocean. At night they opened bottles of cheap wine and drank straight from the bottle. *It's the way life's supposed to be,* he'd said to her. *It's the good life.*

He heated the kettle over the stove and rinsed two chipped cups in the sink. His daughter sat at the table – awkwardly, now, because her legs were too long. (It had been a while.)

He smiled as he set the cups on the table.

– I remember, he said, – the first time we brought you here. You were only little.

She turned her head and looked out the window to the sea. On the stove, the kettle whistled shrill.

– We came out every year after that. He lifted the kettle from the stove. – Every summer. Glorious summers, weren't they?

– You should clean the windows, his daughter said quietly. – You can barely see anything past them at all.

He shrugged as he poured the steaming water carefully into the cups. His hands were unreliable now, some days steady and some days not. He tried not to dwell on this, just like he tried not to dwell on the folds of skin that gathered around the knuckles, transparent and fragile as crumpled paper.

– It doesn't bother me, really. It was your mother who looked after all that.

There was a moment of stillness, of silence so complete that he felt even his heart might pause for the breath of it. Beat *hush, hush* gently against his chest. He sat down.

– It's the nature of the place, he said gruffly. – That's what I like. The sea and the wind and all that.

His daughter didn't seem to hear. She lifted a hand to her face and tucked a stray curl behind her ear.

– Dad, she said. She tilted her head and stared at him. Her expression was unreadable.

– When are you coming back?

– Sugar! He said quickly. – How could I forget, I know you never have your tea without sugar, do you? And he got to his feet, turned his back to her while he looked through the old cupboards for the sugar. Inside the cupboards smelt like salt.

– You can't live like this.

He almost expected the smell to cling to his hands, his unreliable shaking hands. He held the sugar in both hands when he put it on the table. (just in case). Found a spoon. Rinsed it, wiped it. Sat back down. As he passed her the spoon he began to smile.

– Do you remember, he said, that year we forgot to bring the milk?

When she raised the cup to her lips he saw that her hands were shaking too.

– Dad, she said and there were tiny tremors in her voice.

He stirred sugar carefully into his tea. – I thought, he said, – I thought it would be a good idea if I had some alone time. Thought I might write those histories I always talked about.

– Oh. His daughter rested her chin on one hand. Voice soft. – Oh.

– I mean, I'm not going to live forever. Might be a bit risky if I leave it any longer, now, mightn't it? And he chuckled, dryly, as if laughing at your own mortality meant you weren't scared of it.

– You could write just as well back home.

She said it quickly. (not looking at him).

– Oh, that may well be, but –

– Hiding out here doesn't change anything. You know that, don't you? She's gone. You can't just … you can't hide from that.

He stared at his hands on the table. The paper-thin folds of collected years. The veins that lay too close to the skin these days, a heartbeat too easily tracked.

– I'm sorry, his daughter said. – But you can't.

He looked up from his hands.

– Do you remember, he said, his voice faint, – our last summer here? You didn't want to leave.

She met his gaze. – We want you to come home, Dad.

– I can still see you, standing in that doorway with the tears down your face –

– Dad, she said with the tremors in her voice again. – Dad, please listen to me.

He frowned.

– I don't know why we stopped our holidays here after that.

She exhaled sharply, turned and stared back out to the sky.

– We stopped our holidays here because the place is horrible and small and boring and I hated it.

Silence. Still. Heart went *hush, hush.*

He spoke slowly.

– I thought, he said – I thought you loved it here.

She stared, fixedly, past the grime on the window. Outside the afternoon was fading quickly into the coming rain.

– You loved it here, she said quietly.

Still.

– I cried, she said, almost apologetically – because I stung my foot on a jellyfish down the bay. Mum wouldn't let us come back after that. Don't you remember?

In the moment that followed they could almost feel the wind in their bones. Outside it cried.

When she left he made no promises and she made no more pleas. He stood in the doorway and watched her walk away. The wind was blowing with even more fervor now and she stumbled into it all the way down the hill. Behind her the shirts cracked from the line into the wind. (*save my soul! save my soul! save my soul!*). When he couldn't see her anymore he turned and went back inside.

It was the same afternoon that he finally sat down at his desk with his paper and his pen. On the shelves on the wall he had arranged his books from A-Z, easy reference, history pressed tight between the pages like flowers kept for posterity. He wrote.

The History of the Empire begins where all histories do. There is an uncertain territory spanning the geography of memory and myth. There are dark canals between what we think we know and what we just think. Even Rome, with its many histories echoing in the wake of its fall, remains a city of the collective imagination. The Rome you think you know is not the Rome that was – that is gone forever. Rather it is a Rome of myth and rumour and stories of things that may have happened but maybe didn't

He couldn't get further than that. He couldn't move his pen to stretch towards the wolf that mothered two human babes, tiny and mewling and wet. He couldn't think even as far as the Etruscan kings waiting off, stage-left; couldn't imagine the flames that devoured the city of Veii, let alone the brutalities and the victories and the glories of the Republic or the Empire. He stared at the sentences, scratched out words, added more, ripped out the page and folded it carefully into squares before dropping it in the bin. It seemed suddenly strange to try to write the history of a people already written. Why bother, he wondered as he stared at the pock-marks across the desk, when their skies were such a different blue to his?

His mind fell silent. Still. He listened to his heart whisper *hush, hush* in his chest. He wondered if he should sell the bach. They'd bought it the year after they married, because his wife had loved the sea as much as he had. Or maybe he had loved the sea, and only imagined that she did. They are dark canals that lie between what we think we know and what we only think.

Hush, hush said his heart. *Hush, hush.*

That night he dreamt of Julius Caesar. They were standing together at the top of cold grey steps, looking out and across the lazy stretch of roads and buildings and shadows of Rome. Voices carried distantly on the wind. A turret of smoke rose from between far-away roofs. Light glinted off Caesar's tarnished breast plate. They stood there, waiting, watching. In the distance a quick flight of birds wheeled up into the blue, blue, blue of the arching sky.

Water Bores

Linda Niccol

When my world spins out of orbit (this time, thanks to a certain woman, it's way beyond Pluto) I head up the coast to the old family bach. I grab a couple of beers and go out to the weathered wooden plank balanced on breeze blocks under the wind-bent macrocarpa. I sit, gazing out at the sea and the island called Kapiti – say it 'cuppa tea', if you're concerned about the correct Maori pronunciation – until I am ready to re-enter the stratosphere, using the bridge this water-locked town provides.

On the surface it's the ideal place for a break, or in my case a bit of marital soul-searching. It's only when you spend more than a weekend here you realise the relaxed atmosphere is transient, like a petrol rainbow on a puddle. Sure, people greet each other with a polite 'good morning' or 'afternoon' when they pass on the beach or the street. They know their neighbours, their neighbours' children. They meet up at parent teacher evenings or socialise at barbecues but again it's a superficial thing, if you go deeper you'll strike a feeling of unease. I think it's mainly to do with the water.

Unless like our family you'd been coming here for years, this used to be a place you would drive through on the way to somewhere else. Now it's thick with fish-out-of-water Spanish adobe castles, hemmed in by made-over

Lockwoods and run-down baches. Waterfront property anywhere in the world is at a premium, and this place is burgeoning with wannabe life-stylers happy to commute in order to secure their little piece of beachfront.

Building permits are issued by the council at the rate of around sixty a month but no provision has been made for the amenities, especially water, to support the flurry of subdivisions. The new houses include on average three toilets, a jacuzzi and occasionally a swimming pool.

It hasn't rained for nearly three months.

There's no excuse for the council's lack of action, according to anyone you talk to. The 'water bores' in particular. These guys have solved the problem over and over and out loud to any one who'll listen. You can hear their theories any given evening at the Beach Inn.

There's Doug, the between-shifts fireman; Phil, the ex-cop turned landscape gardener and Eric, the car salesman. Three single guys connected by middle-age spread, broken marriages and talk about water. They have a regular table facing the sea and the setting sun, which tonight is putting on a pyrotechnic display in green and red worthy of note, or at least the page of a scenic calendar. I've never once heard them acknowledge this beauty. But they're more than happy to comment on the barmaid's looks or lack of them – making a new judgement with every raising and lowering of their beers.

Because I turned forty a few months ago and because I'd already bought myself the 911 Porsche that a man who owns an advertising company should drive, years ago, when business was good, there seemed nothing to do but have an affair. Well that's how it might have seemed to anyone watching. It wasn't that calculated. I don't believe these things ever are. It would have probably just blown over if Zoe hadn't taken it upon herself to tell my wife.

Connie's fury blasted white-hot at my betrayal, my downward slide into 'Advertising fucking cliché-land,' as she so eloquently put it.

Finally, when Connie said she trusted me again, I knew I didn't deserve it. Forgiven but not forgotten, the whole sordid mess lay between us like a dirty creek just that little bit too wide to jump across. It made no sense that I should be the angry one but I continued to feel indignant and out of sorts.

*

So here I am at the Beach Inn having a drink or five with the water bores. For once they're not re-solving the water crisis for the ineffectual, overly-cautious council, whose hands seem tied by worn-out legislation and conflicting opinions from the experts they have spent thousands of hours and dollars consulting.

Tonight's topic of conversation centres on the demise of a certain Norfolk pine and Victor Ambrose who just sold his cruddy bach in excess of $750,000, a high price even considering the escalating property prices. The magnificent unimpeded view, sans the Norfolk pine on the adjacent property, definitely helped.

The bores are onto their second pints and ready to point the finger.

'Who had the most to gain?' Eric says, fingering Toyota badge on his lapel as if it were some sort of talisman that would tell him the answer.

'Can't prove it though. Not now it's all ashes,' says Doug, hand under the chin of his once handsome face in an effort to stop it collapsing under the weight of sun-bed tanning and cigarettes.

'Victor would have known the owners only use the place on the weekends.'

'Yep. He would have waited for a high tide. And a northerly – that's the key – the sea roaring so loud you can't hear a thing. Then he would have ring-barked it.'

Much of the petty crime that happens in the area occurs on such windy nights. Next morning the pavements are covered in drifts of window glass from cars smashed open like oysters so young men could get at the sweet meat of car stereos.

Victor used to drink with the water bores but since he'd sold up he hadn't been seen at the Beach Inn.

He'd owned the bach next to ours for a couple of years but he and I only really talked the one time.

Victor had waited until his wife was a way down the beach with their enormous dog and then he'd leaned over the fence.

'Beer?'

I accepted, the sun was low; the long shadow of the Norfolk pine fell across the lawn as I crossed the beachfront bank running along the front of the properties. Victor raised his bottle and I did the same. We each took a long swallow. Victor wiped his mouth with the back of his hand.

'Remember that caravan, parked here, day before yesterday?'

I did. It was red and white, a humpty Kiwi classic from the 60s, decorated with old car badges. Victor glanced at the spot where it been.

'Belongs to my brother and his friend,' he said, with an emphasis on 'friend.'

'Is that right,' I said, wondering where this was leading.

'Did you see them?'

'No,' I said.

'They just turned up,' he said, taking a gulp from his bottle. 'I never even knew I had a brother till he phoned from Ozzie last month. My worst nightmare was that he'd be a poofter. Or a greenie.'

Victor's laugh gurgled into a choke. I slapped him on the back.

'Turns out he's both.' Victor gouged a strip through the middle of the bottle label with his thumbnail. 'They said they'd drop in again on their way down South.'

Victor looked out to sea and shook his head. 'Right out of the blue.'

We finished our beers and I went inside and pulled the blind down in an effort to block the stare of the flaming eyeball of the setting sun.

*

Victor's forward planning regarding the Norfolk is artful, Machiavellian.

'He'd have known it wouldn't die straight away,' said Phil.

'Time enough to spruce up his property ready for sale,' wheezed Doug, though a curl of cigarette smoke. 'And wait for the October storms.'

And that was exactly how it had happened. Victor's place was repainted and the garden tidied up and the next week a violent storm hit. The wind was so strong it blew in one of our bach's loose windows. A large shard of glass landed on the table where Connie sat to do the weekend crossword. The bucket-style dining chairs filled up with water. The same wind snapped the Norfolk. Its 50-year-old crown fell, missing the houses, down onto the beach. The next day it was quickly sawn up and carried away for firewood. The stump stuck up like a sore thumb until it was finally razed to the ground.

'When you look at the trunk of a tree like the Norfolk, it seems pretty damn solid, but most of what you see is dead wood.' Phil's new expertise and the fact he was about to take his final arboreal examination brought him to the forefront of tonight's debate. 'The only living part of a tree trunk is the outermost ring,' he went on. 'Called the cambium. Water and minerals move upward. Sugars, growth regulators etcetera move downward. If the bark is badly damaged the tree can't heal itself. Scrape the bark off right around and it literally starves to death.' Phil draws his forefinger across his throat.

It was only a tree but the talk of its death makes me feel queasy. I say my goodbyes and go back to the bach. As I lie in the sweaty throes of an impending hangover I imagined large blue jellyfish – Pacific Man o' War – floating on top of the waves like bubbles of molten glass, their stingers streaming out, carried to shore and left to shrivel in the morning sun.

The crash of waves against the seawall wakes me. I get up and gulp water straight from the tap. I wonder how the bores were sleeping. I remember the night Connie christened them.

We'd been at the Beach Inn drinking till late. The guys were on their pet subject and I could see Connie's patience was dissolving.

'Can we go, please,' she hissed in my ear, as Phil launched into his theory on why drilling bores was only a quick fix and how they'd threaten the water-table. Doug was all for some kind of catchment pond. Eric shook his head.

'Dam the river,' he said. 'All that water just running out to sea.'

'The guy up at the pet shop, he said seawater could be made drinkable. That's what they did in Romania anyway.'

Connie rolled her eyes.

'Yeah, but can you imagine it? The endless dispute between us and the Maoris about who owns the seawater?' Doug snorted.

'You want to know who owns the water?' said Phil. 'We all do! It's the exact same water our great-grandfathers used a hundred years ago, the same water that has been here for approximately four billion years since the earth was formed. The same water, in fact, that keeps going around and around in cycles.'

Connie gave me a sharp kick under the table.

We hurried along the dark beach, our shoes in our hands, trying to dodge the incoming tide. A wave caught and Connie scrambled up onto the rocks. The next one came up to my knees. I waded over to where Connie was teetering and scooped her up. I carried her along, the tide tugging at my pant legs, her arms tight around my neck.

'One more minute with those water-fixated bores and I would have gone out of my mind. Is that all they talk about?'

'Pretty much. It's a big deal around here.'

Lurching inside I dropped her on the unmade bed. Our eyes swimming in and out of focus as our faces and then our mouths then our bodies came together. When Connie got up to pee there was an imprint of the mattress stitching on her butt. We fell asleep in a tangle of sheets and blankets. In the morning her cheeks were flushed like a child's and her breath smelt of last night's wine. That was the last time we really kissed.

*

Having successfully drowned the hangover during the night I get up early and walk along the beach to the shops to get the paper and milk. A slice of tightly curled bark lies on the sand next to some roughly sawn logs from another felled Norfolk. Smooth and crimson where it was once connected to the trunk, the outside of the bark is rough and flecked with bright green lichen. I put it in my pocket and sit for a while on a flat-topped rock.

A woman, face pinked by the early sun, dressed in a karate-style outfit stands on the shore facing the sea. She stretches her limbs slowly, waves her arms out like a crab

A local councillor and her friend nod to me as they stride ahead of their bouncing black Labradors, heads bent slightly against the prevailing wind, unmindful of the hot piles of excrement that steam on the sand in their wake. They don't see the sign with the guilty-looking cartoon dog and the message 'If your dog fouls clean it up $200 fine!' A by-law drafted in a stuffy office, administered by some other council, at some other time. It cannot apply to this morning, to this beach, the tide-washed sand stretching before them and the sparkling waves dancing in and out.

A big dark shape bobs on top of the water. At first I think it's a seal but then I see it's a big log, sailing into shore like a longboat.

*

Connie and I began to come apart when I stopped kissing her. I stopped because I'd started smoking again. Just the occasional one when I'd had a few drinks. I'd blame the smell on clients I'd been entertaining. I'd shower as soon as I arrived home. The film of nicotine would slide off my face but my breath, even though I'd scrub my tongue with toothpaste, still stank when I huffed into my hand. So I started kissing her quickly on the cheek and pulling away before she could get a whiff. This seemingly small cessation of intimacy, after fifteen years of faithfulness, left me open to a much bigger deceit.

Zoe smoked. That's how that all started. At this point I'd like to apportion some of the blame to the smoke-free office policy. I met Zoe on the cold, uncomfortable balcony set aside for those in the building who couldn't or wouldn't quit.

I'd gone there because I was tired and stressed about a pitch for a new client and just wanted to get out in the air. Zoe was just putting a cigarette into her mouth. She smiled with her teeth clenched around it before touching the match to the end and drawing in the smoke. The way she slowly blew the smoke out highlighted her cheekbones and lent her ordinary face an exotic beauty. I got hard.

Responding to what must have been a hungry look on my face, she offered me a cigarette. She touched my hand as she lit it for me. The smoke burnt on the way down. I coughed.

'Sorry, haven't had one for a while.'

'Once a smoker…'

'… always a smoker.'

We chatted about our places of work. Zoe was a legal secretary for the patent firm two floors below.

A few days later we met on the balcony again. She offered me a cigarette. I started off protesting but then took it.

It soon became a regular thing. We'd chat and smoke. She had a bitter, ready wit, which seemed wasted in her dull job.

One blustery day when she was helping to ignite my cigarette she touched my hand again. We kissed. The taste reminded me of my first. I have forgotten her name, that tipsy girl swaying on the front step of her parents' house, her cold nose pressing into my cheek.

And so it began.

We did it mostly in her office after hours. We smoked before and after. We kissed in the lift, our tongues hot and acrid with nicotine.

We'd meet on the balcony and look out over the city rain or shine and smoke. The hand that wasn't holding her cigarette would brush my thigh – our combined exhalation of smoke a screen against the rest of the world.

We'd meet at suburban restaurants and bars – the ones where smoking was encouraged. I would continue to smoke hers, as if the act of buying a packet would signal everyone that something more sinister was up.

We screwed and smoked until suddenly I felt sick.

So sick that I thought I'd better end it. Zoe's reaction was measured. She lit a cigarette. For once I didn't get hard. She blew a perfect smoke ring towards me and then turned her face away.

'Well I didn't expect you to leave your wife or anything like that. But why now?'

I struggled to think of something to say.

'It's nearly Christmas. Connie and I are going away.'

'Well now you won't have to buy me a gift,' she said, dropping her cigarette butt, squashing it with the heel of her boot.

I went home and headed straight for the shower. I'd been standing there for nearly ten minutes when I sensed Connie was in the room. I wiped a hole in the steamed-up glass of the shower stall and looked out. She was standing arms folded staring at the heap of my clothes on the floor. She saw me looking and said in a voice flat as an ironing board, 'You're smoking again aren't you.'

I didn't bother trying to lie. I thought if I admitted to this smaller sin I'd confessed the bigger one.

Connie was the reason I'd stopped smoking in the first place. She couldn't stand it and I was so in love with her it was easy to cut down. But that wasn't quite enough to fool her. She caught me out one night after a deep, prolonged kiss.

'You're too beautiful to smoke,' she said, laying her head on my chest. 'And I was hoping you'd be around for a while.'

I didn't touch a cigarette for the next fifteen years.

Connie's face as I admitted to the smoking this time didn't, as I had expected, become dark and angry. Her look was long and cool. Like she was tipping a glass of iced water over my head.

'How many a day?'

'Does it matter?'

'No. Yes. But I can't stop you.'

She never mentioned it again – until she found out exactly who and what the cigarettes were linked to. Zoe subscribed to this need people currently have to confess all no matter what. Magazines are full of it – celebrities admitting their private falls and foibles as if readers are God, invested with the power to forgive.

I must have somehow transferred my guilt about the affair to the smoking because I never really felt bad about it. Only once, in the very beginning, when I'd just woken up and the details of the sex surged in my head like an ugly beast. But as long as nobody knew, or spoke of it, it existed on another plane; it wasn't real until it had a name, a voice.

Zoe didn't write or call; she invited Connie out to lunch. I am not sure under what pretence. A new charity perhaps – Connie is always raising money for this or that worthy cause. 'Giving something back,' she calls it.

'You risked our marriage for that?' Connie screamed at me. 'She's not even pretty!'

Like I said, Connie's rage blazed, so contemptuous, so utterly justified, I just had to get out of the way. I didn't know if everything was burned beyond repair. But to figure it out I had to leave her for a while. Work out if I could ever cross the muddy creek.

It still hasn't rained. Large shrubs are drooping. Most lawns are brown including ours. Suspicion hangs like a pall over any patch of green. Neighbours are dobbing in neighbours. The water police patrol the streets at night in Leak Detection Units; vans with flashing lights trying to flush out an illegal sprinkler or two.

Window cleaners are out of business. Only the very young dare to write 'wash me' on dusty cars.

The local papers and then the national ones are clogged with stories on the area's deficit. Letters to the editor are full of suggestions, which have quickly become demands. One of the more militant letters recommends overthrowing the council, or at least defying any rules they will try to put in place. Just keep using the water until an emergency is declared. I have to say I'm inclined to agree as I drive through town past badly designed signs that tell me, payer of exorbitant rates, that it's ESSENTIAL WATER USE ONLY.

*

I come back from the gas station and assemble my purchases – a carton of cigarettes, a box of matches and a can of petrol – on the old Formica table in front of the salt-blurred window.

I go down to the beach for a bit of wood. The purple bulk of the island is flat and indistinct. Only first thing in the morning does Kapiti appear three dimensional – furrowed with shadowed hills, covered in thick green bush. Some days it disappears altogether in a blanket of mist. It's easy to see why the Maori chief Te Rauparaha once used it for a fortress.

The low sun glitters on Sonny's place – a house built on one of the tiny outlying islands. One night when Doug was a few sheets to the wind, he told me he talked to Sonny every day. Sonny and another mate drowned in a boating accident a few years ago. Their bodies were never recovered, so it's entirely possible that Sonny is alive. But in the likelihood that he is dead I like to think it's his spirit flashing on the window out there.

I find a nice log of smooth silvery wood and drag it up to the bach. It's heavier than I thought it would be – must be waterlogged. I attempt to cut into it. The chisel's a bit blunt and shears off. After a while I get into the rhythm of it. The wood's dry enough, just denser than I thought.

In between nights spent drowning my sorrows with the water bores and mornings recovering, it takes me a few days to carve out a rough boat. It floats fine – apart from a bit of a list, which I remedy by taking more wood off one side.

When dusk falls I load it up. I wedge in the carton of cigarettes, tuck the piece of Norfolk pine bark, now dry and brittle with bit of fluff clinging to the dead lichen, into the prow. I glance out towards the hulking shadow of Kapiti just as rain hits the window in fat oily drops, which in the sudden boisterous wind begin to lash the glass like a carwash. So much for grand gestures, the Viking funeral will have to wait.

Then Connie phones. She will be here in an hour. Even though I know it's time for us to talk I'm not sure I'm ready.

'Are you sure? It's bucketing down,' I say.

'Well it's okay here. Just spitting a bit.'

Which is not unusual. The geography is such between Wellington and Kapiti that it's possible for it to be fine here and raining there or vice versa.

I rush around tidying up. Vacuuming up the chips of wood. Washing a week's worth of scummy dishes. I sniff the pillowcases and the sheets and decide I'd better change the bed. The storm gets worse. The temperature drops. I turn the heater on.

Still no sign of Connie. I watch the TV news. A man is wading in thigh-deep water, buffeted by gale force winds, towards a half-submerged car. A reporter says that motorists are being warned not to attempt to drive through Mana on State Highway One.

If Connie had a mobile I'd call it but she's never trusted technology. She resisted microwave ovens for years until she found out 'microwave' was a misnomer, dreamt up by some liar in advertising.

Another reporter, wearing a yellow coat, water dripping off the end of his nose, says the roads are flooded from Wellington to Paraparaumu. The news crosses to Paekakariki where a massive slip of rocks and mud has stopped the train just before the station. There are no casualties but all traffic is at a complete standstill.

Two months' worth of rain has fallen in a few hours.

I rest my forehead against the cool glass of the window. A few metres away the sea froths over the seawall. The loaded boat sits on the table. I consider leaving it there for Connie to see – let it do some talking for me.

Instead I do battle with the door, which the wind is doing its best to hold shut. I win. Clutching the boat and the garage remote I squelch across the lawn down to the garage. The roller door squeals up. The garage is awash. I drop the boat and splash through ankle deep water to the cardboard boxes stacked on the floor at the back. (Shelves slipped off the 'things to do' list when Connie and I reached a stalemate – Lundia vs. Dexion.)

I grab one of the cartons marked 'Photos' in a familiar black felt-tipped scrawl. The soggy bottom gives way and Connie and I, kissing, circa 1985, float across the floor.

Connie took the photo. We were in bed. She held the camera with her outstretched arm and clicked the shutter just as we closed our eyes and pressed our mouths together. She must have known, with the insight accorded to new lovers, that such a kiss, such perfect happiness, might never come again.

Back in the bach I open the lid of another box and take out a soggy yellow envelope. I peel the clump of sticky images apart. At first I hardly recognise that slim handsome young man, raising his beer to the woman behind the camera. Five boxes later my life with Connie is hung out to dry with miniature green and red pegs and nylon string once used to display Christmas cards. I kneel amongst hundreds of photos of us lining the skirting boards, on the mantelpiece, spread out on the table; the place is a laundry, a gallery. No, it's a shrine.

Swimming to Australia

Lloyd Jones

Warren was first into the water. He lifted his knees and kicked out over the shallow surf and dived beneath a breaker. Warren made it out beyond the breakers and lay on his back. Any moment he would call out 'Marilyn' as was his wont when underneath a car and needing something from his toolbox. In that way of fat women at public swimming pools, Mum squatted – a slow immersion in the water.

We caught up to Warren – Tess, Bron and myself – and Mum, covering the last few metres underwater, surfaced next to Warren and surprised him with a kiss. Then Warren spoke up and said, 'Australia is out there.' He pointed with his hand and we tried to make out the exact place on the white horizon. Tess began to say how she couldn't see a thing – but lost the confidence to finish the sentence, or say it loud enough for Warren to hear. 'Yep,' said Warren. Australia, he meant. Our mother stared over his shoulder to the horizon with a dreamy smile, as if it had just become clear to her what the rest of us could not make out.

Well, Warren had seen what he wanted to see. Without a word he just swung around and headed for shore, and the rest of us obediently followed. We picked ourselves up out of the shallows and wiped the salt from our eyes, and the first thing we saw was Warren sitting on the wet sand, pulling on the wet ends of his beard. 'Same old place,' he said, and to Mum as she bent down for the towel, 'I'm the abo with the spear. Watch out.'

We drove to McDonald's – Warren ordered nothing for himself which confirmed that he was upset, and at some point, either in the car or in the doorway at home, Mum kissed him on the cheek and said, 'Maybe some day.' But that was Warren, we told ourselves. Like a child when he couldn't get what he wanted.

Other times we drove to the end of the quarry road and watched in silence the sun deliver itself to that place Warren had pointed out, and felt ourselves to be fools for not following.

'Keith says formwork is a hundred-dollar-a-day job there now,' he said.

It grew awfully quiet. We could hear our own breathing. Finally Warren said, 'Yep. I don't know for the life of me why we need to stick around here.'

Then, a week later, 'How would the Musters like to team up with the Gilberts and travel over to Oz?' Warren happened to be cutting his meat, which he kept at as if nothing controversial had been uttered. We exchanged looks but were slow to comment. Then Warren put down his knife and fork, and got up to leave, slamming the door to the kitchen. We heard the car start up, and the spit of gravel as he reversed out to the road, and Mum said Warren had got a bit antsy.

We travelled out to the West Coast beaches this particular afternoon, the last week in February. Warren was in a serious state of mind. There had been some shouting from the bedroom, after which Warren emerged and rounded us into the car. I didn't care one way or the other, but, of course, choice didn't enter into it.

He drove faster than was comfortable. Every other car was an arsehole, and usually Mum would have said something like, 'Warren, better late than dead,' but she didn't and I knew it was killing her not to say anything.

Warren's mood had not improved any when we got to the beach. He pulled off his T-shirt and kicked his slippers inside the car. It was up to each of us to keep up; to get out of the car so he could lock up. He was in no mood to be delayed.

Tess complained of scorched feet so I picked her up and carried her as far as the wet sand. We were all business.

A bunch of kids were playing on a log, and a man wearing goggles swam side-on to the waves with a painfully slow 'crawl' action. Every now and then a wave gently lifted him up, inspected him, and put him gently down again.

Warren dived and smacked his fists. He bullied his way out beyond the breakers. Further out he lay on his back, staring up at variable skies. None of us felt like swimming to his exact whereabouts, but since we were seated at the same table as it were there wasn't much else to do but to look the other way. Mum had a race with the girls to hurry them along. We duly fell abreast of Warren. We were a good distance from shore but none of us gave it a thought. We had hit a warm seam in the current. 'Warm as bathwater isn't it,' said Warren. And once to Bron, 'This way' – as if she had veered off course.

Mum said it wouldn't surprise her if we bumped into an oil tanker way out here. Bron immediately said she wanted to go back.

My mother laughed. 'Just a little further, Bron. You are doing fine. All of you.'

Then she put in a couple of powerful strokes to where Warren was shuffling along on his back. I heard her say, 'We need to talk.'

'I'm all ears,' he said.

'Not out here.' But then she said, 'Supposing we did, what about the children?'

I heard Warren say, 'We've been through that one enough times already, Marilyn.'

'What about Tess – her friends? And Bron? Jimbo just about to start high school…'

'New friends. New schools,' he said.

'Fine,' said our mother.

'Fine is what,' he said.

Some spluttering from Tess attracted attention. She had swallowed sea water. So Warren rolled over on his back. He idled there while Mum swam back to Tess. She wiped away a trail of snot for Tess to say she wanted to go back. She was cold.

'Go back to what?' called out Warren.

'We're on an adventure, sweetpod. Yes, we are,' she said, nodding her head, I think to reassure herself of the idea. She called back to Warren,

'I've just told Tess we're on an adventure. Isn't that right?'

'Pretend. Pretend,' he said.

'I hate Warren,' Tess said quietly.

'Warren loves you,' Mum said.

Warren paddled his feet and blew up a spurt of water like a whale. 'That's right. Mollycoddle her, Marilyn. Every time that girl sniffles the entire company has to pack it in.'

'Tessa is fine, aren't you sweet?'

Tess nodded, allowed herself to be placed back in the water under her own power. She put her head down and swam furiously, out past Warren.

'Dawn Fraser,' he said, now sitting in the water. 'That's another thing, Marilyn. We would have new heroes. More of them. And he began to reel off the names of famous cricketers, tennis and league players. 'The Great White Shark,' he said, because he knew I had done some caddying before Christmas.

'Not to mention climate,' he added, and we stared out to sea.

Back the other way the beach had sunk from view. We seemed to be bobbing above the tops of farm scrub.

Suddenly Mum asked, 'What are we doing out here, Warren?' Her brave smiles had been deceptive after all. And of course. She must be worried. Probably she had been worried the whole time. But Warren pretended innocence.

'I don't know,' he said. 'You tell me. I know what I'm doing. Jimbo, what about you?'

I said I did.

'See. Jimbo knows what he's doing. What about you, Marilyn?'

Then Bron piped up that she didn't want to go to Australia. She was young enough to say what she felt, and I for one was pleased she had, even if it was just to say that she didn't want to leave behind her dolls.

'We'll buy more. Better dolls in Australia,' said Warren.

'But I want Hetti.'

'Hetti can come too. Jesus,' he said. 'What a party of sadsacks. Sing a song somebody.'

When nobody did Warren started to sing 'Advance Australia Fair'. He lay on his back as effortlessly as before and sang at the top of his voice. Barely noticeable at all, Mum had started to hum 'God Defend New Zealand'. Why, way out at sea, did I feel so embarrassed? In between Warren's bellows we could hear Mum's fragile tune. I don't think she was particularly aware of what she was doing, at least not until Warren had finished and she was still carrying on.

'Well, well,' said Warren, as Bron joined in with breathless gasps. I could see Bron's feet and arms scrabbling to tread water, to stay afloat, and her face growing red with the struggle of getting out the words. I wished she would stop. It was a stupid thing to be doing way out here, without anything solid underneath us. At the completion of 'Advance Australia Fair' Warren might have turned and stroked for the New South Wales coastline. But when Mum and Bron finished I felt as though we were all about to sink to the bottom, that there was nothing in this world to keep us afloat, other than this old Victorian prayer.

'You silly bugger, Warren,' Mum said then, and swam over to where Warren floated secure as a log. She was halfway there when Bron said she had had enough. She was tired, and was heading back to shore.

'Bron. Please honey.' But Bron did not appear to hear. She was breast-stroking for the beach. Mum turned around to Warren who was singing in a silly voice a few more bars from 'Advance Australia Fair'. He was enjoying himself – anyone could see that. Then Mum turned back to me and Tess. She said she wanted us to stay out here. 'I want us to stay together,' is what she said, but below the waterline I could see her legs quietly propelling her towards Warren. For the first time it occurred to me that her problem had become our problem. She reached Warren, and the two of them smiled back at us. Warren had one of his hands inside Mum's togs and they were looking at us, pretending that there was nothing for us to see that might cause alarm.

Maybe Warren was right after all. Even in late March summer hung on – women and girls wore summery dresses – a fringe of surf stretched to the white cloud, and beyond. There was a lightness here that included all manner of possibility, whereas, at home, everything had seemed anchored to the ground.

Warren's friend, Keith, a man in shorts, long tanned legs and desert boots, was there to collect us. He was pleased to see Warren. Tipped his hat to Mum. But the rest of us caused him to scratch his brow. Mum and Warren squeezed into the front; me, Bron and Tess sat in the back of the ute.

The air was bone dry, and Bron complained her eyeballs were drying out. Soon we were driving away from the city and the air smelt of bark and leaves. And suddenly of hot road mix, where we slowed for a road gang. Then for a long time we were on a highway. Driving to where – none of us knew. A few times Mum looked back over Warren's arm, which was slung along the top of the seat, to see that Tess wasn't hanging off the end of the tray.

Bron woke Tess soon as we hit the sea. We had entered a stream of traffic and were making slow work of it along a beach esplanade in the shadow of tall buildings. We stopped at the big M. Warren ran across for burgers and shakes, and we set off again, heading inland, away from the coast until the tops of the buildings marking the beach had grown small to the point of vanishing.

There were times in the days ahead when each of us thought we could smell the coast. Perhaps it was simply a longing to be where other people were. In the dusty quiet of the country it was a lot to wish for. Sometimes we sat on the porch and followed a red dust cloud across the flat scrubland, which traced the progress of a four-wheel drive. At night Keith put roo bars on his ute and from our beds we heard it smack through the undergrowth; the rip of rifleshot, and the high whine of a vehicle held in low gear.

Warren and Keith went out shooting most nights. Friends from school it turned out. They took it in turns to hold the spotlight and shoot. Another man did the driving, a fellow from the Danish 'steelie' gang with whom Keith and Warren were contracted to help build the retirement village – 'Ocean View' as it was called – in the foothills. Warren sometimes returned home and reported having spotted the sea. On clear days it was possible – as well, it was comforting to know it was there; that there was this edge, that is to say, a limit to this new life of ours.

Our house for the time being was the former headmaster's house in the grounds of an abandoned country school. We were saving ourselves a bundle living here, according to Warren. It was that, or drive to and from the coast each day.

'It doesn't bear thinking about,' Warren said, after a few weeks of our being settled. Although Mum did say that she felt able to chip in were we on the coast, where jobs were to be had cleaning out motel rooms and apartments. 'For that matter,' she said, 'I might even teach piano.'

'Oh I can imagine that,' Warren said. He walked to the fridge, took out two beer cans, and tossed one to Keith.

We were into our second month and everything new had become familiar and practised. Warren couldn't think why Tess had to land awkwardly after all the times she had landed perfectly okay. Most times Warren slapped the side of his door and we jumped clear, like hunting dogs, from the back of the ute outside the school gates. This occasion the ute started to roll away, then stopped. Warren got out angry at the noise Tess was making. She was screaming and it was hard to know which part of her hurt. Warren stroked her hair and pinched her cheek. But it turned out to be her wrist, which he then held and kissed. He babied Tess until Keith called out something like, 'Time!'

But Tess was complaining that her arm hurt. Really hurt. Warren took another look. He gave it a waggle and pronounced it okay. He had done the same thing plenty of times in his younger days on the rugby field – at worst he had sprained his wrist. And there was nothing you could do about sprains other than exercise patience and let nature take its course. At the same time he wandered back to the ute with a troubled look.

I think Bron, as much as myself, was prepared to believe Warren. Tess was prone to over-reaction. And already her tears had dried. She didn't mention it to her teacher and had no further complaint until that evening when she said it was hurting again.

Warren and Keith were watching the league on the box. Warren stretched his bare foot forward to the TV dials and with his big toe turned up the commentary.

But Tess was crying hard. Everything she must have held in all day was coming out. She hated Australia. Her arm hurt. And as much as Warren leant forward to concentrate he wasn't succeeding. Finally he had had enough, and yelled so he could be heard, 'Marilyn, will you shut her up for chrissakes!' Then he shook his head and I heard him mutter to Keith, 'Every time you can bet your bottom dollar that little…' He shook his head again and shivered, got up and walked over to Tess. He stroked her hair. 'What did I say this morning, Tess? I said, "It's a sprain."'

Mum wondered aloud whether we had gotten ourselves travel and health insurance, which only further aggravated Warren.

He said to Keith, 'Can you believe this? A small girl falls over and suddenly we're looking at airlifts to hospitals. Tessa. Tess! Listen to me…'

But she was crying too hard. Sobbing her eyes out. Mum led her to the room where she and Warren slept, and Tess's sobbing carried on in there, through the doors, in competition with the league.

Warren returned to the sofa and shook his fists before his face.

'What have I done to deserve this?'

'I give up,' said Keith.

Then Warren noticed me lurking, and ordered me to the couch.

'The guy with the ball. See him! There! That's Bella. He's crunched through more bones than you've had hot dinners.'

'That would be true,' said Keith.

Then Warren said to Keith, 'It's still all new to him.'

I heard them shooting later that night. I lay with a sheet over me, listening to the crack of the undergrowth and Keith's ute. It was going on later than usual. Mum came and sat on the end of my bed. 'Still up?' she said, trying to be jolly. A light from the hallway found her face; a full cheekbone of smile that with a little prompting, I felt sure, might turn to something else. 'I suppose it all seems a bit strange. A new school. New country,' she said, and I knew she was waiting for me to say it wasn't that at all. She was daring me to speak her thoughts for her.

'Oh well,' she said. 'Tessa seems to have gone off all right.'

In the morning Tess was very quiet. She had no colouring. It was impossible of course but she appeared to have shrunk, as if each tear she cried had contained a piece of flesh. She sat at the table with her bad wrist in her lap. Warren and Keith were still asleep, so we tiptoed around like shadows. After breakfast Mum told us to get dressed – she had an idea, and hurried us along to brush our teeth. We were leaving the house when Bron allowed the fly screen to snap back on its hinges – and the fright stopped us in our tracks.

Out on the road the plan faltered again. Mum took Tess by the hand and looked to the road behind. There was no traffic for a hundred miles – at least that is the way it felt. 'Has everyone a set of legs?' she asked.

We walked along without making a race of it. The one car that came along, stopped. The farmer was headed a short distance, to the store where we got our groceries. He was surprised to hear we were headed for the coast. Mum told him, 'We have a young lady here with an arm that needs seeing to.'

The farmer scratched his nose. He wished it were tomorrow. Sunday he was taking his family to Southport. Tell you what, he said, if we were still on the road on his return from the store he would drive us to the coast. Otherwise we might as well stay on the road and try our luck.

Luck took the shape of Keith's ute. It crept up behind: its fat wheels sucking up the tar.

Warren sprang out. A light joke on his lips, he said, 'Now where is this lot of nomads headed? Same place we are, I hope.'

Without a word Mum lifted Tess into the back of the ute, among the bits of animal fur and clotted blood from last night's shooting. She hauled herself in – me and Bron followed.

I barely remembered anything of the passing landscape which we must have passed all those weeks earlier. Tess lay in Mum's lap. Her hand flopped on the end of her wrist and she held it up not so much because she wished to show it off, but because it was more comfortable that way. Mum stroked Tessa's hair. Otherwise she was lost in her thoughts.

Soon we entered the outer suburbs. We struck the first set of traffic lights and, after that, the malls. Again there was the sniff of the coast. A light breeze that we never got further inland. Bron said she wanted an ice cream, but we passed the ice cream parlour on the green light and drove to a newish building with tinted windows where Keith, I later heard him tell Warren, had been treated for the clap.

The x-ray revealed a clean fracture. Now that it was pointed out, the bend in Tessa's arm seemed obvious and we wondered how we could have missed it. Warren said he could have sworn it was a sprain. The nurses took no notice. If anything they were short with him – and Warren was asked three times by as many nurses how it had happened. Then I heard one of them behind the curtains quietly ask Tessa for her account.

The arm was to be set that afternoon. Mum stayed with Tess. Warren gave me and Bron ten dollars. He pointed out the hotel where he and Keith planned to hole up, and left us to roam.

That evening as we drove back towards the foothills it seemed to me that we were driving away from everything that was sensible and sane. There was Warren's work, and home, and no overlap, and no way of anticipating what was to happen next.

It was a week later that the ute pulled up early afternoon. Keith didn't come inside the house. It wasn't worth thinking about at the time; only a clue in hindsight. Warren rough-housed his way through the fly screen, gave each of us a filthy look and made his way to the refrigerator. He took his time in telling, and when he did he stared at the floorboards and jabbed angrily with his hands to make the point that we would hear it told once, and that was all.

The company developing 'Ocean Views' had gone bust – or been placed in the hands of receivers – and for the time being cash was on hold. I didn't like the sound of 'for the time being'.

I heard Mum and Warren, later that night, making plans in the living room. Mum was doing most of the talking and for once Warren was listening.

'This is no place for children. How much have we saved up?'

'A thousand … twelve hundred,' said Warren.

'We will need a car. Not a ute mind you, Warren,' she said. 'My children have travelled in the back of that thing for the last time.'

That was the end of Keith. We didn't see him again.

We bought an early model Holden inside of which the whole family and Warren could sit. Warren changed the points and plugs, rustled up a retread from somewhere – and we were roadworthy, heading back for the coast, where we turned south, stopping along the way at building sites for Warren to go and enquire after formwork or carpentry. We stayed in camping grounds and did our washing in laundromats. Mum got work house-cleaning, so we would stay in a place for a few days – never more than a week – until we had petrol money.

It made no sense. Buildings were going up everywhere, but at every site Warren went to the back of the line. Further south, and men gathered outside the sites; they sat on the fence like a line of still vultures, waiting for a job to come free. We pulled along outside, and Mum sent Warren across to the foreman's office. The men watched without any talk in them; sawing grassblades between their teeth. And they watched Warren's return the same way.

'Guess what? Last month they wanted formworkers,' he said, getting back in the car. Always last month. I wondered how long, how much longer this was going to go on, and why we didn't just pack up and fly home.

Then one night we had to make a choice between somewhere to stay and petrol; Mum just kept driving south through the night, and the new day dawned in Taree.

Me, Bron and Tess untangled ourselves from the back seat, and sat up to find we had arrived in a park or public domain. We were parked on the edge of a field. Near a huge tent were elephants and horses. A man in tights walked along a rope. I looked at the map and found we were in New South Wales. The doors cracked as we tumbled out, and from the front seat Mum stirred.

Then we saw Warren coming towards us from one of the caravans parked in line. An older man in a white singlet and braces followed after Warren, who looked keen and ready with news.

'Wake up your mother,' he said. 'I think I may have something.'

But he did it himself; leant in the driver's door and said, 'Marilyn. Payday.' He shushed up then because the man in braces had drawn near. Mum got out of the car. She tried to smooth out the creases in her dress. There was the matter of her hair too, and as she sneaked a look in the fender mirror, she said, 'Jesus. Heaven help.'

The stranger nodded at her, and took each of us into account. Then he made as if what he had to say gave him no pleasure at all. Turning to Warren he said he had misunderstood their earlier conversation. He had been so long in the circus business he had forgotten what a formworker was.

'I had in mind juggling, the wire, something of that order,' he said. 'But what you are about to tell me is that you're not a circus performer.'

Warren nodded, and studied the ground. He raked his toe back and forth in the grass.

The circus man seemed to be taking stock of the situation. He looked at each of us, again. And nodded.

'Still,' he said. He had a thought. He twirled a finger in his ear, and while he was doing that he gave Warren a good going over. Walked around him twice, before finally he said he might have something. Mum smiled at Warren, and he took her hand.

Many years ago, in Italy, the circus man had seen a useful sort of stunt which he had, for some time, meant to introduce to this hemisphere. Maybe that time had arrived; if Warren, of course, was interested. Warren checked first with Mum. She nodded, and Warren was given the privilege of saying, 'Okay then.'

We were travelling north again, through towns we had passed in a single night – Port Macquarie, Kempsey, Coffs, Ballina.

Warren had his own tent. On its side was a picture of a strong man with curly hair and black moustache, and the words 'Man of Steel'. Kids up to the age of twelve paid two dollars for three punches to Warren's stomach. Clearly the man who hired Warren had not been telling the truth. Bron and I had gotten friendly with one of the acrobats who said the last 'Man of Steel', a Hungarian immigrant, had developed kidney trouble, and the circus had left him in hospital in Scone, New South Wales.

'Light hail on a tin roof,' was how Warren described his day's work. But at night our caravan reeked with the liniment Mum rubbed into his stomach and sides. Slowly he began to soften, like one of Keith's skins after a steady beating. The job was taking it out of him. No sooner were we in a new town than he suffered the runs. And the rest of us had to put up with his irritability.

At such times we left Warren in the caravan, alone, and Mum led us on a walk in a strange town.

'Luckier than most kids your own age to be seeing the world,' she said. We didn't feel lucky, but of course she was trying to put the right spin on things. We knew we should be in school, and in a strange kind of way it was unsettling not to be found out, or even feel as though we faced that risk.

In Ballina Warren said he didn't know for how much longer he could keep this up. We heard him groan at night when he rolled onto his sore ribs. He had become a nervous man. The drop of a pin turned his head. The circus manager came to our caravan to say he was pleased with Warren's work, and to ask whether the kids needed something to occupy their time. Mum herded us under her wing and told the man the children were her concern.

'We want to go home,' Tess blurted, and the man chuckled. He poked his head inside the door and took it all in in a sweeping glance. 'This looks homely enough to me,' he said.

'Excuse Tessa,' Mum said properly, but the man waved a hand at her, and walked away.

'We will be out of here by June, Tess,' Warren said. 'June I feel will be time enough.'

We were prepared to believe it. We had something to look forward to; a means by which to mark progress. It was only three weeks off.

But June arrived, and nothing happened. None of us even had the heart to mention the fact of it being June. Not even Tess. We were in Southport, very close to where we had set out. Some of the terrain I recognised from the times we had ridden in the back of the ute. Not only had we lost our place on the calendar but we appeared to be going around in circles.

We had certain games and rituals to push ourselves on. At night, as we lay on our mattresses, Tess asked Bron to describe her teacher, Mrs Marshall, whose class Tess was to have started this year. Then she asked Bron to describe all the kids in her class, which Bron did, fitting out a name with a set of eyes, hair and skin colouring, and habits, so no two were the same. It ended this night when Warren sat up in bed at the other end of the caravan and sent an empty liniment bottle crashing against the wall above our heads. Mum yelled at him to control himself, and Warren slapped her.

I showed up at Warren's tent the following afternoon. I had to push through a flap and Warren looked up, saw it was me, and went back to reading his newspaper.

'Jimbo. What do you want?'

What I wanted was not easily put into words. A short while passed before Warren glanced up again and cottoned on.

'Chrissakes,' he said.

'I paid.'

'So you paid, Jimbo. That's a dollar to the circus, and a dollar to me.'

It didn't make any difference, and he shook his head. He was leaning against a table, rolling back and forth a small pebble underfoot. Then he said, 'Never. Not in my wildest dreams did I ever think it would come to this. Your mother and I, Jimbo ...'

He looked up then, and said, 'What the hell. Let's get it over with. Three shots.'

He stepped onto a small raised platform, the kind a conductor might use. I tried to see him in the same light another visitor to the tent might, but I couldn't get past the fact it was Warren.

'Do you want the full works?'

I said I did, and Warren said, 'Okay then.' He folded up his newspaper and slapped it on the table. Steadying himself he closed his eyes and concentrated for a moment. Then he started to recite with a strange accent, 'My name is Saffrez, last of the desert tribe of Assyrian strongmen ...' I noticed his hands bowling into fists at his sides, and was concerned that he might be forgetting who had paid here. But he collected himself, and carried on. 'Hit me, the great Saffrez. And watch your sickly knuckles turn to dust...'

Warren's elbows fanned out from his sides and he tensed his stomach muscles. He waited with his eyes closed for the punch, for me to get my money's worth. Perhaps all along I had known I wouldn't throw a punch, but what surprised me was my total lack of desire. And at some point when Warren realised that nothing was going to happen, that he had tensed himself up for nothing, he sat down where he had stood. 'Chrissakes,' he said, dropping his face into his hands. Then he shoved his hand out. 'Go away Jimbo. Don't look at me. Leave me please. Go to the beach with your mother.'

I nodded, and said, 'Okay.' In a sense still listening to Warren. On the other hand I think we were all glad to be walking away from it all, the yawns of the sedated lions, the pink candyfloss and the alcoholic clowns.

The shadows from the buildings had almost reached the line of dried foam above the wet sand. A knot of swimmers looking for excitement kept between the flags but well shy of the heavier waves. Me, Bron, Tess with her cast wrapped in plastic, and Mum, stuck together in the same channel, bobbing like corks, taking it in turns to check the arrival of the next breaker. There was no way out beyond the waves. No calm for a horizon to sit along like a painted line. Nothing but movement and foam as far as the eye could see.

And then, without warning it seemed, we were being dragged along a channel parallel to the beach; fighting it at first, then not bothering. None of us was unduly concerned. 'Look, Egmont,' Bron said, of the spit of sand jutting out from the beach, where we might scramble ashore. Meanwhile we did just enough to keep afloat. There was no question of us getting cold.

In time Warren showed. Mum was first to spot him by the parking meters above the beach. I think we had all expected Warren and were nervous at the prospect of his trying to wave us back between the flags, to where he imagined safety lay. He was still in his circus outfit, and we watched this wild figure try to stay abreast, burning his feet on the hot sand as he stepped gingerly between the tidy Japanese sunbathers. None of us said a word. We were comfortable for the moment to just tread water. We were waiting to see if Warren would join us.

At Waimama Bay

Annamarie Jagose

1

Very early morning. Full light but the mist not yet burned off, the world revealing itself in pieces as you passed, the flax clump at the bottom of the driveway as always, the chainlink fence of the tennis courts, the half-barrel house with its wishing well. At this speed, the wind punched your ears, the *shuck-shuck-shuck* as you swept along past parked cars and behind that the murmuring of the sea or the highway, the one the same as the other however you cranked your head, both lost in the mist just now drawing back from the daytime ordinariness of the settlement, three streets wide from the highway at the foot of the hills to the sand dunes and no more than a quarter-hour walk from the north headland to the south. At the top of the rise, standing up on her pedals, Maddy leaned from side to side, steering between the dotted white lines that marked the middle of the empty street. The sound of new rubber curved up from the asphalt. On her old bike she had been able to ride no hands but this one was balanced different. She could probably be a trick rider if she practised. That would come in useful if she ever had to rescue anyone. Say she put out a burning house with a fire hose while riding in such fast circles that she was barely scorched. Or pulled someone from quicksand with a rope tied to her carrier. How her parents would stare at her when she was brought home, as if she were a marvellous stranger.

Darling, her mother would say, we never knew, and even Alice would sit up and take notice.

At the far end of the settlement, Maddy rode over the juddering planks of the boardwalk to look out over the beach. She couldn't touch the ground from the saddle but balanced well enough with a foot on the railing. The cliffs stood pink in the morning light. A fisherman had been swept off the rocks the day before, Boxing Day. Drowned actually. The twins told her that part of it. The sirens had cried out from the surf club and the next-door neighbor, Mr McIntyre, who lived in his house all year round, came over on his croquet-hoop legs to tell her mother.

It's a fisherman been swept off the rocks. It was as if he expected as much. An old man, bad news was his last pleasure.

Oh, her mother said, a winded gasp as if the news had sought her out particularly. She paused a moment, kneading a tea towel, then with a quick pecking glance over her shoulder to where Maddy hung in the doorway, ushered Mr McIntyre out of earshot. The two of them stood on the deck, heads bowed, but it was only later that Maddy understood the news.

Well, said Regan, where did you think he was swept to? His right ear had been pierced since last summer and he had a new habit of tossing his hair back on that side to show the tiny green stud.

Ay, he's sleeping with the fishes, all right, said Ryan. He put on a funny voice like a cartoon dog but Maddy didn't know who he was being. It was often like that with the twins. Not so much that they were older but that there were two of them. Regan had a mole on his left cheek and Ryan one on his right. It was where they had squashed their faces together before they were born.

Creepy, said Alice. Maddy so looked forward to their company each summer that it was the same as being frightened of them. Her heart clambered in her chest when the car came round the last bend in case their house was empty, no hammock and the back door clear of boogie boards and flippers.

We'll probably go to Europe for Christmas next year, Regan had said.

Or Swaziland, said Ryan.

Down at the surf club, the orange inflatable was being put out to sea, sawing its way out the back across the surf break, the chainsaw sound of the motor travelling clear across the water each time it jumped in the air at the crest of a wave. Two lifeguards, one holding the rope at the front and the other steering from the back, came along as far as Maddy, a little further, to nose around the rocks. *Swept off.* It reminded her of cleaning the blackboard, all the words lost forever in a fall of useless dust. When the Zodiac hauled around in the water, ready to run back down the beach, Maddy spat on her palms, rubbed them together and raced the sound of the outboard motor the length of Kontiki Road until she tasted blood in her throat. *Shuck-shuck-shuck.* Someone was up at the twins' place, the sliding doors open to the deck, but Maddy didn't stop, only gave three rings on the bicycle bell and a Tarzan yell, and pressed on, past the club and the main road in, the doctor's house and the lending library with sand in all the book spines, down to the dairy at the edge of the reserve. The venetians were pulled and here was Edith in her slippers, dragging the takeaway signs out to the pavement, her gray bob falling either side over her eyes like broken bird wings.

New bike for Christmas, said Edith in her dreary voice. The twins called her E-Death. A childhood accident had paralyzed her face, they said, leaving her unable to smile all her life.

The dairy was next to the reserve, tucked under the sprawl of a wind-bent pohutukawa, but it could have been anywhere since it had no windows on the sea side, its dusty frontage overlooking the street. It looked like a house from the front with an ordinary wooden door, a lion's head knocker and a panel of thick yellow glass you couldn't see through. As Maddy came in, the buzzer sounded in the back room where Edith cooked fish and chips in the evening, the colour worn off the lino where she tracked back and forth. Edith's husband, who nobody ever saw, sat back there somewhere. He wasn't well – dropsy, said the twins – and the doctor called once a week to suck fluid from him with a needle. The lights weren't on yet and, past the clarity of the front windows, the shop swam in murk. Edith prided herself on keeping something of everything, her shelves stocked tight, the smoke yellowed ceiling hung with strings of fishhooks and tap washers. Bales of potato chips, wax and twine, a life vest, tins of spaghetti and condensed milk, a rack of birthday cards, zinc sticks, onion soup powder sachets, blu-tak, spinning tops, sun hats. Down the back by the bait freezer, there was a dented tin of kippers that had a dancing fish in a top hat on the label that summer after summer no one ever bought although a stream of children made a pilgrimage to it each year. Edith sold loose sweets too, a glass-fronted cabinet on the counter glowing with gummy bears, milk bottles, gobstoppers and sour drops. She never served a child if an adult was waiting and sometimes you could stand a half hour in your togs, breathing in the sherbet fizz and making over your fifty-cent order ten different ways before she got to you.

Maddy rode home slow, the promise of the sun's heat already enough to make the chocolate fish tacky in her hand. The flags were up although the sand looked damp still. No one was in yet and you could get goosebumps thinking about swimming with the dead fisherman rolling about beneath the waves like a capsized kayak, his lonely seaweedy arms stretching out for someone. At the bottom of the driveway, she sucked her teeth clean. The curtains were open and her mother's towel was already hanging over the FOR SALE sign screwed to the deck railing so that you could only read

FO LE

2 BED 000+

The sun hung in the sky like a plate and with all the sparkling and twinkling the place looked as it always did, everyone cooking breakfast or pegging washing or pulling on the string of a motor-mower and a stream of cars arriving from the city until Maddy couldn't remember why she was special, in hand-me-down shorts with a sunburn she could feel when she rabbited her nose, a nine-year-old girl, nine and three-quarters almost, that no one would look at twice. The day belonged to everyone.

2

No sign of Graham yet and no call from him this morning either. Originally he was to have joined them Boxing Day, then the day after and now, even as she listened out for his arrival, her eyes pinkly closed against the mid-morning sun, Celia half-expected him to ring and say he was still tied up in his office with his sign-offs and wouldn't make it until Wednesday, the day his brother was due to arrive. Half a dozen times already Maddy had ridden as far as the surf club to see whether his car was coming down the last stretch of road before the beach turnoff. Determined she wouldn't hang around waiting, Celia had taken herself for a morning run as far as the estuary along the low-tide sand where the first children were already wandering in broad-brimmed hats with buckets and spades like tiny demented explorers as the search and rescue helicopter came low around the headland, still looking for that fisherman she supposed. She tidied away the breakfast dishes, rehung the living room curtains where they had long ago come off their hooks, squared off the board games in the cupboard under the television, until she caught herself, drifting empty-handed from room to room, bumping up against the windows over the driveway like a summer blowfly. Taking herself in hand immediately, she changed into her togs and laid herself out on a deckchair alongside Alice, who, at fifteen, had the genius of indolence.

It was the summer of Alice's first bikini, although this milestone had passed unremarked, Alice appearing on the deck in her new costume the day after Christmas, her scowl daring her mother to make something of it. Already she had the beginnings of a tan, a paler crease of skin tugged back inside the elastic of her pants when she rolled on to her stomach. Well pleased with it, Alice had not yet grown into her body, its new breasts, the blond down on her arms and legs, the one neat horizontal seam at her belly button when she sat as now, reading a magazine.

What? said Alice, dropping her *Cosmopolitan* to her lap.

I didn't say anything. Celia closed her eyes against her daughter's loveliness but the after-image still played on her eyelids. *Six Sex Tips That'll Keep Him From Straying!* She had left her sunglasses inside, her novel also, but wouldn't get up for them. Maddy could fetch them for her next time she came by with news of the highway. She supposed Graham was seeing someone. That would explain why he had not been himself lately, working late, fond as ever but no one could say ardent, making a furtive phone call from the garden on Christmas Day and now missing the first two days, perhaps three, of their holiday.

That was last night's slow realization. Graham had called late and they talked inconsequentially for fifteen minutes but afterwards, reviewing their conversation in the deep of the night, she thought she detected a guardedness in him, a kind of shutting down against her, that she recognized as the self-protective shape intimacy takes in front of someone else. She could imagine him hunched into the receiver on his side of the bed while, over his shoulder, someone she had no interest in visualizing too specifically waited prettily, pretending not to listen. Ridden hard by dreams, she slept badly, woke early to throw the sheets and pillowcases in the washing machine before setting off on her run, as if she were the one with something to hide.

There was his car now, crunching up the gravel driveway in low gear, and Maddy skidding behind in a pale plume of scoria dust, her new bike dropped to the lawn, front wheel still spinning. Alice sat up at once, catching at the open ties of her bikini top and fastening them capably behind her back in a move at once so novel and yet familiar that Celia felt her head heat up with impossible tears. Graham got out with a little stoop and a straightening of his shoulders, the self-consciousness of the one who arrives last and late.

I saw him first! I saw him first! Staggering back against the car door, he caught his younger daughter as she launched off the lowest step of the deck, nearly too big to be carried now but not old enough to care. Maddy slung across his hip, Graham went to muss Alice's hair but she caught his hand in hers and held it to her cheek, the three of them near perfect for a moment, her family, smiling down at her like a Christmas photograph while she lay, milked of suspicion and suddenly happy, her vision swarmed with tiny blotches where she had closed her eyes against the sun.

You're late.

You're lovely, said Graham. They were unpacking the car, everything smelling of tomatoes, the case he'd picked up at the market gardens. The traffic was mad. A truck broken down in the gorge and everything backed up for miles.

Lunch first or a swim?

I had a milkshake at the Copper Kettle on my way through. Have you been in yet? The this and the that of it, said Celia to herself as she waited for Graham to get changed but, although she gave it a minute or two, breathing deeply as she had learned at Pilates, her thoughts went no further. The lawns were overgrown. After lunch she should call the man who did them or they wouldn't get mown before New Year. Down the beach access they went, not quite holding hands but grazing the backs of their knuckles, salt-crusted towels off the line warm over their shoulders, a green and yellow kontiki kite flying high over the dunes and Maddy, already in flippers, walking backwards behind them with a crazy pedaling gait, *I can hold my breath for ages, Dad, you count while I'm under,* her voice carried on the sea breeze back to the house where Alice sat, refusing to look.

Further down between the flags, the sand was crowded with sun umbrellas and the undimmed brightness of new beach towels but just in front of the access path they had the beach to themselves.

Let's swim here, said Celia and when Maddy looked uncertain, Just a quick dip. Kids were like that now. They got it from school, a deep allegiance to the rules of wearing seatbelts, swimming between the flags, crossing on the lights but all without any sense of their own vulnerability, that bird-boned fragility which could arrest Celia with a breath-stopping clutch.

Have you got block on? Celia thought to reassure her daughter by extending another set of safety regulations and immediately she came forward like a penguin, her arms stretched out for the sunblock and her flippers pitching sprays of dry sand. She caught Maddy to her, kissing the top of her head, rubbing in the lotion and continuing to rub, comforted by the solidity of her daughter's arms and legs, until she wriggled from her grasp with the limber muscularity of a fish.

The water was cold enough to make the bones in her feet ache. Standing ankle deep with the wind raising gooseflesh on her arms and legs, Celia couldn't think how she had been hot ten minutes earlier. A small swell rolled up to her knees and she took a step out, another. Maddy was thrashing about in the channel that formed between two sandbars, bug-eyed behind her swimming goggles.

Dad, said Maddy, count how long I stay under, but Graham was out of earshot, sitting on the first rise of sand with their clothes, waving when they turned to look at him.

Don't splash me, said Celia, edging past on tiptoe as the next wave slid by at thigh height. Her hands held out of the water, she pressed through the channel to stand on the other side, scanning the water behind the breakers. Nothing. Years ago, before Maddy was born even, she had once seen a pod of dolphins cross the bay, only fifty metres or so from where she was swimming. She had swum after them but as they increased their lead, she put her face in the water and called to them, a shrill burbling cry such as she imagined they might use to communicate with each other. Foolishness, of course, and she was already half-laughing at herself, when they wheeled around and came for her, cutting down the face of a wave not three surfboard lengths away, as big as cattle at this distance, their skin not hot water bottle smooth as she'd expected but creased and pitted like a baseball glove. Back on shore, Graham was wrapping Maddy in a towel and sitting her between his legs to shelter her from the wind. Out here, it was all slosh and fizz, the squawl of a distant gull, not a human sound to be heard. She was treading water now, her hair still dry, waiting for the perfect wave to ride to shore. Really, it wasn't too bad once you were in.

3

After lunch, the beach was nearly deserted. Everyone had decamped but for a leatherish group of women who always sunbathed topless a little distance from the patrolled beach, in the scant privacy offered by a fallen tree, washed up in a winter storm some years previous and every season a little further sunk in sand. The twins called them The Thongans. There were three of them now, sometimes as many as seven, sometimes just one. Year after year they came, like the sand dotterels. They hung the salt-blasted branches with their towels and angled their foldable recliners to follow the sun's course, ending the day with their backs to the sea, looking over the dunes at the far hills while the shadows lengthened. No matter the heat, they never went in the water. They smoked incessantly, tossing a lighter between them, one or other of them never without a cigarette, their butts buried an arm's length from where they sat. Graham had no idea which house they belonged to or even whether he'd recognize them after dark. You didn't look, of course, but even not looking he had a fair sense of them, tight and oiled like a clutch of sausages on the barbecue, their breasts hanging brown as the rest of them, worn down by their public life, inoffensive as elbows. He kept his head down as he drew level with them and felt his shoulder blades crawl with their looking once he was past. With the sand shimmering empty as far as the estuary, Graham went on his way, lonely and righteous in his slides and board shorts, a *High Noon* feel to the heat of the day.

Celia had sent him out to see whether there was any chance the lawnmower man could get to them that afternoon.

Look at it, she said. He had been sleeping nearly, his feet in the sun but his head under the shade of the eaves, the unread paper folded open over his chest, an odd tangle of dreams strung up on the sounds of the afternoon, the voiceless wheezing bark of George McIntyre's dogs and the scrape of lunchtime dishes next door. Almost at knee height and throwing up seed heads, the grass should have been mown before Christmas.

It needs to get done before Paul's tent goes up, said Celia. Paul was due sometime that afternoon, driving up with his new girlfriend, Angelique.

He won't mind.

What do we care if he minds? It was the mean voice Celia used to keep herself from crying. He's selling the bach from under our feet. She stared at him a blank moment and went to have the nap he needed. Graham looked in on her as he was leaving. The red curtains bellied into the room as he opened the door and were sucked back, throwing a brothel light across the afternoon bedroom that clenched and relaxed like a lung.

Anything else while I'm out?

Mmhmm, she said, feigning sleep, although she could only that minute have put her head on the pillow. Her shoulders and calves had freckled up in the last few days but there was still the underbelly pallor of her city feet. It came to him with the force of a proverb as he set off down the beach access: a summer wife is not a winter wife.

The lawnmower man lived somewhere on Dolphin Drive. One block back from the sea, the houses here mostly favoured motels, two-bedroom blocks with the cars parked off the street in front of the ranch sliders, the occasional two-storey place going up for the view. It felt more raw than over their way, the gardens not yet established, few trees taller than the pitch of the roofs. In the last ten years a lot of infill housing had gone in, many places sporting a second driveway that ran down to a newer place at the back. Subdivided in the late 1960s, the settlement had once been farmland. Their own place was a Lockwood model home, relocated from the city and put on the small rise where Kontiki Road curves on its approach to the south headland. His parents had bought it at his mother's urging, his father never a beach person, preferring to keep to the pavements in his weekend shoes. He had some of their early photographs, the view from the kitchen window a clear paddock out to the offshore islands where now there might be a hundred houses. Paul didn't care much for Waimama, preferring the marina down the coast, and Barb never got over from Sydney now, so the two of them had insisted it go on the market. He hadn't told Celia in case it came to nothing but he had called Barb on Christmas Day to discuss putting it off a year or two so he might have half a chance of buying them out. She was thinking it over, figuring all the angles. He'd have to talk to Paul too. They had been coming here since he was a boy, the nearest thing he had to history.

He needn't have worried about missing the house with its advertising shingle and a lawnmower mounted on the garage roof. From its picket fence to its net café curtains, it was determinedly suburban, as if its being at the beach was an accident. Graham waited at the panelled front door while the doorbell played *Fur Elise*. On the last note, a woman, about his age but with an older air, opened the door. Carpet, a hallstand, dried flowers. She had the practical, open face of a social worker and had clearly been expecting someone else.

I'm Graham Trout. From 31 Kontiki. I was wondering whether – Graham hesitated a moment, made awkward by not knowing the lawnmower man's name – whether your husband…

He's not here. He's out with the other men. There was something disturbing in the way she said this, as if he were somehow less than a man, standing on her porch in his slides and sunglasses. Graham supposed teams of men might be needed to keep the lawns down at this time of year, what with the weather and everyone wanting to look their best for the holidays.

Any idea when they might get around to our place? The woman looked bored, as if she wished he'd go. I wouldn't usually ask, only we have visitors arriving.

Who is it? A woman called through from another room.

It's nobody, Angie, said the lawnmower man's wife. I'll be with you in a minute. It's his brother, she said to Graham and, when he still looked blank, added through the crack of the closing door, Ted's brother, we lost him off the rocks on Boxing Day.

At first, it was just the social embarrassment that heated his cheeks, the blundering awfulness of it, but once he was back on the street, the wagon-wheel gate snicked shut behind him, he was seized by such a severe impatience to be home that he broke into a run, awkwardly pitching himself down the street, fearful of a turned ankle or knee as his slides clopped against the soles of his feet, his breath laboring in his ears before he reached the first corner. He would have liked to be shooting the breeze with Alice, although he didn't know quite who she was this summer, or explaining something to Maddy. More than anything, he wanted to be curled behind Celia, a hand at her breast, sleeping out the afternoon behind the red curtains, the bifold doors open to the deck and, beyond that, the radio static sound of the sea. At the corner, he hunched over, panting, hands on his knees, his vision clouded by a film of blood. A car towing a caravan lumbered past. He didn't imagine he looked like a jogger taking a break, more a middle-aged man whose body had fallen away from him, one of those invisible men that nobody bothered looking at until they fell down with an aneurism or some thrombosis. Standing upright again, he looked about and seeing himself unobserved set off, still breathing heavily, counting his steps, a childhood habit. Eleven-twelve-thirteen. An old woman was weeding the bank of succulents outside the white house with the Astroturf balcony, the backs of her thighs below her shorts seersuckered with age.

Afternoon, said Graham.

Afternoon, she said, not looking up. Thirty-nine-forty-forty-one, crossing Kontiki Road on the diagonal, one slide gumming momentarily in melted tarseal, sixty-eight-sixty-nine and there was the bach sitting above the bend in the road as it always had, as he wished it always would.

4

On the reserve next to the surf club, a young man in low-slung jeans with a ruff of boxer shorts at his waist was standing on the picnic table, turning this way and that, his phone to his ear. The high ridge of hills around the settlement, half farmland, half forestry plantation, meant it was mostly impossible to ring out but this was one spot where you sometimes saw people trying.

Any luck? said Graham.

Not today, said the young man and they nodded one to the other, like fishermen. Cicadas cricked in the yellowing grass and the air quivered in a haze of heat coming off the bitumen. The young man pocketed his phone, half-hitched his jeans as he jumped from the table and was off across the grass with the early evening energy of a dog.

From the top of the dunes it was hard to pick his family from the crowd. Not that there were so many people on the beach with an hour to go before the flags came in for the day but everyone looked unfamiliar in togs, as if they were being played by body doubles. Graham thought he spotted Celia twice before he had her correctly, her face lost in the brim of her sunhat but her hands clasped together at her breastbone as she bent toward her knees, a gesture he wouldn't have known as hers until that moment: Celia laughing. She wasn't with the others, which had made finding her more difficult, but was half-tucked beneath the shade of a blue and white umbrella, sitting back on her haunches, talking to two other women whose bottom halves were all he could make out from here. Caroline and Becky, probably.

Down on the beach, he made out Alice, standing on one leg to peel off her wet clothes. This year she'd taken to wearing a bikini, which took some getting used to, but she never swam without a pair of boardshorts. She had come to see him earlier to ask whether she could go with her friends to Wakefield, the next town up the coast, for New Year's Eve.

What friends?

Sarah and Amanda, she said, after an unconvincing pause. So, can I go?

Ask your mother.

She'll say no. You know she will. She ran from him like a child, calling back over her shoulder, I'm never allowed to do anything. Now she lay on her belly, her chin in the crook of her elbow, looking for all the world as if she needed no one's permission to be herself. Stockily competent in her sunsuit, Maddy was digging with the twins, the three of them trying to coax water up a channel to the towel where Alice was lying, flattered to be the centre of their ambition but paying them no mind.

Kids, said Alice across the warm gap of sand between her elbow and Angelique's.

They grow up soon enough, said Angelique, smiling, her eyes hidden behind sunglasses so that Alice couldn't be sure she wasn't talking about her. Uncle Paul's new girlfriend was a lot younger than Auntie Diane. She looked like the pretty woman in a film that you have to pretend is a mole until she takes off her glasses and stops dressing like a librarian. And Uncle Paul was wearing Speedos, just like a pair of underpants really, with curls of hair tufting out from the legs and all his parts knuckled out at the front.

Walking back to her towel, Celia saw Graham standing at the top of the boardwalk and waved out, waiting for him.

How was it? she said. He had been over the hill to Wakefield for supplies before things got too crazy. Already there were queues of cars idling around the block to refill gas canisters at the garage and a couple of paddy wagons on the lawn at the police station for the extra arrests expected tomorrow night.

The usual. Kids tooling up and down the main street blowing their musical horns. He sounded like an old man: worse, like his old man, worn down by other people's fun. I couldn't get any prosciutto.

Don't worry. We'll do something else. It was a big high tide, the waves breaking right on shore but swelling tall and glassy a few metres out, just the other side of the sandbar. Elevator waves they'd called them when they were kids, Paul and him with their hair sleeked like otters and, truth be told, Barb a better swimmer than either of them. If you timed your entry right, you could get through the riot of white water and ride up and down for a half-hour before the tide turned.

Swim? he said.

You go. I'll watch, said Celia, smoothing a few small sand-hoppers from his towel and arranging his slides in a neat pair with the wifely composure that threw him sometimes. He wanted to be out there now, buoyant and careless, but for the moment he was struggling with his T-shirt caught over his head, facing down her surveillance, his chest hair greying and not as flat-stomached as he'd like.

The waves were pounding the shore, the children squealing and rolling in half a foot of foam, the air salted with haze. Graham stood through several cycles of build and break, then waded out decisively, past the kids and their clutter of polystyrene boards, into the dip of the channel, the water rushing back between his legs until he could stand no longer, gathered himself into a neat arrow and dived cleanly through the green face of the next tottering wall of water. Lean and taut, whittled down to youth by the weight of water rolling over him, he kicked to the surface, shaking the salt from his eyes. One more roller, a few lunging overarm strokes and he was clear, sinking deep in the trough of a wave, then cresting high to look back at the shore, Angelique and Celia sitting either side of Alice. The water was so clear he could see right down to his feet, his pale paddling feet, and beyond that more bright water as if it were illuminated from below. How deep it was, he couldn't tell. Ducking over, he kicked out for the bottom, stroking wide through the water, maybe three body lengths before he caught up a fist of sand, still plenty of breath, another wave passing over like wind, rocking him a little in his underwater world until he kicked back up for the spumish light overhead.

Hey. It was Paul, his hair licked to his forehead, grinning to bust.

Hey. He showed his palm of wet sand, then washed it clean.

They rode up and down, kicking strongly to stay upright, staying well clear of the turbulent break between them and the shore where the mass of water was smashing against the sand.

I had an extraordinary dream last night, said Graham. It was hard to make himself heard over the surf and the splatter of water blown back at them from the crest of the waves. And then the dream was not so extraordinary in summary, a high cliff on the headlands and him peering over at the rocks below, but the feeling it had given him in the night. He had woken just after midnight, omnipotent, the house ticking down as the last of the day's heat left its rafters and crossbeams, and gone to stand on the deck under the stars, the hummock of Paul's tent a dark blot against the lawn.

A dream? said Paul. He had drifted a little further out than Graham, his back to the waves so he could catch what his brother was saying.

Hawaii, called Graham, pointing over Paul's shoulder. It was their boyhood name for those big waves that reared out of nowhere, monstrously high but coming at you all the same, the ones that made you ache for your towel. Paul laughed as he caught the reference and turned to look after Graham's finger where a massive wedge of water was arching tall, half as high again as anything they'd ridden so far and already breaking into a curve of foam at its crest.

Sweet Jesus, said Paul, spiderishly scrambling for shore.

Dive through, said Graham as if he were the older brother, dive through, but Paul had lost his nerve and, caught up in the wave's muscular ripple, was pitched over the brink, the crook of his knee the last thing Graham saw before he dropped after him, the world lost in a welter of water. No up or down, just over and over, his knee connecting painfully with his nose, lungs squeezed for air, surfacing at last on a buck of white water, Graham managed somehow to get his feet under him and land running, pushing hard against the fall of water draining back out from the shore before he could be caught in the next breaking wave. Paul was just ahead, getting to his feet in a scatter of children, and they laughed snortily on each other's shoulders, Graham feeling somehow old and young at once, his brother rearranging himself inside his togs before he could face the shore.

5

Almost lost in the tall grass at the bottom of the section, a rabbit sat and chewed, ears swiveling. He had a pink, whiffling nose that reeled in the summerish smells to the counting-house of his skull: watermelon rind and coffee grounds from the compost heap, hot tarmac, dog spoor. There were usually two rabbits, whether the same two each year Celia couldn't say. She sat on the top step of the deck, waving her ankles free of mosquitoes, her bare arms goosepimpling in the sea breeze that came up fresh most evenings. The end of the day and she found herself washed up here, showered and moisturized, the skin on her shoulder-blades tight as scorched cellophane, the gaps between her tanned toes showing white in the last light of the day. Paul and Angelique were in their tent having one of their frequent rests, so recently a couple they had to recharge each other several times a day with the gift of their bodies. From the gurgle of the pipes, she could tell Graham had just turned off the shower. Maddy was with the twins, ranging across the unfenced sections, intent on some game or other. Celia had seen her a moment ago, scraping at the ground under the neighbour's pohutukawa with one of the boys while his swishier brother waited on the beach access, flipping his fine hair over one ear. Not allowed to go over the hill to Wakefield with friends, Alice had shut herself in the bunkroom.

Everyone's going, she had said. I won't drink anything, promise. You can talk to Amanda's mother. I'll have my phone and I can call you every half hour until it had fallen finally to Celia to say, You're not going and that's that.

George McIntyre fastened the gate at the side of his place and came over the lawn between their houses, his two old dogs bringing up slow.

Well, said George, what do you think? He was dressed as always in sandals, shorts and a T-shirt but had a black patch over one eye. If she hadn't known it was fancy dress down at the surf club, she might have thought he had conjunctivitis.

Perfect, said Celia and when that didn't seem enough, A perfect pirate.

That's it, said George, as if his secret was out. When the first dog slouched over, Celia saw George had tied a handkerchief around her neck. We're going as the Jolly Rogers.

Aren't you a bit early? said Celia. What time's the party?

I'm helping set up, said George and was off, his dogs still mooching through the cabbage trees on the boundary long after he had left.

Graham came with her cardigan, which he draped over her from behind, and crouched a moment with his hands on her shoulders under the pop and squib of firecrackers that couldn't wait for true dark.

Martini? he said, producing two glasses, his with a twist of lemon, a fat green olive in hers, both slick with alcohol, a rainbow gleam on the slopping surface.

Cheers.

Bottoms up. A cautious clink of glass and their undergraduate salutes and here came Becky and Caroline over the dunes, cradling the magnum of Gosset they'd promised, Graham throating his drink in one swallow and holding his hand out for her glass, the loft of sky above as she tipped her head back, the clean surprise of the gin still burning her nose when their guests reached the deck.

Happy New Year.

Happy New Year. A sheepish unzippering as Paul and Angelique extruded themselves on to the lawn, Happy New Year, and Graham returned with a tray of glasses, Happy New Year, five flutes and one wine glass, the sixth in the set broken some summers back. Everyone gathered on the steps as Graham worked the wire cage off the bottle, wedged the cork out with his thumbs little by little until it popped into the air. Chased across the grass at that moment, Regan clasped his heart and staggered a few steps before going down in a theatrical death roll.

Happy New Year, Mrs Trout.

There was a moment of perfect silence that grew too long as the six of them stood and sipped champagne.

And what do you do, Angelique? said Becky, meaning to be friendly but hearing herself otherwise.

I project manage, said Angelique, so that no one was the wiser.

And she writes haiku, said Paul, putting a protective arm about her waist while Angelique looked modestly away. She texts them to me all the time.

Oh, said Graham. Let's see: seventeen syllables, right? Celia wouldn't have thought that he knew what a haiku was but it seemed he was right.

Give them one, said Paul. What about Winter Prelude? How's that go? but Angelique didn't need prompting.

The end of autumn

Last leaves cling to chilled branches

Sad cello charcoal, she said and allowed her glass to be refilled. Up the beach access came four young men in toga sheets. It was night at last.

Celia drank more than she should, although didn't have time to notice until she was serving dinner, roast duck breast with fennel and orange salad that Paul had matched with Mt Difficulty pinot noir, the children eating barbecue hamburgers late at the picnic table, heads craned for the roman candles. Alice wasn't hungry but ate the burger Celia brought to her and then, wishing she hadn't, threw the empty plate out the bunkroom window into the karo hedge. Nobody cared about her: they were just trying to make themselves feel better. Celia cleared the table, waving away help, glad for the excuse to be up and moving. No one could manage dessert just yet. Paul fetched a bottle of single malt from his car and, at the sink, Celia watched him pour smoky tots into glasses among the leftover cutlery, his head hanging close to Graham's, the two of them easy and fathomless as the boys they once were. The bright walls of the kitchen pressed in on her unexpectedly and, holding on to the yellow Formica bench while the room reeled about her like a ship's cabin, there came upon her an intolerable feeling that she didn't know how she could get through, a sharp-edged realization of the shortness of life. It was as if she were suddenly revealed to herself as a moth, yes, a moth with a moth husband and moth children, who would all be extinct tomorrow, the world grinding on unchanged.

Everything OK? Becky poked her head over the island bench, Caroline at her shoulder. We're going outside for a smoke. Celia followed them out through the laundry to stand under the clothesline. Among the beach towels, Caroline pulled a badly creased hand-rolled cigarette between her lips a few times before cupping a match to it.

Fantastic dinner, said Becky, taking several sipping breaths at the cigarette.

Mmmm, said Caroline. Fantastic.

Should we have asked Angelique? said Becky.

She's a man's woman, said Celia in seriousness. The orange coal of the skinny joint flared and her throat was plumbed raw.

And what sort of woman are you, then? They were laughing at her, Caroline playing her ribs with her elbow, and Celia, cross and pleased at once, inflated on a breath and magnificent with smoke.

I thought I was a moth, she said.

A moth?

We were all moths, she said and, really, it was hilarious. She had never felt less insect-like. Out at the clothesline with Becky and Caroline, she couldn't resurrect any sense of horror. The sound of surf was always louder at night.

Bands of people were calling and stumbling on the beach access in the dark, making their way between parties, the sky electric with cordite. Elvis went by in a white jumpsuit with a woman done up in metres of pink tulle.

Rex, Celia heard her say, My wings keep coming loose.

Mine too, said Becky and they laughed and laughed, at what Celia couldn't have said, her blood got up in bubbles from the champagne, the whole world mad with effervescence. It must be time for dessert, fried Christmas cake and ice cream, and so returning across the dewed lawn in bare feet, the fishermen's lanterns making their way up the headland track and the stars swooning overhead, the Southern Cross and the pot, the rest indistinct in a phosphorescent blur, Celia missed by minutes Alice's escape from the bunkroom window, in denim turn-ups and her new Max shirt, hair tied back in a ponytail, the sound of a car idling for her two houses away.

6

At the bottom of the driveway, the twins were poking through the clump of flax with a rake and a broom handle. Already they had harvested four crumpled beer cans, a black beanie, and a Stone's Ginger Wine bottle. The flax was like a net, stretched against the currents of the night pavement, spilling its moonlight catch on the morning lawn. Maddy came wheeling her bike over the grass so it wouldn't make any noise. No one else was up. Not a sound from her parents' room and the tent still zipped shut although it must be eight or even nine o'clock.

Have you seen Alice? Her bed was empty when Maddy woke. She had meant to stay awake until Alice came home but somehow slept as usual, lulled to dreaming by the sensation of falling and rising on the day's waves that always rocked her bunk. No one had called her for bed and in the end she had given herself up, coming inside without being told, nearly eleven on the microwave clock when she passed through the kitchen. In the bunkroom, Alice was standing in the dark, tying her hair back.

I'm going out, she said, as if she hoped Maddy might stop her.

What if Mum comes? Maddy had heard their mother laughing in the garden only minutes before.

Cover for me, said Alice like a movie spy and crawled over Maddy's bed and out the window. Now Ryan was thrusting his broom handle into the flax so vigorously that he was almost swallowed up inside the long spiked leaves, one elbow crooked across his face to protect his eyes.

I've got one, he called so that Regan stopped pouring off the ends of the beer into the wine bottle and came around to see. Ryan worked his pole like a flounderer but it was only a kitchen glove, grey with age and the thumb missing. Last year, they had found a condom, or said they had.

Have you seen Alice?

Nah, said Ryan.

Nyet, said Regan. Maddy pushed off on her bike, not sure where she should look but itching to be doing something. It was the New Year, which meant the first day of the first month of the year she turned ten, but it felt tired already and not coming out right.

The first of the runners from the King of the Hill contest were coming along the street, having raced from the surf club up the fenceline of the tall hill behind the settlement and back down the steep tip of pasture to the highway. Although the main road in was closed to traffic, no one stopped Maddy on her bike or much looked at her, the small crowd only interested in the race, the men with numbers pinned to their singlets, emptying their water bottles over their heads as they sighted the finish line. Nearing the intersection, she saw the first lady runner, her head so bandaged in mirror sunglasses she looked like a crazy fly, coming over the last stile on the way down. It hadn't been a plan exactly but at the intersection Maddy turned on to the highway, an unfriendly wind pushing against her, the road much nubblier under her wheels than the smooth tarseal she was used to. Around the first bend before one of the race officials called out to her, she cycled past the faded sign for the Waimama dairy, coasting downhill and over the one-lane bridge before the slow climb up the next hill. Standing off the saddle for the first slope, Maddy had to walk most of the hill, pushing her bike. A car whipped by, buffeting her in its slipstream. The road looked different this close: the ditches deeper than she had supposed, a possum flattened against the asphalt like a cartoon coyote. It was two more hills and her lungs shaking with the blare of a truck's horn before she gave up. She almost made herself cry imagining her and Alice lost on the same day and Mum and Dad orphans the rest of their lives.

Outside the surf club, the pageant was in full swing. The prizes for the surfcasting competition and the King of the Hill race had been distributed and the Little Nippers had been led through their lifesaving demonstration. Now the semi-finalists in the Miss Waimama Bay contest were being announced over the loudhailer from the volunteer fire brigade truck, the final three contestants unknown to the locals but walking the temporary stage in their swimsuits as if they owned the place.

Never seen a one of them before, grizzled George McIntyre, making up for lost opportunity by not taking his eyes off them now. It was the same every year, the big prizes going to the professional circuit-queens helicoptered down from the city with their even teeth and tans. In the burl of noise, a vein behind one of Graham's eyes pulsed painfully.

Can you see the girls? he said. Celia's head felt too delicate to shake.

They'll turn up. She leaned back against him in the crowd, a perverse enjoyment to be had in feeling ragged with him on the first day of a brand new year. Without his having done anything wrong, she had forgiven him.

Maddy limped a little, a frill of dried blood descending into her sock. She had come off her bike in the shingle on the side of the highway and the crimped metal edge of a pedal had taken a gobbet out of her right shin. Ditching her bike in the tall grass, she'd walked back to the settlement, approaching the surf club from the north headland. It seemed everyone was packed on to the lawn in front of the stage, the wah-wah sound of the loudhailer coming at her fuzzily across the distance. Although the flags were up, the beach was empty except for a solitary lifesaver on his stand and, closer to her, a knot of men rolling a surfboard out of the shallows and wrapping it in a cloth. Up the sand they came, three on one side, two on the other making heavier work of it, straight over the tussock toward Maddy. There was a sixth man, it turned out, waiting on the street, who smiled at her in a teacherish way as he drew a fold out stretcher from the back of his green station wagon. Over the dune came the men with their dripping burden, stern-faced but kindly, as if they could save her from the drowned fisherman, for it was him at last, she saw that now, carried in a tarpaulin as pulpy as a bag of goldfish.

They did not shoo her along but let her stand there, their blood-streaked witness, as they packed the car and wound the tinted windows, silent and efficient, with a fisherman's respect for the catch.

Between the surf club and the sea, Maddy walked on behind the turned backs of the crowd. Without looking, she saw Alice, sitting by herself on a fence railing in yesterday's clothes and a borrowed sweatshirt. Maddy climbed up beside her and let Alice look at her a long moment as if she were a difficult maths problem.

Do Mum and Dad know? said Alice. Maddy shook her head.

I came looking for you, she said, displaying for Alice the holy evidence of her wound. Such a baby, thought Alice, loving Maddy newly. Everything looked the same as always but Maddy knew it was different. She was brimful with some feeling she hadn't a word for, a kind of undertow that pulled her out of her depth, far out from the crowd of regular people who huddled together in their holiday clothes. Alice put her arm around her little sister and cuddled her close, so close it broke some safety catch in Maddy's throat and made her cry, sour silent tears for the dead fisherman, for the five years between her and Alice, for her abandoned bike, for all the things she didn't know and would have to learn.

Contributors

Rhonda Bartle was born and raised in New Plymouth. She still lives in Taranaki, in a rural setting which is 'fast becoming just another part of town'. In 1999 she won the BNZ Katherine Mansfield Short Story Award and in 2000 her novel *The Gospel @ccording to Cole* (2000) was published. In 2003 she won the Webster Popular Fiction Award for her novel *The Lie of the Land*, which was published by Hazard Press in 2005. A full-time writer, her favourite beaches are Timaru Bay, south of New Plymouth, where her parents' ashes were scattered, and Mokau, in northern Taranaki – 'so long, so black, so west coast'.

Norman Bilbrough was born in Feilding and educated in country schools and in Wellington. He has published books for children, three volumes of short stories and a novel, *The Short History of Paradise* (Penguin, 2005). His stories have been widely anthologised and he has won the *Sunday Star-Times* Short Story Competition twice. He lives in Wellington where he makes a living as a manuscript assessor and a teacher of writing. His favourite beach is Cheltenham, on Auckland's North Shore, 'a dreamy quiet place where the water can be as warm as a puddle'.

Sue Emms grew up in England, Aden and New Zealand. A published novelist, poet and short story writer, her work has appeared in various literary magazines and she has won or been placed in the *Takahe* and *Sunday Star-Times* writing competitions. The founding editor of the literary magazine *Bravado,* she lives in the Bay of Plenty, where she works as an on-line writing tutor for the Waiariki Institute of Technology. She has two favourite beaches, Waiotahi, near Opotiki, for 'Its long gentle slope, warm water and mass of ancient pohutukawa', and Curio Bay in Southland, for 'its petrified forest, the massive heave of the Pacific and the gales that blast straight up from the Antarctic'.

Charlotte Grimshaw was born and brought up in Auckland. She is the author of three novels, *Provocation, Guilt* and *Foreign City*, and a short story collection, *Opportunity* (2007). The holder of the Buddle Findlay Sargeson Fellowship in 2000, she has also been a prize-winner in the *Sunday Star-Times* Short Story Competition and in 2006 won the BNZ Katherine Mansfield Short Story Award. Her special beaches are Karekare, on Auckland's west coast, where she spent holidays as a child, Whatuwhiwhi in the Far North, where her father-in-law is buried in the Maori graveyard, and Hobson Bay in Auckland, near where she grew up.

Witi Ihimaera was born in Gisborne. A graduate of Victoria University of Wellington, he is now Professor of English at the University of Auckland. A past winner, on three occasions, of the Wattie/Montana Book of the Year Award, his most recent works are *The Amazing Adventures of Razza the Rat* (2006) and a new collection of short stories, *Ask the Posts of the House*. Witi's interests include swimming, sailing, movies, concerts, tennis and reading. His favourite Auckland beach is Long Bay, and in the Gisborne area, Waikanae and Whangara, the latter being where his novel *The Whale Rider* was filmed.

Kevin Ireland was born in Mt Albert, Auckland. His family moved to Narrow Neck, on the city's North Shore, in 1938, then to Takapuna. In his early twenties he moved into the army hut behind Frank Sargeson's house, and began to devote himself to writing. After living in London for 25 years he returned to the North Shore to live in 1984. A poet, novelist, short story writer and memoirist, he was the recipient of the Prime Minister's Award for

Poetry in 2005. His sixteenth book of poems, *Airports and Other Wasted Days* (Hazard Press) was published in 2007. His favourite beach is Cheltenham, in Devonport, because, 'It's handy, it's glamorous, it has free cold showers and it's shallow and safe for my grandchildren. I love it.'

Annamarie Jagose teaches in the Department of Film, Television and Media Studies at the University of Auckland. She is the author of three novels, including *In Translation*, which won the PEN Best First Novel Prize, *Lulu: A Romance* and most recently *Slow Water*, which won the Deutz Medal for Fiction at the Montana New Zealand Book Awards and the Vance Palmer Prize for Fiction at the Victorian Premier's Literary Awards. 'At Waimama Bay' is part of her current project in which she is rewriting a series of Katherine Mansfield's major short stories. Her special beach is Whiritoa, on the eastern Coromandel Peninsula, where her family has a bach.

Lloyd Jones grew up in the Hutt Valley and still lives in Wellington. A novelist, essayist and children's writer, his adult novels include *The Book of Fame*, which won the Deutz Medal for Fiction at the Montana New Zealand Book Awards, and *Paint Your Wife.* His latest novel, *Mr Pip,* is an award-winning, international best-seller and in 2007 he was awarded the Creative New Zealand Berlin Writer's Residency. An ardent surfer, Lloyd's favourite beaches are Wainui, near Gisborne, Ngawi in the Wairarapa and Golden Bay, 'for its tremendous tides. You can walk across wet sand and cross pools and channels to stand where just an hour or two earlier you saw a fishing boat pull up anchor'.

Shonagh Koea was born in Taranaki and brought up in Hawkes Bay. She has published seven novels and three short story collections, including *The Best of Shonagh Koea's Short Stories* (1999). Her latest book is a series of autobiographical essays called *The Kindness of Strangers: Kitchen Memoirs* (Random House, 2007). In 1993 she held the Fellowship in Literature at the University of Auckland and in 1997 the Buddle Findlay Sargeson Literary Fellowship. Shonagh lives in Auckland, where she enjoys going to the cinema. Her favourite beach is at the end of Lansdowne Street, in Bayswater, because it is only a short walk from the house where she lives and writes.

Graeme Lay grew up on the Taranaki coast, first in Oakura, then Opunake, which instilled in him a love of the sea. He attended Victoria University of Wellington and later moved to Auckland. The author of over twenty books of fiction and non-fiction, he also works as an editor and manuscript assessor from his home in Devonport, on Auckland's North Shore. He is also secretary of the Frank Sargeson Trust. His most recent books are the historical novel, *Alice & Luigi*, and a travel memoir, *Inside the Cannibal Pot.* His favourite beach is Hahei, in the eastern Coromandel, for 'its glittering, pink-tinged sands and whorled volcanic cliffs'.

Katherine Mansfield (1888-1923) was born Kathleen Beauchamp, in Wellington, and grew up in the city. In 1903 she travelled to London with her family and spent three years there. She returned to New Zealand for two years, then went back to London, determined to become a writer. In 1911 she published her first collection of stories, *In a German Pension.* Her second collection, *Bliss and Other Stories*, appeared in 1920, and *The Garden Party and Other Stories* in 1922. She died near Paris after a long battle with pulmonary tuberculosis. 'Crescent Bay', in her story *At the Bay*, is modelled on Day's Bay, on the east coast of Wellington Harbour.

Owen Marshall was born in Te Kuiti but has lived most of his life in South Island towns. A novelist, short story writer and poet, he has received many awards for his writing, including the Deutz Medal for Fiction at the Montana New Zealand Book Awards and an ONZM for services to literature. In 2002 the University of Canterbury awarded him the honorary degree, Doctor of Letters, and in 2003 he was in the inaugural recipient of the Creative New Zealand Writer's Fellowship. His most recent book is *Watch of Gryphons* (2005). A keen tennis and hockey player as a young man, Owen's favourite beach is Caroline Bay, Timaru, because 'it has many happy associations with my youth'.

Bruce Mason (1921-1982) was born in Wellington and moved to Takapuna at the age of five, living with his family in a house just above the beach from 1926 until 1938. The local setting of beach, sea channel and Rangitoto Island inspired his most famous work, the one-man play, *The End of the Golden Weather* (1959), which fictionalises Takapuna as 'Te Parenga'. His other plays include *The Pohutukawa Tree* (1957), *Awatea* (1965) and *Not Christmas but Guy Fawkes* (1976). The Bruce Mason Centre in Takapuna commemorates him and recently *Golden Weather* was performed on the beach on Christmas morning. It is not presumptuous to suppose that the writer's favourite beach was Takapuna, below where he grew up.

Victoria McHalick was born in Cambridge, England, to New Zealand parents, and was brought up in Wellington. She completed a law degree and a BA in English Literature at Victoria University. 'The Picnic Virgin' was her first published work of fiction, followed by a collection of stories, *The Honey Suckers* (2001) and a novel, *The Taming* (2003). She is currently writing a novel set on a beach in Fiji. While acknowledging that the Kapiti coast has the ideal sand for castle-building, her favourite beaches are 'the ones where you can see your shadow on the sea floor as you swim'.

Linda Niccol started life near the beach at Raumati and was educated at Epsom Girls' Grammar School and Wellington Polytechnic. Her first book was a short story collection, *The Geometry of Desire* (2005), in 2006 she won the prestigious British Short Screenplay Competition and she has recently completed a second collection of short stories, *The Temperature of Water*. She now lives in Raumati, where she grows cacti and succulents and collects clocks. Her favourite beach is Ladies Bay, Kohimarama, a popular gay nudist beach where in the 1980s 'we'd sit, fully dressed, slurp our wine and munch our baguettes and brie until the sun went down and the tide chased us up the cliff's steep steps'.

Emily Perkins was born in Christchurch and grew up in Auckland and Wellington. She attended drama school and had roles in television before turning to fiction writing. Her collection *Not Her Real Name and Other Stories* (1996) won the Best First Book Award (Fiction) in the Montana New Zealand

Book Awards and the Geoffrey Faber Memorial Prize in Britain. She edited the anthology *The Picnic Virgin* (1999) and in 2001 published the novel *The New Girl*. In 2006 she was the Buddle Findlay Sargeson Fellow and worked on her next book, *Novel About My Wife*. Now living in Grey Lynn, Auckland, Emily's favourite beach is Cheltenham, on Auckland's North Shore, 'for its ease, friendliness and serene view of Rangitoto Island'.

Sarah Quigley was born in Christchurch and has a PhD from Oxford University. She has lived in England and the US and has won several awards for her fiction and poetry, including the Pacific Rim Commonwealth Short Story Award and the *Sunday Star-Times* Short Story Award. Her most recent novel is *Fifty Days* (Virago). She divides her time between New Zealand and Berlin, where she was the inaugural Creative New Zealand Writer in Residence. She confesses to being that rarity, 'a New Zealander who doesn't really like the beach', but pressed to pick a preferred one, chooses Taylors Mistake, near Christchurch, 'because there's little sand and lots of hills to climb'.

Frank Sargeson (1903-1982). Born Norris Frank Davey in Hamilton, he qualified as a solicitor in 1921. After travelling to Europe and relishing the cultural life of London and the Continent, he returned to New Zealand, abandoned the law as a profession and changed his name. Determined to make a living as a writer, he moved into his family's bach in Takapuna. There he lived frugally, growing vegetables, doing relief work and becoming a short story writer, playwright, novelist and memoirist. He also mentored many New Zealand writers, including Janet Frame, C.K. Stead and Kevin Ireland. His house, a short walk from Takapuna beach, is preserved as a literary museum.

Jenah Shaw was born in Auckland. Many of her childhood holidays were spent at Glinks Gully, a small beach just west of Dargaville. This setting later inspired her two short stories 'The History Of' and 'Away', the latter winning the Secondary School Division of the *Sunday Star-Times* Short Story Competition in 2005. Jenah attended Pakuranga College in Auckland and Garin College in Nelson. She is currently studying English and History at

Victoria University of Wellington. Her favourite beach remains Glinks Gully, for 'its privacy, beauty and quintessentially New Zealand summers'.

Tina Shaw was brought up on a farm in the Waikato. She went on to attend three universities, had a daughter and learned to play the mandolin, though not well enough to join a bluegrass band. A novelist, short story writer and book reviewer, she held the Buddle Findlay Sargeson Fellowship in 1999 and the Creative New Zealand Berlin Writers' Residency in 2002. Her fifth novel, *The Black Madonna* was published by Penguin Books in 2005. Her favourite beach is Tawharanui, just north of Warkworth, where her story, 'Holly', is loosely set.

Acknowledgements

The following stories or extracts were first published in the listed publications.

'At the Bay' is from *The Garden Party and Other Stories* (Constable, London, 1922); *The End of the Golden Weather* was published by the New Zealand University Press and Price Milburn in 1962, revised 1970; 'Entanglements' is from *Under the Bridge and Over the Moon* (Vintage, 1998); 'The Tsunami' appeared in the story collection, *Supper Waltz Wilson* (Pegasus, 1979) and in *The Faber Book of Contemporary South Pacific Short Stories* (edited by C.K.Stead, Faber & Faber, 1994); 'Holly' first appeared in the anthology *Crossing*, compiled by Agnes Nieuwenhuizen & Tessa Duder (Mammoth, 1995); 'The Seahorse and the Reef' was published in *Kingfisher Come Home* (Secker and Warburg, 1995); 'A Great Day' was first published in *The Bulletin* on 17/11/1937 and also appears in *The Stories of Frank Sargeson* (Penguin, 1982); 'self-catering' was published in the *Sunday Star-Times* in December 2005; 'Broken Rhythms' is from the story collection *Having Words With You* (Penguin, 1998); *The Lonely Margins of the Sea* was published by Random House, 1998; 'The Picnic Virgin' is the title story of a collection edited by Emily Perkins (VUP, 1999) and was published in the story collection *The Honey Suckers* by Victoria McHalick (2001); 'My Late Father' appeared in the anthology *Spinning a Line* (edited by Owen Marshall, Vintage, 2001); 'Only Waving' was published in the *Sunday Star-Times* in January 2005; 'The Outsider' is from the collection *Motu Tapu* (Polynesian Press, 1990);

'Storms' is from the collection, *Opportunity* (Vintage 2007); 'Water Bores' is from the collection *The Geometry of Desire* (David Ling, 2005); 'Swimming to Australia' is the title story of a collection published by VUP in 1991; 'At Waimama Bay' was first published episodically in *The Press* in Christchurch in 2004-2005 and in *The Best New Zealand Fiction* Volume 2 (edited by Fiona Kidman, Vintage 2005).

The remainder of the contributions to *The New Zealand Book of the Beach* have not been published previously.